ALSO BY A.C. ARTHUR

Seduction's Shift

Temptation Rising

PASSION'S PREY

A.C. ARTHUR

St. Martin's Paperbacks

This is a work of fiction. All of the characters, organizations, and events portrayed in this novel are either products of the author's imagination or are used fictitiously.

PASSION'S PREY

Copyright © 2013 by A.C. Arthur.

For information address St. Martin's Press, 175 Fifth Avenue, New York, NY 10010.

ISBN: 978-0-312-54912-1

Printed in the United States of America

St. Martin's Paperbacks edition / April 2013

St. Martin's Paperbacks are published by St. Martin's Press, 175 Fifth Avenue, New York, NY 10010.

10 9 8 7 6 5 4 3 2 1

To the members of A.C. Arthur's Book Lounge

Your support and unwavering dedication have been invaluable throughout my writing journey. I thank God for each and every one of you.

Glossary of Terms

Shadow Shifter Tribes

Topètenia—The jaguars
Croesteriia—The cheetahs
Lormenia—The white Bengal tigers
Bosnia—The cougars
Serfins—The white lions

Acordado—The awakening, the Shadow Shifter's first shift

Amizade—Annex to the Elders' Grounds used as a fellowship hall

The Assembly—Three elders from each tribe that make up the governing council of shifters in the Gungi

Companheiro—Mate

Companheiro calor—The scent shared between mates

Curandero—The medicinal and spiritual healer of the tribes

Elders—Senior members of the tribes

Ètica—The Shadow Shifter Code of Ethics

Joining—The union of mated shifters

Pessoal—The secondary building of the Elders' Grounds, which houses the personal rooms of each Elder

Rogue—A Shadow Shifter who has turned from the tribes, refusing to follow the *Ètica*, in an effort to become their own distinct species

Santa casa—The main building of the Elders' Grounds, which is the holy house of the Elders

Chapter 1

His mouth opened wide, the scream buried somewhere deep inside him. But it was there. Years later the scream would manifest into a roar that matched the deadliest animal in the rain forest. That made him powerful, stronger and deadlier than his tormentor. It gave him control. And with that control the pain of abuse was buried, the pleasure of the kill was born.

Xavier Santos-Markland stood naked, palms pressed against the Indian-stone-tiled wall of his shower, while water drizzled down over his bowed head. He let its simmering heat ease the tension that seemed forever embedded in his muscles. His teeth clenched as memories poured off him just like the stream of water, his mind forever occupied by the dark clips of his past.

It hurt. That was the first and most prevalent memory. The pain, both inside and out, of that very first time, the first day of his nightmare.

And it was unnatural. Another fact he realized instantly. He'd cried out, his scream loud to his little-boy ears, almost earth-shattering. But no one came to his rescue. Nobody heard him.

He was too small to fight, too weak to do any real damage or even to defend himself. As time passed, the pain increased, lodging itself like a tumor in his chest, growing steadily with each assault. He craved revenge, even then. Not just revenge, but justice. The boy in him hated every breath he took, every sunrise he saw, every morning he rose again. Because they all meant it would happen again. There was no one to stop it, no one who knew.

Then one of those mornings years later, he woke to a change. To his own ears his heartbeat sounded different; his blood pumped a little faster in his veins. His undershirts didn't fit, his pants were too tight on his thighs. In school when he talked, his voice sounded different, deeper. And when it was time for the pain to come again, he was ready.

It happened so fast: In the blink of an eye the tables were turned. The tormentor became the victim, the inflictor became the inflicted.

The rage was released with teeth so long and so sharp, claws so vicious, roars so powerful. Blood rained from all around, its acidic stench filling his nostrils, rushing through his system like a tsunami. Death became the answer to the pain. And he became the killer.

X had the perfect view.

Tits and ass—T&A—were bountiful in Athena's, one of Washington, DC's, premier adult nightclubs. When he'd walked in, the two bouncers standing on either side of the doorway had looked him up and down. They even frisked him to make sure he wasn't carrying a weapon. Little did they know he didn't need one—*he* was a weapon. A hostess, which X thought was a nice touch for the establishment, walked him to his seat. Five feet, ten inches tall, tiny waist, thick thighs, rounded ass, and breasts that made his mouth water—just what the doctor ordered for his state of mind.

Which he'd rank close to being fucked completely up.

He'd consumed an entire bottle of Hennessy while sitting alone in his apartment. But because he was a Shadow Shifter, he wasn't falling-on-his-face drunk. Instead he was mellow to the point of wanting to pull this physically perfect female onto his lap and give her every pent-up stroke his dick had stored for the last few months. He was in that place that he lingered in sometimes after the dream. The lonely dark space that threatened to suck him in if he didn't get ahold of something tangible, something that could handle all that was locked inside him.

X slid into the booth directly to the right side of the stage and watched as the hostess placed a slim drink list and a napkin in front of him, leaning forward so her ample breasts jiggled in his face.

She had a ready smile, thin lips, and eyes that looked like she was used to having sex—*normal* sex. That definitely was not what X had in mind. Not tonight.

No, after the day he'd had he wanted—was at the point now where he desperately needed—something more.

So he ordered another Hennessy, straight, and sat back in the booth, waiting for the next act to hit the stage. He watched with one hand on his thigh, close to his semi-erect dick, all the T&A on display, because as far as appetizers went, Athena's was doing a pretty damn good job.

The lights dimmed, and members of the audience began cheering. The next act was about to begin. There came a flurry of lights dancing around the room in slow motion as the first notes of a sultry tune began to play. The spotlight stopped on the pole, shined to perfection. The crowd went wild, jumping up out of their seats already. X remained perfectly still.

He'd picked up a scent.

Her leg appeared first, a strappy silver number with heels that looked too high to be legal. X's gaze followed

her calves down to her toned thighs as she'd kicked her
leg out to line up with the pole. He shifted in his seat,
adjusting his growing length.

The spotlight spread wider, the music's sexy slow
rhythm pulsing throughout the room. Her thighs were
killer, the plump globe of her ass only slightly covered in
silver sparkling boy shorts as she jumped onto the pole
and made a twisting move that put her entire body upside
down, her legs splitting in midair. The crowd roared, but
X tuned out their sounds. Dollar bills were already flying
through the air, but X didn't reach into his pocket to retrieve any of his own. Instead his eyes stayed trained on
the body. She had a milky, heavily creamed–coffee complexion, the hoop ring threading through her navel sparkling as if in response to the crowd. He had no idea what
the material was that was able to hold her heavy breasts
inside the bra that matched her shorts, but the plump
mounds gyrated with her movement, giving everyone
a view of what could possibly be her most prized pos-
sessions.

His breath froze, his gut clenching when his gaze fixed
on her face. She'd just turned so that she was upright;
long, ebony hair slid down her back like a cloak. And
even though her makeup was plentiful, making her look
like an exotic temptation, there was no mistaking who
she was.

Caprise.

His fists clenched on his thighs as his dick threatened
to break free of the zipper that held it back. Questions
filled his mind, but Caprise alone filled his sight. He
couldn't look away, couldn't move to grab her ass off that
stage, and couldn't open his mouth—now salivating with
lust—to yell at her.

Once again she bounced on the pole, this time extending her legs forward, then opening them so her crotch was

displayed—luckily covered by the shorts, he thought with only minor relief. That was short-lived. In the next second she was off the pole, ripping the shorts from her ass to reveal a tiny string with more sparkles disappearing into the curvy cheeks of her ass.

A man tried to jump onto the stage, money in hand. His mouth was hanging open, eyes all but bulging out. X felt his cat roar and slapped a hand on the table in front of him. A bouncer grabbed the man by the collar and yanked him back, dropping him into his seat. X let out a quick sigh. When his gaze returned to the stage her bra had been removed to reveal pasties on her nipples, more sparkling, as if that were what he was supposed to look at. She was basically naked, he thought, swallowing hard in an effort to regain his senses. When her hands grabbed her breasts and she leaned over shaking them to the crowd, X's sharp teeth pricked his lower lip. He wanted her. The thought hit him like a punch to the gut. She licked her finger, traced it along the small patch of material at her juncture, and X had to drag a hand down his face.

The rest of the show was lost on him as he'd stood and made his way to the side of the stage. There was a bouncer there giving him the don't-even-try-it look. On impulse, X flashed his FBI badge and the bouncer, intelligent character that he was, took a step back. Vaguely he realized her music had ended. He was more focused on the fact that she was sashaying her naked ass off the stage. Because the bouncer had taken a hike, X was able to slip through the STAFF ONLY door and was right there the moment Caprise stepped those sex-on-stilts shoes of hers on the floor.

He grabbed her by the arm. "Don't say a word," he warned when she looked up at him in surprise. "Not one fuckin' word!"

Chapter 2

This was not the career Caprise Delgado had in mind for herself. Truth be told, she'd never given a whole lot of thought to what her career goals and aspirations were. Hence the reason she was buckling the strap on her five-inch-heeled Manolo Blahnik sandals in a costume that looked like it was meant more for the hotel room than the stage. There was a contrast here, one Caprise hoped nobody picked up on. Why would a woman who could afford Blahnik shoes be on a stripper pole?

None of your damn business would be her definite reply.

This was her life and she was going to lead it however she damn well pleased. Even if it meant running from the truth.

For Caprise, complaining had been deemed futile a long time ago. For one reason: There was no one for her to complain to. Her parents were dead, and until last month she hadn't seen her brother in five years. Friends weren't on her list of priorities; generally, any type of long-term connection to people was off limits to her. Why? Because pain was an emotion she was too damn familiar with.

She had a trust fund that she'd come into the day she turned twenty-one. Ten million was hers to do with as she pleased. This meant she didn't have to really do anything. But her parents had worked, both of them. Her father had been an architect, her mother a registered nurse. Her older brother, Nick, even though he'd come into his own trust fund when he turned twenty-one, also had a law degree and ran a very successful law firm with his partner and best friend, Roman Reynolds. Just because the Delgados had money didn't mean they were pampered. And it hadn't escaped her that an architect and a registered nurse were actually millionaires. Just one of those questions regarding her family she'd refused to scrutinize.

"Ten minutes, Cee." Yandy Linch, the night floor manager, opened the door to the dressing room she shared with two other girls, said what she had to say, then closed the door again with a bang.

That's how things went at Athena's, hustle and flow, dance and make money. It wasn't the best place in the world to work, but it gave her the chance to do something she'd always loved to do, dance. It had been one of those hidden indulgences, started when her mother had enrolled her in ballet at the age of seven. From there her love of the solitary art had grown, until now she was willing to put on this ridiculous costume and take it back off again, just for the release of dancing.

She'd auditioned for the Dance Institute of Washington when she'd finished college, and had been accepted. Then her parents had died, and her perspective had shifted. Just recently she'd gone back to the institute to see if there were any teaching or intern positions she could take—anything that would keep her in touch with what was once very important to her. In the meantime, she'd slake her need, her one true love, by doing this.

It wasn't all bad, she'd told herself when she'd checked the mirror one last time and left the dressing room. Here at Athena's they loved the Goddess—that was her stage name. Patrons began lining up at the club at nine just to see her eleven-thirty show. She only did one show four nights a week; that's all she'd committed to once she'd come back to town. The owner of the club, Bam Milton, had known her for years. Actually, he'd been one of the only constants in her life so far. But Caprise wouldn't call them friends—more like associates who bumped into each other a lot.

As she walked gracefully on the heels, clicking through the small hallway that led to the stage, she thought about her brother and what he'd think if he knew what she was doing. He'd flip the hell out without a doubt. Then again, Nick was famous for flipping out all the time anyway. Just recently he'd lost it over his female being kidnapped.

That had been wild—these last few weeks, that is. How Caprise had been drawn into the world of the Shadow Shifters once more she had no idea. She'd never owned up to being a shifter, never wanted to and didn't want to now. Yet she was stuck with Seth, the cute and generally nice shifter guard who clung to her like glue and was right at this moment probably lurking around some corner in the club. She was living at Havenway, the new headquarters for Rome, the head of the Stateside Assembly, and his First Female, Kalina. Caprise was not only drawn into their world, she was smack in the middle of it.

Still, to be honest, she didn't hate it all that much. She got to see Nick almost every day. And she was getting to know her sister-in-law, Ary, who would be giving birth to her niece or nephew in the next few months. So there was some benefit to that hulking goof of an FBI agent and Shadow Shifter, Xavier, keeping her locked in that room at Rome's mansion all those weeks ago. He really irked her, X did. Each time she saw him, each time he opened his mouth to speak to her, something inside her moved. His voice slid through her entire body like something infecting her. She couldn't quite put the feeling into words but hated it just the same. Some days she'd go so far as to say she hated Xavier Santos-Markland even if she didn't have an explainable reason why.

Her music started and Caprise closed her eyes, stepped into the world of the Goddess, the persona that was her alter ego. The woman she really wasn't, but secretly was.

As she danced, all thoughts cleared her mind; there was only the music. She always picked slow, sultry songs with piano or violin solos that pulled at the heart. Reached out and grabbed anyone listening, making them pay total attention to her and what she was giving them.

This gave her power. It made the Goddess exactly who she was. She commanded the attention of every male and female in this room; their eyes could not focus on anything or anyone but her. It was like a drug, and tonight Caprise was flying higher than a kite.

As she grasped the pole and pulled herself up, flipping effortlessly until she was upside down, she wondered fleetingly about the first man to throw money on the stage. It was too dark for her to see his face, but she knew he was there. She'd heard his panting as he'd made his way as close to the stage as he could get before tossing the bills.

Where did he work? What did he do? Was he married? Did he have children? A boy and a girl maybe? Did he fuck his wife while thoughts of her ran rampant through his mind?

That question stuck and Caprise slipped from the pole, moving her hips to the rhythm, easing her body down so that her legs were spread wide, her palms touching the floor. She leaned forward then, using her fingers to simulate a crawling motion as she stretched out on the stage.

Rolling over to her back had the crowd roaring again. The music did things to her, rubbed along her like the fingers of a lover. A lover she didn't have.

With the feeling of appreciation and a gentle tug of lust pushing her forward she stood, danced around the pole for a couple more notes, then stripped away her boy shorts, letting the strangers in the dark see what she'd been blessed with. Inside she laughed: They really couldn't see her at all.

When her breasts were all but bared she could hear the crowd getting more excited. The sound of money moving through fingers grew louder. The scent of lust, need, sex, tinged her nose. Damn the senses of a shifter. In one minute she hated them. In the next they were second nature.

They loved her, the crowd out there. Even though not one of them knew her name, the day she was born, her favorite color, her most detested food. They loved her. The Goddess and the myth she created for them.

The song came to an end too soon, her body still humming with energy, with a need still unfulfilled. She picked up her cash, although she didn't need it. On her way back to Havenway she'd have Zach stop her at the local House of Ruth to make her nightly contribution.

Stepping off the stage put her into a different atmosphere. The temperature changed, and she shivered. Where was Norm with her robe? Norm was the stagehand, a young boy with glasses as thick as a beer bottle, eyes so small she almost didn't know they were there. His body looked like he suffered from malnutrition, his face the victim of a total acne attack. But his voice was soft and always layered over the Goddess like warm rain after her performance.

Tonight, he wasn't there.

She was just lifting her arms to wrap them around herself and preparing to walk down the hallway to the dressing room when she was grabbed.

Warning alarms rang with persistence throughout her body. Every nerve standing on end as if she'd touched a live electrical wire.

"Don't say a word." His voice was deeper than she'd ever heard it before, deadlier. When she looked up at him his cat's eyes pinned her for two seconds, totally stealing her breath and any smart retort she otherwise may have come up with.

"Not one fuckin' word!"

He cut his eyes from her after that order, dragging her behind him down the hall until she almost tripped and fell.

This, Caprise thought with exasperation, was not going to end well.

Chapter 3

"What the hell are you doing here?"

Lips of a medium thickness spread into a smile, a leering and maniacal one. Cool blue eyes stared back at him in a way that said it knew who it was speaking to and didn't give a damn. Sabar felt a tiny bit of pride at the shifter, but an even bigger part of him was pissed the fuck off that these creatures thought it was okay to roll up on him, on his turf, whenever they got the damn urge.

"Payback," he said simply. "A concept I'm sure you're familiar with, jaguar."

Sabar moved forward in his chair, letting his arms rest on his desk. His body still hurt, damn that bastard Faction Leader. Shifters had the ability to heal thirty times faster than humans, but there were still some injuries that could be lethal. Especially to a shifter who was being treated by a human medical researcher instead of a doctor trained to deal with the shifter anatomy. But he was alive; that was a good thing.

"Spit it out, I don't have all day."

His guest's response was to laugh, his upper and lower incisors clearly visible. He was a killer. Sabar could see it in his eyes. And he was on a mission. Game recognized game, he thought with an inner chuckle.

"When I get what I came for I'll be gone."

"And what did you come for?"

"It's *who*."

Sabar figured as much. "Then who?"

"She's here. I followed her scent. Her name is Caprise." He passed Sabar a picture.

Sabar took it, rubbing his fingers over the face of the female. She was a looker. Beside him, Darel stood. His second-in-command had healed from his own wounds, probably because his weren't as extensive as Sabar's. Or at least that's what Sabar chose to believe.

"She works at the club," Darel said.

"Get me inside and I'll do what I need to do then get out of your hair."

"Oh, yeah, you need to hurry up and get out of my hair," Sabar said. "What's she to you?"

His hands came up from his lap, fingers clenching together as he bent them back, cracked his human knuckles. "My business."

"My fucking town!" Sabar yelled. "Now, you tell me what your plan is or we kill you right here, right now. Your choice."

He sat back in his chair, rubbed a hand over thick waves of hair, cut short on the sides, left to curl on the top. "She is my *companheiro*," he said simply.

"And who exactly are you?" Darel asked. "You're not from around here—I'd know you if you were. Where are you from?"

"You people have many questions. My name is Rolando. I am from India. That is all you need to know."

Athena's was Darel's territory. It was where he could be the boss without any interference. He'd thought, as he lay on that fucking table across from Sabar, bleeding like a

stuck pig, that he'd never stand here in the glass-encased
tower room that overlooked the stage and the entire first
floor of the club again.

Yet here he was. In his rightful place doing what he
was quickly coming to love.

Lifting a glass of vodka to his lips, he took a slow sip.
He looked down into tonight's crowd, feeling the energy
in the room. He scented the lust and the greed and the
slovenly nature of the humans who walked through the
door paying their twenty-dollar cover charge to get in. Inside the pockets of the men were wads and wads of cash
that they'd happily dump into the hands of each scantily
clad female who graced that stage. Yandy, the female who
had been in charge of the ladies when Darel took over,
would collect 50 percent of whatever the strippers walked
off stage with. Those were his terms, and they were non-
negotiable. The fact that the majority of the dancers were
also fucking his shifters gave them incentive not to balk
about the money they were losing. The sex was a welcome substitute. Stupid humans.

Tonight, Darel wasn't alone in the tower. It was normal
to have Thunder and Black with him, his two newest
backup shifters. They were both mean-ass, fresh-from-
the-jungle jaguars with a penchant for Italian females and
cocaine. The combination could prove dangerous sometimes, but always entertaining for Darel, who after his
last brush with sex had taken to voyeurism. That doped-
up chick Sabar had told him to watch had gone buck
wild, trying to kill Darel as if he'd been the one to give
her Sabar's savior drug—which coincidentally was now
making them a shitload of money. So no, Darel had decided to keep his dick in his pants or in his own palms
for the moment. Besides, watching gave him a new buzz
that he was just beginning to explore.

This dude said his name was Rolando. He definitely

had the look of a man from India with his dark brown skin and ink-black hair. His accent was here and there, as if he'd taken great time to master the English language. And his eyes, Darel didn't trust them. Not one bit.

The one he called his *companheiro* was a stripper here at Athena's. She was new. Darel had seen her on a couple of occasions. He'd known she was a shifter and was waiting until the perfect moment to let her know that he knew. It seems that moment would be tonight as Rolando was intent on having her.

Sabar had given Darel precise commands in this area. Check them both out to see if the distinctive *companheiro calor* was there, then, if it was, bring them both to him. If it wasn't, kill Rolando and bring Sabar the girl because there had to be a reason this foreign shifter was looking for her.

Darel wasn't totally sure how he was going to handle the situation. As of late he'd decided to play things by ear. Sabar wasn't handling his business the way Darel thought he should be. Especially not since Bianca's mysterious arrival.

When the lights went down, Darel took his seat. He motioned with a nod for Rolando to do the same. Thunder and Black would remain standing, ready at the drop of a dime if some shit should jump off.

For the first few moments of the act all the men watched in silence. Probably all touching their elongated dicks as the Goddess worked her magic on the pole. As Darel inhaled deeply he scented that not only was Rolando excited by the show, he was enraged. Darel couldn't help but smile, figuring he'd be jealous as hell if it were his mate on that pole shaking her ass for all these men to see and toss her some money.

Darel had seen her before, knew her routine, the swell of her breasts and the curve of her ass. She was attractive, there was no doubt, and alluring, he'd say, given the way his fellow Rogues seemed transfixed by her.

But all that changed when Darel caught a whiff of something—no, someone—else in the room. He stood, looking down into the dark crowd. With the night vision of his cat he could see as if it were daylight. And the one he searched for stuck out like a cub in a den of lions. Only this cub had massive balls, probably because he was the second hand to the East Coast FL.

Darel smiled again. Tonight was going to be a good fucking night.

After years of searching, hunting, waiting, he'd found her. Rolando looked through the glass, down to the platform where she stood, moving her body, showing herself, and cringed. She was for him, dammit! Only for him!

His *companheiro*. He'd told her this over and over again, and she'd lied to him. Looking him in the eye, declaring her undying love for him, taking him into her body. Then leaving without a word, taking with her a piece of him he'd ever since craved.

But now he was here and there she was. He would have her. He'd traveled far, had begged reprieve from his leader to search for the one who would complete him. He had only a limited time to return or face the wrath of his leader—a thought that was not desirable. So he would not waste time.

Standing, he turned toward the door in which he'd entered. But the two jaguar shifters moved with him, blocking the exit.

"I must get her," he said with intent.

"Sit down until the show is over," the lead shifter here, the one they called Darel, said without turning around.

He was watching her, watching Rolando's mate with a hunger that sickened Rolando. He wanted to tear that bastard's throat out for daring to disrespect him in this manner. But he had specific instructions from his leader not to cause a scene, not to expose himself here in America. Rolando hoped like hell he could keep that promise.

"I want to go to her now," he restated.

"When she's done making my money, you can have her," Darel said.

The two at the door simply smiled, looking beyond him to see his *companheiro* once more.

"Do you not have any respect? She is my *companheiro*," he told them.

The one with the skin as dark as night smiled, his teeth a bright contrast with his coloring. "She's entertainment right now, homeboy."

At his sides Rolando's fingers clenched and unclenched, his claws stinging just beneath his skin as they pressed forward, determined to break free. He bore down so hard on his teeth, his temples began to ache. With a cool and what he hoped was a controlled gaze, he looked through the window once more, watching as Caprise moved across the stage, just about naked. Taunting him with her betrayal and deceit, daring him to come and get her.

Rolando never turned down a dare.

Chapter 4

The door closed, the clicking of the lock sliding into place echoing loudly in the small room. Caprise immediately wrenched her arm free of X's hold. It wasn't easy and had her stumbling back a few steps. But that was good. Space was good.

"How dare you!" she said through clenched teeth. "Do I come to your job to manhandle you? Big idiot! That's what you are," she raged. Then she made a colossal error, and truth be told, if she'd claimed more of her shifter heritage she would have known better. Her instincts would have been heightened, her nostrils alert to the scent of danger.

He'd grabbed her again before she could say a word. Spinning her around and lifting her off her feet, he slammed her ass down on the dressing table with no mercy.

"What the hell do you think you're doing? You're a freakin' shifter, an elite breed, and you're stripping in front of horny men for money. I should paddle your ass good for this stunt. What do you think your brother would say if he saw you tonight?"

His hands gripped her forearms, shaking her every so often as if to reiterate the words he spoke—which really, with a man the size and build of X, was not at all necessary. But there was something else about his touch, another reaction besides the general irritation at his audacity. It was one Caprise had felt with him before, the one that evoked a feeling in her she did not readily accept—desire.

"If you don't get your hands off me you're going to be very sorry," she told him in a low, serious tone.

All sorts of things were roaring through her body: intense lust, pierced by anger and by the interest that Xavier Santos-Markland had been sparking in her since the moment he'd locked her in that room.

"So I can't put my hands on you, but you'll allow strangers to get their rocks off looking at your naked ass!"

He was angry, his cat's eyes said that much. Yellow-rimmed, with a muted green inner layer and pitch-black centers that narrowed to almond shapes and had her swallowing hard. But his touch, even though she'd told him to get off her, this was what was driving her insane. It was making her skin itch all over, had her nipples puckering, her center pulsating. She inhaled deeply, exhaled slowly, and that only made matters worse.

"It's my ass" was the only reply she could come up with.

His scent confused her senses, pushed her buttons until she felt almost frantically out of control. She should be scratching his eyes out, yelling and screaming for help. But she wasn't. Instead she was looking into dangerous eyes, feeling an embrace that was stern, hard, almost painful, and she liked it.

"What if I told you I didn't like you showing off your ass?" His words were punctuated by hoarse chuffing noises that were loud and scraped against a foreign part of her.

Inside, that beast of hers that Caprise ignored on a daily basis rose from its normal perch and stretched. "Not your call," she told him defiantly.

Then he let go of her arms and Caprise almost moaned with missing the contact so swiftly. She should have known he wasn't finished with her. His thick hands roamed down her back until they were under her cheeks, gripping them tightly. Lust speared through her body at an alarming rate. She bit down on her bottom lip to keep from screaming.

"Really," she sighed then shook her head and added more persistently. "You need to take your hands off me." Her eyes closed because his held her as captive as his touch.

God she wanted to run, she wanted to break away from him, knock down that door and run as fast as she could. Because that's what she did best. When things got too hard, Caprise ran hard and long in a quest for what ... safety, serenity, sanity?

She shook her head, her fingers curling over the rim of the table. Running was not an option, not anymore.

"What I need, you little tease, is to taste you."

His words seemed quietly lethal, his voice laced slightly with dread. Was he questioning his own actions? No, not X. He knew what he wanted at all times and had no problems letting everyone else know. Everything about him screamed attitude, dominance, danger. There was no weakness in this man, nothing he ever did that he would end up regretting.

But when he pulled his hands from her ass Caprise was almost certain he'd walk away. He'd say something about telling Nick and yank her ass off the table to carry her kicking and screaming back to Havenway. That's also what he was good at—telling on her then leaving her to bear the consequences, alone. He'd never stuck up for her, never backed up what she said or did, never supported her in any way. Caprise didn't care, it didn't matter what he did or didn't do because he was nothing, nobody.

Until his hands slid to her knees, pushing them apart. X lowered himself until his mouth covered her center. She still wore the sparkly pasty that matched her costume, but he quickly used his teeth to rip that away. With a growl he spit it across the room then returned his face to the crevice between her legs. He pushed her knees out farther, extended his tongue, and licked her long with one powerful stroke.

Her head fell back, smacking against the mirror as she gasped. Breathing was a task as her entire body trembled. His fingers dug into her skin as if he were trying to break her bones beneath. He wasn't gentle, not one bit as his mouth tortured the tight bud of her clit. Something was building in her chest, maybe a moan. No, Caprise did not moan for any man. Ever.

His fingers moved from her knees up her thighs to pull apart the wet lips of her womanhood. He licked her over and over as if he thought to consume her entirely. Then he speared his tongue into her opening and a sound ripped free of her lips. It wasn't a moan, but more like a purr. As good as his mouth on her felt, she wouldn't touch him, she couldn't. Her knuckles were probably white, she was holding on to that table so tightly.

Caprise felt like an entrée at which he seemed overly pleased. Her mind screamed for her to clap her legs shut and get the hell away from him. Her body protested with the arch of her back and the gentle chuffing of her cat, now fully awakened thanks to X's every lick.

With teeth bared the feline was aroused beyond measure. So long it had waited to be summoned, to be allowed to let loose its aura. Much to Caprise's dismay tonight seemed to be the night.

The one thing X knew with startling clarity was that Caprise Delgado was going to be his tonight.

There were issues, reasons why he shouldn't be doing what he was doing, why he should find Seth Jamison—the guard who was assigned to Caprise—and blast his ass for not keeping her locked down tight. Instead of addressing those issues he was drowning in the exquisite taste of her.

He was wrong on so many levels. And normally that admission would be enough to halt him in his tracks. But this, what he felt when he was around her, wasn't normal, he was convinced of that fact.

She was delectable. X had known the minute he saw her again they would end up in this place. The verbal sparring between them over the past few weeks had only brightened the flame that had been smoldering. Seeing her tonight, surrounded by a sexual air, in a room full of horny men and scantily clad women, had pushed him beyond his breaking point.

X needed right now, he needed this as badly as he needed his next breath. And dammit, he was going to take his fill!

When he finally was able to pull his mouth away from her it was to nip at the soft skin of her thigh. When his sharpened incisors touched the light skin, she gasped, hissed a curse.

She did not push him away.

That was key, because if there was one thing X was not into, it was forcing women to do his bidding or abide him in any way. Whatever he did, he did with the knowledge that his partner was in full agreement. And Caprise wasn't telling him to stop. She was, in fact, no longer telling him to get out or to get away from her. What she was doing was creaming for him as if she heard his silent commands, feeding his steadily growing hunger for her. Looking down at her center as arousal glistened over her plump folds, he growled, ready for more.

His gaze raked over her body as he stood full-length in front of her. X snatched those silly things off her nipples, wanting to see all of her right here, right now. Her breasts gyrated with the action and she made a mewling sound that had his gaze flying up to hers. Her eyes were gold, like liquid sunlight, and mesmerizing to both X and his cat, which now scraped at the surface.

It knew there was another cat close; it scented her and wanted just as badly as X did. It was weird, this being part man and part beast. There were two parts he had to satisfy, two parts that were hungry and needed desperately at this moment.

"You ready to come for me?" he asked in his signature deep voice.

She tilted her head only slightly, as if through these different eyes she needed to study him. He was sure his cat's eyes were alight with the hunger it felt and was rewarded by her licking her lips, her own incisors clearly visible.

"You ready to come for me?" was her retort.

His dick grew harder, threatening to break the damn zipper of his pants. Instead X did the honors, pulling his length free then moving his hands to palm both her breasts. He looked down at his dark skin against her light, and even the contrast was arousing.

When her fingers wrapped around his thick length he didn't suck in a breath—even though ripples of pleasure from the intricate piercing he had along the underside of his dick soared up his spine.

"That's right, sweetheart, hold on tight," he said roughly.

She jerked and massaged his dick with the hands of an expert. As he palmed her breasts, fingering her nipples, X's jaw clenched. She'd asked if he was ready to come for her. He was ready for her, period, and hoped she was for him.

His answer came when she leaned forward, scraping her sharp teeth over his shoulder blade, then licking over the spot with her warm tongue. Inside his cat roared, prompting him to mimic her action. When his teeth settled on her soft skin he bit down harder, to the point where he tasted her blood on his tongue.

This was normally where X pulled back, searched the eyes of his partner for any revulsion or fear associated with his actions. Caprise's back arched, her fingers tightened around his dick, and her teeth once again found his shoulder. X licked her wound then scraped his teeth along the line of her shoulder. He squeezed her breasts so hard, if she were pregnant they would leak. And all the while her purring had continued, her breath growing heavier, her body trembling beneath him.

She was enjoying this as much as he was and for X, that was huge.

He pulled back from her, dropping his hands from her breasts and moving them to her rounded ass once more. Pulling her to the edge of the table, he used his thighs to push hers farther apart, then speared his dick right into her entrance. She bucked beneath him, her arms going around his neck to scrape along his back.

Pumping began immediately because he couldn't hold back. Blood roared in his ears as he drove deeper into her. She lifted her legs, locked them at the ankle behind his back.

"Come for me," she taunted, her eyes glittering with arousal as she held on tightly.

He gripped her ass, his fingers slipping into the crevice as he pulled her closer to him. "After you," he replied.

She pumped back, matching his motions stroke for stroke. Her acceptance of his entire length at one time was phenomenal. No woman had ever been able to take him all at once.

He'd thought her taste exquisite; now the feel of her threatened to consume him. She was so wet, her walls clenching him so tightly he almost couldn't breathe. Years ago when he'd decided that piercings could also offer the stinging pain he seemed to thrive on, X had gone to his old pal Geo—who'd done all of the seventeen tattoos on his body—and explained what he wanted. Geo hadn't bristled, just set to work. The four one-and-a-half-centimeter metal balls that had been inserted just beneath the skin of the underside of his penis created exactly the effect X wanted. At the moment of insertion and for a short time thereafter there had been pain, but whenever he was inside a female the pleasure was damn intense and well worth it.

Right now, as he thrust deep and pulled out of Caprise, he felt like roaring, it felt so damn good. Instead he lifted her into his arms and turned her away from the table. She could only hold on to him for support now. And that she did well. Her breasts were plastered to his chest, her wet pussy sucking his dick like a hungry baby. X pumped harder, faster, wanting her release right now.

She didn't moan his name but her nails were going to make a permanent mark on his back, her signature of sorts. Inwardly he smiled at the thought of walking around with a piece of her with him for all time. When she pulled back from him, X moved a hand to the small of her back to keep her steady.

"Now," she said through clenched teeth. "Right now!"

Her words echoed his thoughts as their thrusts continued, the smacking sound of their connection filling the room. He knew the moment her release hit her because her back arched almost all the way back. If she weren't a cat she would have surely broken some bones with this position. But she was, and she was a beautiful feline at that. Her eyes were bright with desire, her body long, lithe, sinewy.

His dick was buried inside her to the hilt, his own release coming seconds after hers began. X had to hold on to her extra tight as the effort racked his entire body, had even his bicep muscles trembling. He'd barely made it to the wall before he felt like his legs would give way.

But they didn't. X held her tight to him as his dick continued to pulsate inside her. She was releasing her legs, trying to push away from him when he bit the lobe of her ear to keep her still.

"Not yet," he whispered roughly. "Not fucking yet."

She lowered her head to his chest, not lying on him, but her forehead resting against him as she gathered her breath. Her hands were no longer on him and X felt her pulling away second by second. The desire was ebbing, if only slightly. In a minute she'd be ready to bolt or to kick his ass, neither of which he was going to stand for.

He had some really bad news for Caprise Delgado—he wasn't leaving this place without her. And if she wanted to argue about that . . . wait. X paused, lifted his head to the air, and inhaled.

Rogues.

Chapter 5

The foreign shifter was right behind him. Black and Thunder were both at his side, until the hallway narrowed out just before hitting the dressing rooms. Darel calculated the odds of him taking the Goddess and Black or Thunder killing the new shifter, Rolando. Odds were heavily in their favor. As he'd come down the stairs his mind had only half been on Rolando and the look of pure rage on his face. The other part of him had been focused on following the scent that came from that fuckin' Faction shifter. After their altercation on the side of the road he'd never forgotten the three of them—the leader with his pompous ass, the second that walked around like the Incredible Fucking Hulk, and the one who'd tried to kill him. His side still ached a bit from the injuries he'd sustained that night. He was healing, albeit a little too slow for a shifter. But Darel wasn't in the mood to question the whys about that. Now he was out for blood—and the Hulk was on his turf.

At the last door near the end of the hallway Darel stopped. Placing both his palms on the door he lowered his head, inhaled deeply over and over again. "They're in here," he said with a growl rumbling deep in his chest.

"What are we waiting for?" Rolando questioned.

"Shut up!" Black warned.

The air was thick with scents, from rage, to feline, to lust, and finally resting on sex. They'd had sex, of that Darel was sure. He didn't really give a damn if the Faction shifter had sex just before he died. Maybe that would make death more acceptable to the big bastard. Rolando would probably go nuts once he picked up that scent, but Darel wasn't in the mood to care.

He took a step back and nodded at Thunder. Darel hadn't been sure how this shifter had gotten his name until he'd heard his growl, which sounded like a rolling clap of thunder that rippled through the sky. That same sound was emitted from the six-foot-one-inch, 290-pound Rogue as he lifted a foot and kicked the door to the dressing room right off its hinges.

X had never run from a fight, not in all his adult life, nor in his life as a shifter. He'd always stayed and fought to the bitter end.

Not tonight.

He scented the Rogues, knew there was more than one, and looked at Caprise—who was still naked, damn beautiful, and glaring at him as if she, too, would like to clamp her teeth into his neck. The decision was already made.

"Let's go!" he told her while he looked around the room for something, anything she could put on.

There was a bag by the table with clothes sticking out of the top. He reached down and grabbed the garments without even knowing what they were or if she could fit into them. "Put this on."

"You are not in control here," she told him.

X heard her words but was too busy kicking out the window across the room from the dressing table where he'd just fucked her to reply. When he turned she was standing there, arms folded across her generous breasts.

"Dammit," he growled, stalking over to her. "I said put it on!"

Ripping the garment from her he found an opening and pushed it over her head. It looked like a shirt, but it was long enough to cover her ass and that was all that mattered. Of course she fought him the entire time, her arms flailing out, her knee coming up to just miss his unsuspecting groin. But X was used to fighting dirty. He bent forward, grabbed her at the waist, and tossed her kicking and screaming over his shoulder.

"You're a big stupid jackass ogre!" she screamed, the effort to get out as many names as she could almost funny to X. Except for the fact that in about two seconds Rogues were going to knock down this door and most likely either take them captive or try to kill them.

X hated having to leave the Rogues behind, especially since they were the original reason he was there. But the risk of Caprise possibly being hurt was not one he was willing to take.

He pushed her through the window first, his palms giving her ass a powerful shove that most likely had her falling into the alley face-first. She definitely would not be happy about that. Going through the window next, X hit the ground then felt her kick at his side and cursed once more.

"Don't put your hands on me again!" she yelled.

Oh, he was definitely going to put his hands on her again, and soon. But right now he needed to get them out of here.

He grabbed her by the waist and pulled her down the alley to where his black Ford F-150 SVT Raptor was parked. Seth appeared out of nowhere, yanking open the back door after X had found his keys and hit the automatic entrance button.

"Where the hell have you been?" X growled at the younger shifter.

"Giving you two some space" was his reply, accompanied by a smirk that X didn't appreciate.

"Give Eli a call and let him know Rogues are in the area. Tell him I want the area canvassed and guards on a scheduled watch for the next few blocks," X said as he opened the driver's-side door.

His personal guard, the one he hated like hell having, Zachary Villareal, looked at him questioningly. Zach was pure Brazilian with a dark sunburned complexion and thick eyebrows. His hair was shaved crew-cut-style, and his specialty was weaponry. If there was a weapon out there that could shoot a missile out of the sky on the other side of the world in the midst of a hurricane, Zach knew about it. Hell, he'd probably invented it.

"What's doing?" Zach asked him.

"I'm driving. You stay here and find out which Rogues are in residence and report back to me."

"I'm supposed to stay with you," Zach insisted. "FL's orders."

He didn't have to add the last sentence because X didn't care. He was the commanding officer in this situation so Zach was going to listen to him. X would deal with Rome's wrath later. Besides, he didn't want anyone to know where he was taking Caprise.

"Just get the hell out of my truck. I'll deal with the FL. I want to hear from you in the next hour with names," he told Zach as the shadow finally relinquished the driver's seat and X slipped inside the truck.

Zach nodded just as Caprise slapped her palms against the back windows. The doors had been locked the moment she was put inside. As trained guards both Seth and

Zach knew the drill; besides, they both also knew Caprise. She was hell on wheels—the shadow hellion, as they'd taken to calling her when neither X, Nick, nor Rome was around. For the most part all the shadows at Havenway thought she should be locked away on a daily basis.

Tonight, X figured, he'd be giving them all a welcome reprieve.

"Stop banging on my windows," he told her as he backed out of the alley.

"You're a jerk," she spat.

X thought a minute before responding. He didn't blame her; he wanted to curse and roar over his actions in her dressing room as well. He'd lost control. And X never lost control. If there was one thing he'd learned in all his years, it was to always remain in command of the situation. It was deadly not to. Yet with Caprise . . . it wouldn't happen again, he vowed.

Instead he replied lightly, "Funny, you weren't saying that about fifteen minutes ago."

"I wasn't being kidnapped fifteen minutes ago," she shot back.

He caught her eye in the rearview mirror and stared. There was more he wanted to say, but his body was too busy warring with his mind for that coveted control he knew he possessed.

She didn't break eye contact. That would be too submissive for Caprise. No, she would meet him round for round, blow for blow, whether it be a verbal battle or a sexual one. X admired that about her, even though he was sure she didn't know that.

She didn't want to be with him, not a second longer. Giving in was a temptation, one that had been taunting her for weeks. She'd imagined how good a lover Xavier would be—because she'd known right off the bat he would be good. Something about his thick build, his muscled body, and that fuck-you attitude he wore like one of his tattoos had told her sex would just be another one of those things he did amazingly well.

And her intuition hadn't been wrong. He'd been hard and fast and potent, all the components she loved when it came to releasing her own sexual frustration.

For some women it was about candlelight and roses. For Caprise, who had learned long ago that romance was definitely for the birds, it was all about instant gratification. X had given her just that. Her release had come like a bullet out of the air, fierce and deadly as it hit her head-on. Her body had trembled and shook with pleasure and then it was over. Simple as that. His high-handed treatment later was over-the-top and she planned to show him that she wasn't the type of female to tolerate such actions. But she hadn't had the chance. He'd thrown her through a damn window then had her stuffed in the back of this humongous truck—which by the way fit X's big bad attitude to a T.

She wanted to jump out and return to Havenway, but that was most likely suicidal considering how fast he was driving.

"You always kidnap women after sex?" she asked, mainly because she'd begun to calm down and accept that he'd probably saved them from a lethal attack. She sat back against the seat and looked out the tinted windows at the evening streets of DC.

"You always ignore the scent of your enemy planning a sneak attack?" was his comeback. It figured it was another question instead of an answer, the bastard.

"I work in a strip joint, there're a lot of stenches going around in there. Besides, I don't have any enemies that would want to attack me." There was an air of untruth to her words, but she ignored that little tidbit of information.

"There were Rogues in that place. Is that normal? Do you know any of them? Since you work there and all."

He could be snide and ignorant and a pompous ass. But he was a damn good fighter. Caprise knew this because Rome would never have made him second-in-command if he wasn't. She knew they were friends, had been since they were younger, along with her older brother, Nick, but Rome was a top-notch leader who expected only the best from his team. If X was a part of that team, a close part, it meant he had to be the best of the best.

If there were Rogues in the club, X could have taken them, Caprise didn't doubt. So why did he run instead?

"You aren't afraid of the Rogues, are you, Xavier?"

She knew her voice was taunting, had meant it to be just that. But she'd also wanted a real answer. She wanted to know what ruffled his feathers—the fierce but contained FBI agent and shifter warrior. What was he hiding behind that persona he so desperately wanted everyone to believe?

But he didn't answer. She should have expected that. When he took the next corner with even more speed and she slid along the backseat because fastening her seat belt hadn't occurred to her, Caprise cursed.

"I'm not afraid of anything," he answered finally. His voice tight, his gaze straight ahead, shoulders squared.

He wasn't lying. Fear wasn't a part of X's makeup, that she knew for a fact. Still, Caprise couldn't shake the thought that there was much more to this shifter than anybody knew. At any rate, it wasn't her job to find out.

"I don't scent anything or anyone." It was an admission, one she wasn't sure why she'd made. She'd come back to DC to take control of her life, but lately she'd been doing and saying a lot of things she wasn't quite sure of.

"Why is that?"

The interior of the truck had developed a chill, and Caprise shivered. She hated being cold; it made her feel isolated, alone, vulnerable, as she had been all those years ago in the Gungi. In her mind there was a slight debate on whether or not she should answer him, then finally she figured what the hell. "Because I'm a human."

She saw him hit a button on his dashboard and watched as a garage door opened. He drove inside and she was treated to a bright-ass light bouncing off stark white walls. There were six parking spots, each one of them already filled with a car or truck. One was even occupied by a motorcycle. At any rate there weren't any available spots. No matter, X put the truck in park and hit another button.

Caprise jolted slightly as the truck began a downward descent. They were sinking into the floor. She looked around curiously as they were lowered into a darker space. When they were once again on level ground he drove the truck another few feet then parked in a corner near a wall with an elevator and a door. She wondered which one they'd be using.

When X got out he took his sweet time coming back to open her door. The minute he did, she jumped out, taking in big gulps of air.

"I don't like confinement," she told him.

He shrugged. "Most cats don't."

It was instinct to reply, "I'm not a cat."

"You are what you are, Caprise. Words won't change that."

He didn't even look at her as he slapped his palm against the elevator button.

"I'm a human," she said when they stepped into the elevator.

"And a jaguar."

She was about to open her mouth to argue but figured it was futile to argue with X. He wasn't the type to yell at a female but he did step in front of her, grabbing her by the back of her head. He was quick, his lips taking hers swiftly, his tongue stroking hers with a heat that licked and relit the fire inside her. Hungrily he kissed her, his teeth nipping her lips, tongue rubbing greedily over those spots. She would have tried to pull away but there was no mistaking the fierce grip he had on her head. Besides, the duel was enticing. She pulled his bottom lip into her mouth, sucked on it wantonly, and was rewarded by his other hand moving to grab her ass.

Caprise took a step, backing him to the wall this time and pressing her body against his. If X wanted to play the sex game he was going to have to learn that she was a top-notch opponent.

Chapter 6

Every bit of lust that had been pent up inside her since she'd returned to DC came pouring out of Caprise tonight. She felt almost desperate for more the moment he touched her. It would have been demoralizing if she thought for one second X was interested in anything more than sex from her. But this was it and it was basic. Basic was safe. Safe, Caprise could definitely handle.

The elevator stopped. In the distance she heard a dinging sound, and the door opened. X grabbed her by the wrists and all but pulled her down the hall. Arousal punctuated his every step, from the way he moved his legs to accommodate the erection she'd felt pressed heavily against his thigh, to the deep rise and fall of his breathing as he tried to keep a lock on things until they were behind closed doors.

Caprise could not deny the characteristics of her own arousal. For instance, she knew for a fact her nipples were hard enough they might actually cut through the fabric of the shirt she wore. She wasn't even going to think about how instantly her juices had begun to flow upon that succulent elevator kiss—but walking down this hallway so quickly produced a cool breeze that was heaven to the heat between her legs.

He had a keycard to open the door, which she thought

was kind of strange since this was clearly an apartment or condo building, not a hotel. Then again, it was even more out of the ordinary to pull into a garage then sink through the floor to another hidden garage.

X was an FBI agent, so who knew what type of gadgets he had. Still, it made her feel like what they were doing or where they were going was some incognito spy nonsense.

X entered the apartment first, then pulled her in behind him. It was dark, but Caprise could see him just fine. She even saw the frown that marred his face when his cell phone rang.

"Is that your girlfriend? Should I leave?" she asked in a teasing tone.

He did not have a girlfriend—at least that's what Ary had told her. She'd acted as if that was the last bit of information she'd wanted to receive, but truth be told there'd been a small pinch of relief when her sister-in-law had made the announcement.

There was no answer from him, just a frown; then he was clicking off his phone. He reached up an arm and touched an almost imperceptible pad on the wall behind him. The room became illuminated.

Caprise turned around instantly, curiosity overriding her questions about his phone call. This was his home. She didn't know exactly how she knew this, just had a feeling—a feeling that was weirdly reaching out to her. Walking away from him slowly, her feet slapped against glossy hardwood floors. The walls all around her were white, sickening white like a hospital or insane asylum. There was a sofa, a love seat, a coffee table, a flat-screen television on the center wall above a fireplace that looked as if it had never been lit, and four framed pictures on the wall. That was it.

She shivered involuntarily but resisted folding her

arms over her chest. That was her protective stance but here, standing in the center of X's living room, Caprise doubted she needed protection. The brooding shifter across the room from her would protect her from any harm. He'd feel obligated to, considering it was technically his job. It was useless, however, since Caprise was perfectly capable of protecting herself. She'd been doing so for years. As far as protecting herself from him went, Caprise knew exactly what she was doing.

"You live alone with hardly any furnishings. It's cold in here." She was making simple statements, acknowledging the facts as she saw them. X looked at her as if she were giving him the time of day and he'd already checked his watch. "I don't like the cold."

"Then I'll keep you warm," he replied immediately coming to stand in front of her.

"What if I say no this time?" she asked, wondering what he was thinking. He looked closed off, as if his body was here but his thoughts might actually be someplace else.

"Then you'll sleep on the couch and continue to be cold."

He didn't shrug, but the implication that he didn't care either way was ripe in the air. So was something else in the air, she thought.

Caprise moved away from X again, exploring his personal space with him not so much as uttering a word. Through an archway was his dining area, a long rectangular space with floor-to-ceiling windows making up one side, more white walls on the other. There was a table about six feet long, marble-topped with thick legs and six chairs to match. There was nothing else.

She peeped into the kitchen and almost smiled at the repetition of design. White walls, stainless-steel appliances, dark granite countertops that matched the dining room table, on the floor large slate-gray tiles instead of glossed wood. His bedroom—that's what had been reaching out to her, she figured, as there was still a tugging in her gut.

He wasn't behind her when she turned, which was only a minor surprise. Usually a good host gave a new guest a tour of his home, or at the very least followed the guest while they made her own impromptu tour. X did neither. Caprise was not shocked.

There were two bedrooms, one she knew instinctively was not his because the door was wide open. Inside there was exercise equipment and another large flat-screen television. In one corner was a U-shaped desk with two desktop computers; one laptop was closed on the end of the desk. The bathroom was huge, decorated in the same slate tile from the kitchen, its shower in the center of the room in a circular shape with glass doors and an overhead showerhead. All around was the color gray: towels, walls, the tub, the toilet, like some higher being had deemed this place a perpetually cloudy day.

In the hall once again she touched a hand to the closed door, knowing this was his personal space. A whiff of dominance assailed her and she looked to the left, where X stood at the end of the hallway, hands fisted at his sides, legs spread partially, chest and head held high. He was daring her and giving her permission all at the same time. She didn't falter, but opened the door and stepped inside.

Here the monotony of the decor was broken. His bed was huge. Then again, it would have to be to accommodate him comfortably. Four thick posters held up the king-size mattresses to a bed that had to be at least a couple of feet off the floor. It looked as heavy as his truck, she thought as she moved closer. There was a huge armoire in the corner closest to the door. All the furniture in here appeared heavy and ornate, like something out of a time warp. It was dark cherrywood and had intricate designs carved inside. The floor was bare and so were the walls, but in this room, amazingly, Caprise was not cold.

"As you can see there's space for two," he said in a gruff tone from his spot in the doorway.

She'd known he was there, had felt his presence close, overshadowing.

"Do two often sleep here?" She was asking about the girlfriend thing again and berated herself for it. She already knew the answer, or at least she thought she did. Furthermore, it didn't really matter. Or it shouldn't matter.

"No female has been here before" was his answer just before there was a knock at the door.

It was a low knock, she knew, but she heard it and so did X.

"Get comfortable," he told her before leaving her alone.

"Yes sir," she mocked him when he was gone.

Touching one of the bedposts, she thought with a bit of smugness, *No female has been here before.* Why did that please her?

Caprise was not into fairy tales. She didn't want any type of happily ever after, with any man or shifter. Not anymore. That was the trouble with first relationships, they had a tendency to leave everlasting scars. She resisted the urge to touch the physical scar left over from said relationship, letting her mind ripple over the mental ones before shaking her head clear of it all.

She climbed onto the bed and was sitting in its center with her legs crossed when X returned.

Innocent, that's how she looked sitting on his big bed, with her slim frame and wild hair hanging past her shoulders. The shirt she wore was huge and hung on her like a curtain. Long luxurious legs were folded together and tucked neatly. Yeah, she looked like a high school kid instead of the alluring stripper he now knew her to be.

"Seth brought your things from the club," he said, putting her purse and the bag with her clothes and shoes in it near one of the dressers on the opposite side of the room.

"He sucks as a guard, you know," she told him when she'd scrambled off the bed to grab her purse. "You shouldn't have been allowed to get near that stage or me, for that matter."

"I'm his supervisor," he told her. He moved to his dresser, taking his cell phone from his pocket and putting it along with his keys on the surface. "And you should have stayed at Havenway."

X had thought the same thing about Seth earlier, but after seeing the shifter already near his vehicle he realized Seth had known he was there all along. And maybe the shifter was doing just as he'd said: *giving them space*. Although X had no idea why Seth would think that was necessary.

"I can go back now if you'd let me out of this gray cell you've created for yourself."

He turned to her then. "You think my house is a cell?"

She was reading something on her phone, her brow furrowed, and for an instant, just a quick second, X scented her fear. In the next moment it was gone; she'd squared her shoulders, put the phone on the dresser closest to her, and flipped her hair over one shoulder.

"You're kidding, right?" She shook her head. "No, you don't kid, nor do you laugh. Okay, yes, this is a cell. It's cold and impersonal and clearly designed to keep people out."

X frowned, hated that her assessment sounded damn close to the truth. "And you were named psychotherapist when?"

She shrugged. "Just an observation. So look, I'm tired. I need a shower, then I plan to sleep. How long do you plan to hold me captive this time?"

He hadn't held her captive before. Sure, he'd locked her into a room at Rome's house, but that was for her own safety. X could say that keeping her here tonight was for the same reason. Rogues had been to Athena's before. X knew this for a fact, because Sabar's savior drug was being sold there. Diamond, the stripper he'd met a few weeks ago and who'd subsequently been killed, had worked at Athena's. She'd recognized the drug with the mysterious symbol on its package. Yet tonight, of all nights, they'd come straight to Caprise's dressing room. Why?

That was a good enough reason to keep her here, in his house, in his bed. But if he were totally honest he'd admit that this was where he'd wanted her for quite some time. Fate had just played into his hand. Since she'd been back Caprise had become his one weakness. Sure, he'd denied that fact for the first few weeks of her return, but X wasn't in the habit of hiding from the truth. He wasn't in the habit of hiding at all. In fact, he hated like hell that he couldn't go back to Athena's and kick some Rogue ass. But for tonight he'd have to leave that to the guards.

"Take your shower then you can sleep in here."

"You don't like to answer questions, do you?" she said with a tilt to her head as if she were actually studying him.

He folded his arms over his chest, not trying to avoid the hardening of his dick at the sight of her long bare legs and nipples poking through the cotton of that shirt. However, he was definitely trying to keep her busy little mind off him. Because it was one thing to want Caprise in his bed, another to want her in his life. Especially that part of his life he didn't even want to claim himself.

"You ask too many," he snapped.

Her gaze dropped, rested on his crotch, and X felt an

extra burst of arousal. She was tempting him, daring him to cross that room and fuck her again. And he could do it. He wanted desperately to do it. But he didn't.

"Get your shower and get some sleep."

When he was walking past her to leave the room she stopped him.

"You don't scare me, Xavier. Your big badass routine doesn't scare me," she told him.

As thoughts of what he wanted to do to her played like a movie trailer in his head, X could only sigh. "It should."

Chapter 7

I KNOW WHAT YOU DID AND I KNOW WHERE YOU ARE.
SEE YOU SOON.

X frowned as he read the text message that had just come through on Caprise's phone. Because it was his nature, he picked up his own cell and punched in the number the text came from. He also emailed it to himself with a note to do a trace first thing in the morning.

The sound of water still running in the shower gave him an extra few minutes. And while X knew it was probably one of the biggest breaches a man could inflict on a woman, he looked through her purse. Among the variety of female things she also had a small handgun and a tube of Mace. As if she knew she needed to protect herself. But from whom? The person who was sending her this text, most likely.

Suddenly he wanted to know who this person was, what he or she was to Caprise, and what she'd done that they knew about. And X wanted to know right now. Putting down both phones, he left the bedroom and entered the bathroom. She hadn't shut the door all the way, part of her I'm-not-afraid-of-you stance, he figured. So X pushed his way inside.

Through the lightly steamed glass he could see her silhouette. His body tightened. She lathered the soap in her hands then rubbed those hands up and down her arms. Her long nimble fingers scraped up her neck. She held her head back and let her hands cross her shoulders. When they came down to cover her breasts, X's breath hitched. She was gorgeous, there was no other accurate way to describe her—even though that seemed kind of cliché.

He took a step closer, his fingers moving quickly to undo his pants. Cursing because his boots were still on, X bent quickly to untie them and kick them off. When he stood again she was facing him, her luminescent eyes staring at him through the glass. Slowly he pulled his shirt over his head, pushed his pants down, and stepped out of them.

She stepped under the showerhead then and let the water sluice over her body, rinsing the soap suds away. Knowledge that he was watching her was alive in her gaze, the fact only making X hunger more. Every inch of his body was taut with need, his dick jutting outward as if it were reaching specifically for her.

When she switched off the water X reached for the door handle. He opened it and she stepped out, coming to stand so close her nipples brushed over his chest, his dick slapping against her stomach. His hands went immediately to her neck, his thumbs rubbing along the line of her jaw.

"You're such a tease," he whispered.

She touched a still-wet finger to his bottom lip, rubbing along its contoured edge. "And you can't resist me" was her soft retort.

Her body was a wanton sex machine, just humming with desire. If he put his hands between her legs at this very moment he'd bet everything he owned that her plump folds would be wet and waiting for him. He could lay her on this floor right now and fuck her brains out and she wouldn't do a thing to stop him.

Yet her eyes, even alight with her feline heritage, said something just a little contradictory. She was studying him, watching everything he did, hearing every word he said with extra-sensitive ears, dissecting this entire situation with a formula only she was familiar with. What did she want from him? Was this all she expected? He hoped so, because it was all he had to give. Questions assailed him as her finger traced his top lip. He extended his tongue to lick the pad of her finger, and she smiled.

"You don't know what you're getting yourself into here, Caprise. I'm not who you think I am."

Her response was to toss her head back and chuckle. He watched long sheets of hair dripping to the floor, flowing behind her. Just as she'd said, he was unable to resist, so X lowered his head and kissed along the exposed line of her neck. When her hands slapped against his shoulders, her long nails scraped along his skin, she whispered in a husky aroused voice, "And you have no idea who I am. That makes us even."

No, X thought as he pushed her down to the floor so that she was on her knees in front of him, they were not even. She was a well-bred, beautiful woman even if she had denial issues. And he was more dangerous than she knew.

He leaned over her, put his palm to the base of her back, let his fingers trickle down between the crevice of her bottom. He stopped at her anus, felt the tight bud and the persistent jutting of his dick. On a coarse oath, he squelched that thought, figuring she was nowhere near ready for him that way. Using both hands to spread her wider, X thrust his dick inside her ready opening.

Caprise screamed with the stretching of her skin and

simultaneously arched her back, pushing back to take even more. This was how she liked it. She wondered how X knew. Soft and slow didn't work for her, hadn't in a very long time. Now she craved fast and hard, long deep strokes that she felt throughout her entire body, vicious climaxes that took her breath away. This was what she needed. Especially tonight.

Through the shower door she'd seen him stripping, watching as every inch of his deep brown skin was exposed. That skin was covered with beautiful artwork that she suspected he took time and consideration to select. Every tat would mean something to a man like X, would symbolize some part of his life, some part of the man. After she'd stepped out of the shower the front of his body was even more alluringly visible. Across his chest was a tribal-type tat with its swirling lines coming to a sharp sword-like peak. Lower, on the left side of his abs, was a jaguar, long and sleek, majestic. His biceps sported more tribal insignias that wrapped completely around the width. She'd noticed them specifically because she was into tat work as well. What she hadn't seen was the emblem of the *Topètenia,* but she knew it was there; somewhere on his body would be that icon, the human marking that her brother and his two friends had gotten as a symbol of their loyalty to the tribe. A symbol of the animalistic part of themselves—the part Caprise continued to deny.

His body was as gorgeous as she'd imagined each time she saw him. Thick, toned muscles, oozing masculinity and power. He was exactly what she thought he was, despite what he said; she knew this man, had known him for years. He was the one of the three who was least expected to be smart and cunning. While Nick and Rome had achieved good grades and headed straight to college, Xavier had graduated with minimal honors and

immediately dedicated his time to the US Marines. Upon
his completion of those four grueling years of training—
as she remembered him explaining to Nick one night—
he'd applied to the FBI. Three years in the field and X
was elevated to special agent status. That wasn't the
norm, but then again, neither was X. And it was no mistake that Caprise had paid close attention to him, even
then.

As he lowered her all the way to the floor, covering her
from behind, something primal was unleashed in her,
something as natural as breathing as she arched her back
and accepted him inside her. She reared back, her head
lifting, mouth opening wide as she screamed his name.
Against her bottom lip, sharp incisors pricked and her
body sizzled with desire.

On the surface it might seem strange that she was here,
in this position, with this man she hadn't seen in years.
But she and X had been making their way to this point for
a long time now. She wasn't surprised, nor was she disappointed. He was an excellent lover, and that's all she
needed.

"Your cat is hungry. She's been asleep for much too
long."

His voice was deep, as deep as his strokes inside her.
She didn't care much for what he'd said but wasn't in the
mood to argue.

"Fuck me!" she ordered instead. If she stayed focused
this would go just like before and she would survive
again.

Strong hands clasped her hips, holding her while he
pounded inside her. She kept her palms flat on the tiled
floor, her knees planted firmly, and rotated her bottom to
match his strokes. Every brush of his dick made her
tremble. There was something on his shaft, she'd felt it

when she'd held him in her hands at the club, some sort of barbing or piercing that rubbed along her sensitive skin with precision and pushed her closer and closer to the brink.

Her nails scraped along the tile as her breathing hitched and her breasts slapped together, matching the sounds of their sexes meeting. Their combined scent was heady, and permeated her senses so that when she licked her lips she swore she could taste him; closing her eyes she could see his warrior's body strong and powerful behind her. He surrounded her, not only because she was in his bathroom but because his aura was that strong, that all-consuming. That was unanticipated.

They reached their climax simultaneously, again. Both of them trembling, taking precious seconds to catch their breaths. Caprise's heart pounded in her chest, sweat peppering her forehead. She focused on her breathing and growing steady enough to stand and walk away from him. But that wasn't working out too well.

"Let's go," he said, wrapping an arm around her waist and pulling her up.

"I've already showered," she said when she saw that's where they were headed.

"Yeah, but you need another one now."

"Thanks for the compliment," she replied snidely, taking the loofah she'd just used and reaching for the soap as he turned on the water.

Like her, he liked the water hot, almost to the point of pain. There were more than a few things she and X had in common, but Caprise wasn't about to comment on them. Saying them aloud might allude to something . . . something she didn't want to think about.

"You're too thin" was his next compliment.

She tried not to bristle, really she did, but it just wasn't in her nature. "You're just full of nice things to say to me tonight. Is that how you usually treat a woman you've had sex with?"

Turning her back to him, she lathered her front and waited for his response.

It didn't come in the form of words, but his strong hands grabbing her shoulders, turning her to face him.

"You're not like them" was all he said.

Caprise didn't take that to mean a good thing, but didn't reply, either. To keep this line of conversation going would mean she cared what he thought of her, or of what they'd done together. And she definitely did not want that. Caring would make this so much more than it was. So much more than Caprise figured she was ready for. Her get-it-together plan didn't include falling for a man, especially not for X.

He'd never slept with a woman before, never wanted to. Having sex with them was like a ritual he'd practiced over the years. Whether it was a hard intense session, or a quickie, X always left first and he always returned home to his own bed where he slept alone.

Yet here it was, a little after two in the morning, and he was lying in his bed, staring up at the ceiling. Beside him Caprise slept with her long, lithe body curled into a fetal position facing him. Her hair was only partially dry, spreading across the pillow like tentacles. She was lovely when she slept—and that was a thought X had never had before. With only his night vision to go on she had a soft glow to her skin; thick eyebrows were arched perfectly, framing alluring eyes even in sleep. Her nose was small, lips pert; she had high cheekbones and a soft jawline.

Something inside X shifted, as if his cat, too, was trying to acclimate itself to this new experience. A thought crossed his mind—he could touch her. Right now, at this moment, as thoughts of her filled his head, he could reach out and touch her cheek, or her arm, or her leg and she would feel him. She'd probably awaken hurling smart-ass words or cursing at him, her eyes sparking with anger. X's dick hardened at the thought.

Her anger, as well as her angelic sleeping trance, intrigued him, touched him on some level that was probably foreign to them both.

With a grunt, X abruptly turned his head so that he couldn't look at her. He remembered the text he'd seen on her phone and the fact that he'd been so distracted he'd forgotten to ask her about it.

More predominantly, X remembered . . . he remembered everything about his life. Every moment that made him the man he was. And he cursed because that man could never reach out and touch a woman like Caprise, or any woman for that matter. He could never afford to simply lie and watch her sleep, to even dream about a life with her.

It simply wasn't possible with a man like him.

Chapter 8

A man like Xavier Santos-Markland should never have been allowed into the Bureau.

He was a liar and a fraud and now, Special Agent Dorian Wilson had reason to believe, a murderer. As a professional courtesy he'd tried calling Markland a couple of times yesterday and last night. Dorian figured he'd set up a meeting, toss out a few questions, and get a feel for where Makland's head was. But he'd never reached him; voicemail picked up every time. If he was a guilty man, that was probably on purpose; if he was innocent . . . well, Dorian wasn't really considering that.

Admittedly the evidence he had against Markland was circumstantial. Still, his gut told him whatever had happened to Diamond Turner was connected to Markland. It was also likely connected to the murder of Senator Baines and his daughter months ago, and those two prostitutes. In addition to these brutal killings, there had been half a dozen other deaths in the last three weeks involving an unknown drug. The DEA wanted to know if Roman Reynolds was somehow linked to the development and distribution of this killer substance. After their initial investigation into Reynolds's law firm they'd found nothing connecting him directly to any cartel in Brazil. But there was definitely a lot of movement coming out of South America. One cartel they were specifically watching was Cortez, even though informants couldn't pin this new drug to that long-running drug empire. It had to be Reynolds, and Markland was one of Reynolds's most trusted confidants.

Some would say Dorian was obsessed. He wouldn't quite take it that far. So what, he'd had this growing file on Roman Reynolds and the law firm he owned, Reynolds & Delgado, for almost three years now. It didn't matter that he'd made a point to get a copy of the Metropolitan Police Department's file on every murder that had occurred in the city in the last twenty-four months. Hell, it was a stroke of luck that his sister was married to a lieutenant in the homicide division or that wouldn't have even been possible. And just because he worked for the Drug Enforcement Agency didn't mean he couldn't also investigate a murder, especially if that murder may very well be connected to a homegrown drug cartel. But none of that meant he was obsessed. Just really, really interested in what Reynolds and his crew were doing.

He parked his car across the street and walked toward the high-rise condominium building that had only been built about three years ago. It was twenty-five stories of glass and steel and futuristic in its crisp and angular design. Reportedly it had cost more than ten million to build and was touted as the new direction of the city. Dorian thought it was a waste of space and money. Why couldn't they have built another school or a recreation center? In his mind there were at least ten million other more sensible things to do with this space and that type of money than to build more homes for the rich.

That fact, to Dorian, solidified Markland's unlawful involvement with Reynolds. He lived here, on the top floor.

How did an FBI agent afford such sweet digs? he thought, slipping one hand into his pocket, using the other to open the double glass doors at the entrance.

His shoes made a clicking sound as he crossed the glossy marble floor. He liked dress shoes, liked dressing up for work, period. That was something that had been instilled in him when he was younger. Yolanda and Stuart Wilson made sure he and his two sisters dressed impeccably for church and wore only the cleanest starched uniforms at the strict Catholic schools they'd attended. Besides, Dorian knew he received more respect than a lot of the other agents because he was always professional about his work and his appearance. This morning, visiting one of his own on suspicion of murder, was no different.

Flashing his badge at the young attendant, he said simply, "Xavier Markland."

The attendant was shaking his head negatively before Dorian could finish saying his name. "No guests after midnight or before eight AM."

Dorian almost chuckled, but he wasn't really in the best of moods right now. "What's this, a frat house?"

First response was a shrug, then he said, "Rules. Besides, you've got to be on Mr. Markland's approved list of guests or we're not to let you upstairs anyway."

Dorian nodded, pulling a wad of money out of his pocket. He wasn't rich, but he tended to carry some extra cash just for situations like these—when, as a sign of the times, the badge wasn't working as well as it should.

He lay three twenties down on the counter with his badge, then pushed his jacket lapel back to expose the nine-millimeter sitting quietly in its holster.

"Let's try this again. Xavier Markland," he said, his voice low and hard as steel.

With a lick of his lips a slow smile began to spread

across the attendant's face. He reached for the money but Dorian slapped his palm over it.

"Mr. Markland?"

"Take the second elevator up to the nineteenth floor. There are two elevators all the way to the back of that hallway. Take one of those to the penthouse. He's the only one on that floor. And if he asks, tell him I wasn't at the desk when you came in."

Moving his hand away from the cash, Dorian retrieved his badge, pushing it into his pocket. "Won't you get in trouble for not being on your post?"

"Probably get written up," the attendant told him. Then he looked straight at Dorian, a serious expression marring his face. "But Mr. Markland will kill me if he finds out I took money to let you in."

Dorian nodded, letting the words *Mr. Markland will kill me* play over and over in his mind as he headed toward the elevator.

"Where the hell is she?" Nick Delgado asked Eli and Ezra Preston the moment he saw them in the dining hall.

They were the twin guards assigned to Nick and Rome. Last night, however, they'd been called away from Havenway to assist at some nightclub in the city named Athena's. Nick hadn't grumbled too much because it was two in the morning when he'd received the knock at his bedroom door and the announcement that there'd been a Rogue sighting. On any other night Nick would have happily climbed out of his bed and headed out with the two Lead Guards, but Ary was just entering the sixth week of her pregnancy and since neither of them had ever experienced this miracle before, Nick was inclined to stick as close by her as he could.

It wasn't until this morning when he'd spoken to Rome that he'd learned the full extent of the story. Rogues had indeed been sighted at Athena's, where Caprise had apparently been working as a stripper.

That last fact was still hard for Nick to swallow, and his temples throbbed incessantly with the effort. Rome was sitting at the desk in his home office. Both of them lived at Havenway now, their refuge from the city and all the attention that had come to Rome's estate just about a month ago. The facility was still undergoing construction, but to date was coming along nicely. Nick, however, did not plan to stay here indefinitely. He wanted his own house for Ary and their family. And he definitely did not want to remain in hiding from the world they deserved to live in just as much as the humans. Still, he understood that, for now, the safety of his wife and child came first.

"She's not here. We checked her room and she didn't come home at all last night," Eli replied, slipping his aviator jacket onto broad shoulders covered by the fitted T-shirt he wore.

Eli was the more somber twin. While his green eyes, mocha skin tone, and cleft chin mirrored Ezra's, he wasn't as flamboyant and outgoing as his brother. That was most likely the reason he'd been assigned to Rome as soon as he'd been appointed Faction Leader. With Nick's enigmatic personality and previous popularity with the females, Ezra was the best pick for his guard. Even though, right now, Ezra was keeping a tight lip, probably because he knew Nick was very close to going off totally.

"Where the hell is Seth?" he asked, keeping a tight rein on his temper. Once upon a time this would have been a task for Nick, but since finding Ary again, his temperament had taken a less volatile edge. Today remaining calm was proving difficult. And who could blame him? Caprise was his little sister. Before a month ago she'd been gone for five years and he hadn't known where she was or what she was doing. Then she just showed up, with secrets in her eyes and a chip on her shoulder as big as a damn boulder. Now she was missing. They couldn't blame him if he wanted to break something or someone in two to find out where she was.

"Seth checked in already this morning. He says she's safe," Ezra told him.

The guard stood across from Nick, about four feet away. He wore black slacks and a white silk shirt. His jacket was probably in the car. Since Ezra accompanied Nick everywhere, he tended to dress for the occasion. Today being a workday, he would be in a suit going to the office. The diamond studs in both his ears sparkled even as his gaze toward Nick was serious.

"Did he say where she was? Where they are?" Rome asked sitting back in his chair.

Rome had been the Faction Leader for almost ten years now. He'd been Nick's best friend for even longer. Rome knew Nick's moods just as Nick knew his. Right now the FL was concerned for Caprise and reserving judgment on this current situation.

For about two seconds Ezra looked uncomfortable. The guard exchanged a look with his twin, and they both finally shrugged.

"If you know something, you're bound by your duty as Lead Guards to tell me now," Rome said tightly. "Not to mention the fact that you're as close to us as brothers. Nick deserves an explanation if you have one."

Ezra nodded. "You're right, boss. Look, Seth called last night or early this morning, and said that X had taken her to his place. When he checked in this morning he said they were still there, had been all night."

The room was quiet and still except for the buzz of irritation that filled its space.

"Okay, she's with X so she's safe," Nick said, even though something about that statement seemed a bit off to him. "So get X on the phone and find out when they're heading to Havenway."

Ezra nodded. "Right."

When the two guards left the room Nick stood for a few moments at the slim window looking out to the Great Falls National Park. That was where Havenway was located, deep within the park, hidden by dense trees and a small creek that almost gave the impression of their home in the Gungi. Well, not almost, but probably as close as they were going to get. The Virginia location was about an hour and a half away from their law firm in DC.

"What are you thinking?" Rome asked.

"Something's not right," Nick replied immediately. "Why didn't he bring her back here? Why keep her in the city? And what the hell is she doing stripping?" He figured he'd be the one to approach the subject since he knew Rome was probably thinking it.

When he turned to look at his friend he was rewarded with a look of relief on Rome's face.

"I wondered that myself. Do you know where she's been for the last five years?"

Nick rolled his neck, listened as muscles cracked with the effort, and tried to let his shoulders relax. "She didn't say, I told X to look into it but he hasn't gotten back to me with a report. I know she's always loved to dance and was even enrolled in dance school before she left. This just doesn't sound like Caprise."

Rome nodded. "She seems different now. I've noticed it in the weeks she's been here."

"Ary's been talking to her. She thinks Caprise is starting to adjust. But I don't know," Nick admitted.

"She's still not happy about being a shifter, that we all know for sure."

Nick shook his head. "She's never been happy about

that. I thought at least she'd come to terms with it by now. But she's still in denial."

"Which isn't good for us if there are Rogues roaming the streets, out for shifter or human blood," Rome stated.

"X was investigating Athena's because Sabar's savior drug was reportedly circulating there."

"You think she may be taking the drug?" Rome sounded skeptical but the question still stung.

"No," Nick replied adamantly. "She's not on any drugs. I would know." Or at least he thought he would.

For the last few weeks he'd seen Caprise every day. Some days she looked almost happy and others she was sullen and agitated. Yesterday he remembered she'd made some remark about their parents and everyone having secrets. He'd been running late for work and so hadn't stopped to ask her what the hell that meant. Now he wished he had.

"It's just a thought, man. I know she's your sister but we've got to keep an open mind about this. I don't believe in coincidences," Rome said.

"So the fact that Caprise was stripping at the same club X was investigating for the savior drug and they run into Rogues there is all connected?"

"What do you think?" Rome asked.

Nick sighed. "You're right. It's connected. I just hope—"

His next words were cut off as his cell phone rang loudly. Reaching down to the case at his waist, Nick pulled the phone free and answered, "Delgado."

"Nick, it's me, Caprise."

She was talking fast and she was whispering. Nick was instantly on alert.

"Where are you? What's wrong?"

"I'm locked in the bathroom at X's place. Some cop just came in talking about arresting him for murder."

"What?"

"Just get over here as soon as you can!" she said. Then the line went dead.

Rome had already stood and was glaring at Nick when he clicked off his phone.

"What's up?"

"X is being arrested for murder," he replied quizzically. Then he turned and quickly left Rome's office.

The pounding at his door was incessant and irritating as hell. X rolled out of the bed cursing fluently as he moved through the condo, heading toward the door. He wasn't wearing anything but the scowl he knew was on his face, and whoever was at his door at this ungodly hour deserved to get a damn eyeful.

After disengaging the locks he pulled the door open and was shocked to see Agent Dorian Wilson standing on the other side.

Agent Wilson was likewise shocked to see X in the state he was in, as witnessed by the widening of his eyes then the setting of his features.

"Mornin', Agent Markland. I need a word with you," he said. "But I can wait until you're a little more decent."

X stepped to the side, letting the agent into his home. No apologies, no words. He just let him in and stalked back to his room to throw something on. Caprise was still asleep, thankfully. The last thing he needed was her questions on top of asking himself why Agent Wilson was here in the first place—which, by the way, was a good goddamn question.

He remembered this guy as the one Kalina had been working for to look into Rome's financial dealings. His entire profile had come up in the database search he'd done on Kalina. He was a thirty-three-year-old native of the DC metropolitan area; single, two siblings and parents still living. Eight years with the DEA, army four years, three years MPD, and elevated to DEA after one major drug bust. Those were the immediate details coming to X's mind. The question of the hour still remained: Why was he here in X's apartment, right now?

Upon his return to the living room he saw the agent studying one of the black-and-white pictures on his wall.

"It's South America," he offered, crossing the room to take a seat on his couch.

Agent Wilson nodded. "Been there recently?"

"I've got family there" was X's reply. "What can I do for you, Agent?" he asked because this small talk wasn't going to work well for him.

Wilson turned around, keeping his eye on X as he crossed the room to sit on one of the remaining chairs.

"I have some questions for you, Markland."

Not *Agent* Markland, X noted. Suspicion wasn't a scent X smelled often. But he knew it when it was circling around him like vultures over a carcass. With practiced ease X kept his face and emotions blank. He stared back at the agent and said, "Ask your questions."

"Do you know a woman named Diamond Turner?"

X remained perfectly still while inside his cat paced, watched, and waited. "I met her about a month and a half ago. She was standing outside of Athena's."

"Did you see her again after that?"

"No."

"Did you have any contact with her after that night?"

"No."

Wilson didn't believe him. X could see it in his eyes, never mind the ever-growing stench in the room like rotting vegetables.

"Why?" X asked in return.

Wilson waited a beat, sat back, and rubbed a finger over his clean-shaven chin. "She's dead," he said matter-of-factly.

Again, X was sure not to show any emotion at all. Of course he knew Diamond was dead, had seen her body himself at the morgue. None of that came as a shock to him. The fact that Wilson was here in his living room asking him about it was.

"And you're here telling me because?" X asked.

Wilson wasn't any superior of his; they were both special agents working within their own government agencies. For years X had worked in the human trafficking department in an attempt to stop the ever-growing trade. It also gave him time to work off the anger that still boiled in his system at the thought of helpless females being repeatedly abused by men who were supposed to be their saviors.

Wilson, on the other hand, worked with the DEA, in the international drug trade. Diamond's neck had been bitten almost in half. She had nothing to do with international drugs. At least X didn't believe Wilson knew what her link to international drugs was. Otherwise, he wouldn't be sitting in X's living room looking as if he were really about to arrest him. Then again, if Wilson had some idea of what drug Diamond had taken and if he knew about Sabar and his twisted gang of shifters, then it might lead him back to X. But X doubted the latter very seriously.

"This was found with her things," Wilson said, flicking a business card between his fingers.

He didn't extend it for X to see and X didn't need him to. He knew it was his and almost cursed. Instead he did what he always did when faced with bullshit. He shrugged.

"So she had a business card."

"She had *your* business card. A special agent with the fuckin' FBI. You want to explain that to me?"

So Wilson's calm, cool, and collected exterior could be ruffled. X had figured as much. They'd both been taught to bluff with the straightest face possible, to play everything close to the vest and remain professional. X would hold up his end of the bargain.

"No. I don't want to explain it to you. I told you I met her one night and didn't see her again after that. There's nothing more that I have to say."

X stood as he spoke. "Now if that's all you wanted to ask."

Wilson stood as well. "You're really going to make me take this route?"

Again X shrugged. "What route would that be?"

"I can get a warrant, search your place. Then I can arrest you, have you indicted in a capital murder case. You'd lose your career, your life as you know it now, everything."

"Or," X said, taking a step closer to the agent, "you can put that card back in your pocket and walk your ass out of my house. I'm done talking to you."

"If it was personal, I can try to help you. Maybe we can work something out with the director," Wilson insisted.

Dorian Wilson was about six feet tall. He had a deep brown complexion and dark, generally honest eyes. His frame was strong; he worked out regularly. He was a damn good agent. X was also willing to bet his next paycheck that Dorian was here with more than suspicions about Diamond Turner's murder.

"I don't need to work anything out. But you definitely need to go."

Wilson shook his head. "This isn't going to go away just because you don't want to deal with it. I'm going to keep digging because I know something's going on with you."

"Then get out your best shovel and have at it" was X's flip retort.

He was very close to losing his cool with this guy. How dare he come up in his house asking him everything but if he'd killed Diamond himself? Obviously he had nothing besides that business card to go on, so X wasn't giving him the time of day.

Just as they reached the door and X opened it, Nick was strolling down the hallway, sporting one of his designer suits and a royally pissed-off look on his face.

Chapter 9

"Do you have a warrant?" Nick asked Agent Wilson.

"Not yet" was Wilson's tight reply. He wasn't looking very pleased with the new arrival.

Nick nodded. "Then you were just leaving. Here's my card. If you need to speak to my client again you go through me."

Wilson took the card Nick extended to him, giving both Nick and X a very pissed-off gaze.

"I'm not through with you yet," he told X.

"Fine. But you're wasting your time," X told him with a serious glare.

"Like I said, get in touch with me if you need something else from my client."

Nick was using his best lawyerly voice. X would have laughed at how polished and professional his friend sounded, when his usual dialogue was about kicking somebody's ass. But he refrained.

"Right," Wilson said, giving Nick a nod, then walking out the door.

The same door that Nick subsequently slammed so loud X thought the windows that lined the entire side of his apartment might break. He didn't bother to stand there and wait for Nick's tirade. Instead he walked into the kitchen and reached into the fridge. It was still early, but he definitely needed a drink to deal with what was about to take place here.

X pulled out a bottle of beer and twisted the cap off, taking a deep swallow as about two minutes later there came a quiet knock at the door. On a curse he heard Nick's dress shoes clicking across his wood floors. Then he heard the door open and close once more. X began counting, had only gotten to five when Nick and Rome walked into the kitchen.

"What the hell's going on?" Rome asked first.

Nick was shaking his head. "More important, where the hell is my sister and why didn't you bring her home last night?"

X rubbed his free hand down his bald head and took another swallow of beer. "Number one, I don't know what's going on. I suspect they think I killed Diamond Turner, the stripper from Athena's I met a while back."

He was already walking out of the kitchen, a very angry Nick and a perplexed Rome following behind him. When he was once again sitting on the couch, X emptied the beer. "And two," he stated, looking directly at Nick, "I wanted to keep Caprise safe. So I brought her home with me." Not entirely the truth but he figured if he'd said, *I wasn't finished fucking your little sister, that's why I brought her home with me,* things were going to go to shit pretty fast.

"Safe from what? What were you even doing at that club?" Nick asked, standing directly in front of X.

Rome touched a hand to Nick's shoulder. "The fact is that Caprise is safe. Right?" Rome asked, looking around the room.

"She's still asleep," X said, then thought about his words again.

Nick was shaking his head. "Negative. She's locked in your bathroom. That's where she called me from when she heard somebody talking about arresting you. That's why we used Rome's helicopter to get here as soon as possible, to keep your ass out of jail."

"Fuck!" X stood and placed the bottle on the coffee table. He was about to walk back to his bedroom when Nick grabbed him by the arm.

"Whoa, you have some explaining to do first."

"Get your hands off me, Delgado," he said, a rumbling in his chest signaling his cat was damn tired of sitting on the sidelines.

"Just calm down, both of you clowns."

That was Rome, always the negotiator, the problem fixer, the fucking Faction Leader.

Both Nick and X stood still. X looked down at Nick's hand on his arm then back up to Nick.

Begrudgingly and with a look that clearly said this wasn't finished, Nick yanked his arm away. "You and I are going to have a conversation," he told X.

X thought about flipping Nick off, which wouldn't have been out of the ordinary. It wasn't as if they were planning some big-ass shifter wedding in the rain forest like Rome and Kalina had, or even a quiet ceremony at Havenway like Nick and Ary had shared not too long ago. No, he and Caprise had just had sex—some damn good sex, but still, just sex. Nick was X's friend; they were even closer than friends; the three of them were like brothers. They'd been there for him when he needed them and hadn't asked any questions. For that X would always be grateful. And it was that gratitude that wouldn't allow him to disrespect Nick by brushing him and his concern off totally.

"First, Caprise is obviously okay because she was able to call you, Nick. Second, I want to know everything that happened at Athena's. Then I want to know what that

cocky-ass DEA agent who used Kalina in his sham of an
investigation was here questioning you about."

Rome had taken off his suit jacket and thrown it across
the back of the love seat. He was loosening his tie as X
came to stand by the fireplace. With his arms folded over
his chest, he looked directly at Rome, who had now sat
down.

"I wanted to see what was going on inside the club. We
know Sabar's running his drug through there, so I wanted
to check it out. When I got there, Caprise was dancing,"
he said, casting a glare at Nick. He wasn't sure if Nick
knew about his sister's occupation. No, X was certain he
didn't. And the curse that came from Nick the moment he
said it confirmed that notion.

"I waited for her to get off stage then took her back to
her dressing room to question her." He omitted the rest
for everyone's sake.

"Question her about dancing or the drugs?" Nick
asked, as if he had to in the first place.

They were like family . . . except Caprise wasn't related by blood, which meant he could sleep with her and
remain loyal to Nick. Or at least he hoped so.

"I questioned her about the dancing. Up to that point I
hadn't seen any drugs—or any Rogues, for that matter.
Then the scent came. They were coming to Caprise's
dressing room."

"For what? Does she know any of the Rogues that fre-
quent the club?" Rome asked.

"She wouldn't associate with Rogues," Nick said.
"She'd kick 'em in the balls and laugh in their faces."

X did chuckle at that, even though he was feeling anything but happy at this moment. "You're right about that.
But no, she said she didn't know who could have been at
the door. And I didn't stick around to find out. My first
concern was getting her to safety. So we jumped through

the window. Seth and Zach were already waiting at the truck. I left them there to keep watch and brought Caprise back here."

"And at no time did you think it was necessary to call me and let me know?" Nick questioned, jamming his hands into the pockets of his dress pants and staring at X as if he could pounce on him at any moment.

"Last time I checked I was a grown-ass man. I don't have to check in with anyone" was X's heated retort.

Rome held up a hand to stall Nick's next comment. "Okay, so Caprise has been dancing at the club. Has she seen anything useful to us?"

X shook his head. "I don't think so. Then again, she's not really looking for Rogues. She's sort of doing her own thing."

"Yeah, shaking her ass for the public," Nick chimed in.

"I'd tread lightly in that area if I were you," X warned him. "She nearly bit my head off when I commented on her occupational choice."

"That's because it's none of your damn business," Caprise said, entering the room wearing skintight jeans and a T-shirt so tight it made X's mouth water.

"It's my business if you're out there trying to get yourself killed," Nick fired back. "What is this stripping thing you're doing?"

Caprise made her way to the center of the room with one hand on her hip, the other pointing a finger at her brother. X could only shake his head. Whatever she was getting ready to say, she meant business. How they were all going to deal with that, X had no idea.

"I'm an adult. I can do whatever I please. And for your information it's called exotic dancing, not stripping, you idiot."

Rome covered his mouth and gave a fake cough to hide that he was chuckling. X stood behind Caprise.

"I don't think they were coming after her. If I scented them it's believable that they scented my presence as well," he said, trying to take the heat off Caprise. He'd never defended a female like this before. Sure, he wanted to protect all females, especially shifters. But this, it was a little different.

"How long have you been dancing there?" Rome asked.

"About three weeks," she replied evenly.

For as candid and sometimes rude as Caprise could be, she always respected Rome.

"Has any Rogue ever approached you?" the FL asked.

"She's not on the lookout for them like we are," X replied.

Rome stood. "But she can still scent them if they're near. Have you ever been near a Rogue at that club?"

"I don't think so. But he's right, I'm not looking for them. I go there twice a week, do my dancing, collect my money, and go. I don't hang out there on a regular basis, and I don't socialize with anybody while I'm there."

"They could have scented you," Rome agreed, looking at X. "And if so, they're damn bold to come after a commanding officer."

"Probably figured he was alone so they had a good chance of taking him down," Nick said.

His voice sounded deceptively calm. Then again, X doubted that Nick had put two and two together to equal that he and Caprise had actually slept together last night.

"Well, if you guys want to continue talking about your secret society crap that's fine with me. But I'd like to go home and get changed. Is Seth here to take me?" Caprise asked.

Rome nodded. "Seth's downstairs."

"I'll take you back to Havenway," X replied.

"That's not necessary," she said with a toss of her hair over her shoulder.

It was the first time she'd looked at him since she came into the room. Yet it felt like she was looking right through him.

"I said I'll take you home," he insisted.

"And I said it's not necessary," she said, slower, more intensely. "Look, don't get any fancy ideas about what happened last night. You and I are on the same terms we were before. Okay, so maybe we're not total enemies, but I'm not into the possessive shifter crap all you guys have a habit of pulling."

Before X could reach out to stop her Caprise headed to the door. And a strong hand on his shoulder told him he wasn't finished with the conversation with Nick and Rome just yet.

"You fucked my sister!"

There was no escaping Nick's fury, and X didn't really try. It happened and it was done, just like Caprise said. Nick would have to accept that and move on.

"We're adults, Nick," he said with a sigh.

Rome had sat back down, shaking his head, using his cell phone to most likely alert Seth that Caprise was coming down. The guard would be in the lobby the moment she stepped off the elevator. From that point on he wouldn't leave her side again until they hit Havenway.

"She's my sister, X. You don't just do your friend's sister and think that's okay."

He had a point there, but X didn't care. He wasn't explaining himself to Nick or to anyone else. For him, explanations had died the day that dirty bastard Jeremiah had.

"Okay, Nick. I slept with your sister. Now can we

move on?" He'd really wanted to be able to tell Nick about last night himself, but Caprise apparently had other ideas. He should have known she would.

"No, we cannot move on. You don't have a mate, X. You have sex and it's not even casual sex. You have fucking escapades that could easily leave the other person hurt. My sister is not one of your playmates. She's not some whore for you to screw any way you like."

And there it was, X thought with growing fury. Since he'd had his first shift at the age of fifteen, X had known he was different. He'd felt it in the air he breathed. When he began feeling the gnawing sexual urges of the *Topètenia* he knew that he'd be different in that respect as well. His history had already pre-ordained that fact. Finding willing partners wasn't easy at first—young females tended to be afraid of his darker sexual urges. But as he'd grown older it seemed more doors had opened. Anal sex wasn't taboo anymore—whips, chains, stimulators, nipple clamps, role playing, none of that was out of the question. It was the norm for him and for those who kept his company. Nick and Rome knew all this and had never said anything about his preferences. Until now.

"It was consensual, you bastard. And I'd never hurt her," he told Nick through clenched teeth once he'd gotten right in the shifter's face.

"She doesn't deserve to be treated like that," Nick retorted.

Rome stood then, moving to separate the men. "All right, let's take it down a notch. X is right, Nick. Caprise is an adult and she looked just fine to me when she strolled out of here."

"That's not the point," Nick said.

"It's the point for now," Rome told him. "What they do is their business."

X didn't back down, but he did look away. He hadn't

wanted this confrontation with Nick, hadn't wanted to walk down this road with him. But not touching Caprise had not been an option. So he'd deal with the repercussions.

"I asked you to look into her whereabouts for the last five years. Did you do that or where you too busy thinking about how quick you could get into her pants?" Nick asked tightly.

"I'll find out where she was and what happened," X said. He'd already decided that would be his priority today, especially after he'd seen that text message on her phone. But that was before Wilson had made his appearance.

"And keep your hands off her," Nick stated adamantly before walking to the door. "Don't talk to Wilson without me present, either," he yelled on his way out.

The door slammed again and X ran a hand down the back of his head.

"You've had one hell of a night," Rome said, his voice much lighter than Nick's had been.

"Tell me about it," he said, sinking down onto the couch.

Rome looked down at him. "It had to be Caprise, huh?"

"Man, I couldn't have prevented that even if I wanted to. You ever had someone that just got under your skin, instantly, like a disease?"

Rome smiled, nodding. "Yeah, I've had someone like that."

"No," X replied quickly. "Don't get it twisted, I'm not falling into the mate and joining trap like you and Nick have. I just meant, it was like a hunger that I had to feed."

"And are you full now? Have you had your fill?" was Rome's question.

X didn't reply. Something told him that whatever he

said wasn't going to be perceived the way he meant it, so he remained quiet.

"Look, you know how Nick is. And I know how you are. We've got some serious shit going on around us, so I'd like for you two to keep this personal thing on the down low while we figure out what to do about Sabar."

X nodded, understanding that as the FL, Rome had priorities. "Diamond died at the hands of a Rogue. Probably someone close to Sabar's camp because she had a lot of that savior drug in her system. She didn't look like she was carrying the type of money needed to buy it. I'll try to talk to those other females at the club."

"No," Rome said quickly. "You stay away from Athena's. That's just ammunition for Wilson to get that warrant for your arrest. I'll have a couple of other guards start hanging around down there, see what they can find out."

"And I'm supposed to do what? Sit around here and wait for Wilson to make his next move?" X asked, not liking the sound of that.

Rome nodded. "I've got a hearing at ten, then a meeting with a client this afternoon. You call Bas and find out if his captive has started talking yet."

"I can do that," X told him. He'd make the call to the Mountain Faction Leader, Sebastian Perry. Afterward he'd head out to Havenway because the answer to Rome's question was—X hadn't gotten his fill of Caprise Delgado.

Chapter 10

The ride back to Havenway seemed ten times longer than it ever had before. Caprise sat in the back of Seth's silver Jeep Wrangler, which had been redesigned and fitted with top-notch technology and weaponry on Nick's orders. It wasn't just for her safety; all the guards were now being given these vehicles complete with tracking devices and self-destruct commands in case any of the vehicles should ever fall into the wrong hands.

Nick was in charge of security for the East Coast Faction and because Rome was now the head of the Stateside Assembly, his ideas were usually implemented throughout the four zones. The Shadow Shifters were assuming a strategic role in the States, unbeknownst to the humans who believed they were the ruling species here.

Laying her head back on the seat, Caprise fought to push those thoughts from her mind. She didn't give a damn what the shifters did. She wasn't one of them. Or at least she'd never wanted to believe she was. It hurt too much to be different. Having your classmates hate you because you can outrun them in gym class, or because you could smell their backstabbing lies before they had a chance to catch you in their traitorous trap, wasn't fun. The decision to stay to herself after tenth grade was one Caprise made to keep her own sanity, as well as to keep from hurting someone with the unnatural instincts she possessed.

As time progressed she realized that being different caused pain on more levels than she ever could have contemplated. Her parents, for instance, died young. In a car accident—which seemed innocent enough, but there were secrets and whispers and reasons for Caprise to believe that their differences were what had really led to their deaths. After the funeral she found herself despising her genetics even more than before.

Which was why the fact that she'd run to the Gungi was still a mystery to her.

The jeep came to a stop and she hurriedly pulled on the door handle to get out. Seth was at the door when she stumbled from the backseat.

"A lot of help you are. Leaving me with crazed shifters when you're supposed to be my guard," she was muttering to him as she stalked up the stone path that lead to the side entrance of Havenway.

The front of the facility looked like an old abandoned warehouse, even though it had been almost completely rebuilt from the inside. Discretion was key, so they'd opted against remodeling the outside. Nobody entered through the front door, and the place was secured by an alarm system as well as being sensor-protected. There were two side entrances and one underground entrance accessed from the back.

Most of the jeeps parked along the back side, or went underground to the garage there. But Seth had parked in the trees. Caprise knew this was for her sake, so she wouldn't have to walk the distance to the door or take the elevators from the garage. Still, she was too pissed off to even thank the guard for that consideration.

For all intents and purposes she had no problem with Seth. He was just above six feet tall, with a strong, wiry frame and dark, intense eyes that she figured some female would find alluring one day. Right now, however, he wasn't so alluring as he followed her up the walkway.

He didn't reply to her remark. He never did. Which kind of irked her because Caprise loved a good argument, or even just a heated exchange at least once a day. It made her feel like her life wasn't as out of control as it really was. When she was close to the door she heard him mumbling and figured he was speaking into the two-way communications link all guards wore in their ears 24/7. There was a loud click and then what sounded like a boulder being dropped slowly from a cliff as the heavy reinforced steel door opened.

She stepped inside and was welcomed by the cool air-conditioned environment of Havenway. Somebody said good morning; Caprise didn't reply, just kept walking. Havenway consisted of lots of long halls, with doors everywhere. She still had no idea what was behind every door and didn't really care. Her room was on the second floor, down another corridor. She took the stairs at the end of hallway number two and walked with quick strides. Her goal was to get inside her room without having to see or speak to anyone. As soon as she punched in the code to her own private quarters and pushed into the room she began to breathe a sigh of relief.

Too fast, too soon.

"Oh, Caprise, I'm so glad you're back. Were you hurt? Should we go down to the medical center to have a look at you?"

Aryiola Delgado with her beautiful amber-colored eyes, long streaked hair pulled into a ponytail, and protruding belly, stood in the center of Caprise's bedroom rattling off questions as if this was the start of some great inquisition.

Caprise dropped her bag and purse and pushed her door closed tightly. "I'm fine, Ary," she told her sister-in-law.

In the weeks since she'd returned and moved into Havenway, she and Ary had become friends, somewhat. For Caprise, female relationships were just as hard as male ones. She'd been on her own without any ties for five years. And before that, her dealings with people not in her family were minimal. That was all due to her differences as well, and she'd refused to bond with the female shifters as her parents had suggested. It seemed, quite miserably, that Caprise was destined to be alone.

No, that wasn't true. Not if her sister-in-law had anything to say about it.

"Are you sure? Nick didn't want to tell me what was going on, but I got most of it out of him anyway. When the helicopter arrived and he and Rome left so quickly I knew something bad must have happened. But Kalina came to see me and said that X was fine, that he hadn't been arrested. She said you'd stayed with him but I told her I'd find out everything from you personally."

Caprise nodded as she passed Ary to open the wardrobe where her clothes hung. This was how most of their conversations went—Ary talked, Caprise nodded or gave one-syllable answers until Ary grew weary and gave up. Something told her today Ary wasn't going to give up. And there was something that was bothering Caprise; maybe it wouldn't hurt to talk about it. What if she gave this sister thing a try? No, not with Ary. Even though she didn't like talking to her sister-in-law, she did care about her and the baby she carried. Unloading all her issues on Ary wasn't a good idea.

Still, she didn't really have the energy to keep dodging her questions, either. As usual, sleep hadn't come quickly to her last night. But it had come eventually, which was still a little baffling.

"X and I had sex," she said bluntly. Then she pulled

out a dress and threw it over her shoulder. "I'm going to go in and change."

Ary looked stunned and for a moment Caprise thought she might make a clean getaway.

"Wait, you did what with who?"

So much for the clean getaway.

Instead, Caprise figured, she might as well just get this over with. She moved to the king-size bed, which at first seemed utterly foolish for just one person, but then she'd fallen in love with its extreme comfort, even on those nights that sleep eluded her.

"X and I had sex. He showed up at the club being all bossy and controlling as usual. Then one thing just led to the other and we did it." She shrugged but even she realized that what she'd just said wasn't that simple.

Ary came to sit on the other side of the bed, taking a moment to adjust herself and her growing girth. Pregnancy for Shadow Shifters was a bit different than it was among humans and full-breed jaguars. Ary would carry the baby for twelve to eighteen weeks max; then she'd deliver what would look like a human but after going through puberty would become a full-grown jaguar shifter. So right now, she looked like she was about four months along in a human pregnancy, complete with the swollen ankles and face.

"You don't even like X" was Ary's next comment. She'd folded her arms so they rested on top of her stomach, and Caprise resisted the urge to reach out and touch her.

In fact she turned away, looking across the room instead.

"He's arrogant and high-handed and obnoxious."

"Okay," Ary said. "That may be true. I guess the next question would be what's he like in bed?"

To that Caprise couldn't help but chuckle. Ary was a *curandero,* a former healer to the *Topetènia* tribe and current director of the Stateside Medical Center. She was also a little bit naive about the way things were done in the states considering she'd grown up in the Gungi. So her question seemed more than a little off to Caprise.

"It wasn't that big a deal," she started to say. "But then he gets even more macho-man on me and tosses me into his truck, because he says Rogues are coming. We end up at his place, where—" She sighed. "—we do it again."

"Again?" Ary asked. "Well," she added, barely holding her own smile in, "I guess that means he was pretty good in bed."

No matter how contrary her nature, Caprise smiled right along with her sister-in-law. "He was good. But that's not the point. It wasn't supposed to happen."

"So why did it?"

That was a simple question, one Caprise had been avoiding since the moment X pulled her off that stage.

"I don't know" was the only reply she could come up with. And surprisingly, it was the truth. She didn't know why she'd had sex with X when sex had been the farthest thing from her mind since she'd made her way back to the United States. No, to be even more honest with herself, sex hadn't been what Caprise had shied away from— intimacy was. And what she'd shared with X wasn't intimate, it was basic and good. Damn, it was good.

"So let me get this straight. You and X were at a club together and then you had sex. Rogues appeared, then you ran away to his house and had more sex. Does that sound about right?"

"The facts are there. But let me fill in the blanks because you're going to find out anyway. I've been working two nights a week at Athena's. I dance there because I haven't heard back from the school about getting a job dancing or teaching or whatever. X was there last night and he saw my routine. I don't know, I guess he got turned on, and when I came off the stage he dragged me back to my dressing room. Then he smelled Rogues and things got all crazy."

"And you ended up in his bed again?"

Caprise frowned. "Why do you keep going back to that point?"

Ary laughed. "It's a pretty hard point to get past. No pun intended."

Caprise could see she was enjoying this way too much. "You've been around Kalina too long. Speaking of which, where is she?"

Ary shook her head. "Don't try to change the subject. She's in some training meeting with the newly hired staff. I don't know if she really likes the new duties of being First Female of the Stateside Assembly, but it's keeping her plenty busy. And now back to you and X and the Rogues. I know he's been investigating the club. We actually saw the girl who was killed there at the morgue."

"That's the girl they think he murdered?"

"X would never murder anyone, especially not a female. That's not what shadows do," Ary said adamantly.

It took valiant effort not to roll her eyes. "He's a man, Ary. He was born in the states and raised here. So he's visited the Gungi, that doesn't make him a part of the tribe."

"You're wrong. The Gungi is in our blood, no matter where we're born. *Topètenia* are from the Gungi and will always return to their home in times of need. Isn't that why you went there when your parents died?"

Caprise opened her mouth to speak then clapped her lips shut again. She took a steadying breath and clenched and released her fists. "How did you know I went back?"

"I saw you."

"I didn't come to the village. I stayed away."

Ary shook her head. "I left the village every morning to visit Yuri. I saw you one morning. You stayed on the western side, down by the river. I recognized you because you look like Nick, even in cat form."

Shit. The Gungi probably hadn't been a good place to hide anyway. Yet Caprise had been drawn to the forest regardless of what her mind thought was best.

"Why didn't you ever say anything?"

"It wasn't my place. Besides, I had no contact with your brother so I had no way of knowing he was looking for you."

"And you figured he'd dumped you so why speak to his sister."

Ary didn't reply.

"Sorry. I'm just agitated." She sighed and laid her head back against the headboard. Hearing her cell phone chirp from across the room in her purse where she'd left it just made her mood worse.

"Agitated because you slept with X or because you don't have an explanation for why?" Ary asked.

"Both," she replied quickly.

"Sometimes there is no explanation. Things just are the way they're meant to be," Ary stated.

Caprise didn't like the sound of that, but her temples throbbed now and she figured that was a sign that she'd done too much talking. Ary, in her quiet, know-it-all sort of way, had taken the unspoken hint and left her alone.

On the floor Caprise's phone went off again. Without preamble, a low growl sounded in her chest. She wanted to curse, but hissed instead and stomped into her private bathroom to change. The last twenty-four hours had been a complete headache for her. She could only hope the next hours would prove better.

* * *

When Caprise stepped out of her bathroom she wanted to scream. Her day was getting worse.

"The next time I tell you I'll take you home, I want you to wait for me to do just that," X said from across the room where he leaned against the wall beside her dressing table.

"I'm not under your command" was her retort. She almost told him to get out but knew that would be futile. "How'd you get in here?"

"I told Nick those access codes were bullshit. I cracked it in two seconds," he replied simply. "You can't lock me out just because you want to."

"I can and I did. But since you clearly want to act like the animal—"

Her words were cut off as X moved across the floor with lightning speed. In the next second he'd grabbed her wrists, pulling her arms up above her head. With the barest push he had her flat on the bed, his strong body pinning her down.

"Don't," he said through clenched teeth. "You and I are the same."

She should have been afraid, suspected a normal person would be. But since she'd never had any real claim to "normal," that didn't include her. "I'm not like you."

He stared down at her for a long time, his dark eyes almost absorbing her in their intensity. His bald head glistened, beckoning her fingers to touch and explore just as she'd done when they'd had sex. She grabbed a handful of the comforter beneath her instead.

"You can get off me now. Playtime is over." It was so much easier to be flippant, to act like he was having absolutely no effect on her. When the truth was—and up until now Caprise had always prided herself on confronting the truth head-on—Xavier was making her feel things she just wasn't used to.

"This is not a game," he told her sternly.

"I'm back at Havenway safe and sound. Seth plans to guard my every breath for the next millennium so there's no need for you to act like my personal bodyguard."

"I'm not finished with you."

He'd said it so matter-of-factly, like it was something she should have known and if it wasn't he would make sure she did. Caprise didn't know why that both irritated and turned her on. The irritation was slightly conquered by the intense look in his eyes. It was like a storm there, brewing steadily; Caprise had to wonder what would happen when it finally exploded. When everything this shifter kept so bottled up would erupt. Better still, she wondered if she would stick around to see the results.

"Look, I can face the truth. That's the type of person I am," she told him. "So here it is, last night was a shock to both of us. But it happened and today's a new day. Can't we just move on?"

"I can't" was his reply.

To Caprise the admission almost sounded tortured. As if X really meant what he'd said but didn't like it any more than she did. Her cell phone picked this exact moment to chirp and before Caprise could even think about going to retrieve it, X was up off the bed.

"Well, if I'd known that was all it was going to take," she quipped in a much lighter tone than she was feeling.

He grabbed her purse and unceremoniously dumped its contents on the bed. As soon as she saw the phone, Caprise reached for it. He snatched it just an inch from her grasp.

"Who the hell is this?" he yelled into the phone after he'd answered.

Caprise held her breath. She'd been receiving text messages for the last two or three days, but never had she received an actual call.

"Whoever you are I'll find your ass. If you're smart you'll stop dialing this number. If you're stupid I'll slit your throat the moment I see you."

X pressed the OFF button so hard Caprise thought he would break the phone in two. When his gaze returned to hers she saw something she'd never seen before. No, she'd seen it before and had taken that warning by running so fast she didn't even know where she'd finally stopped. Today she had no place to run. X stood in front of the door he'd broken into. There were two windows on the opposite side of the room but they looked like they belonged in a mental institution—too slim for any human or shifter to slip through, but just big enough to offer some sunshine and fresh air.

No, this time, Caprise realized she'd have to stand and face the beast staring back at her.

"If you know who that is that keeps calling and texting you I'd advise you to tell me right now," he said in a tone so tight, so lethal she actually shivered before straightening her back.

"No," she said, taking a nervous step toward him. "That's my phone and whoever calls or texts me is my business."

"Don't play with me, Caprise. This is serious."

"It's my business, Xavier. I didn't ask you to get involved and I'd actually prefer if you didn't." She reached out a hand for the phone.

Her limbs didn't shake although she felt like she wanted to. Inside her cat paced, watching to see what would come next. It was eerily drawn to the cat within X, the beast that had warranted his swift eye-color change. Caprise pushed back, daring her cat to make a move. She'd kept her other half on a tight rein all these years; she wasn't about to stop now just because he was around.

"Someone is threatening you," he said, his voice a lower timbre than it had been before. "I don't like it."

"It's not your concern," she replied quickly.

He took a step toward her and she had to demand her feet remain still. Lifting her head to stare up at him she said, her voice just a tad lower in compromise, "It's no big deal. I can handle it."

His gaze searched hers for what seemed like endless moments. Then he did something that shocked and confused her. X extended a hand, touching the edge of her chin softly with one finger. The very motion looked awkward on him, yet felt surprisingly soft and whimsical to her. Then he spoke and awkward took another turn.

"I'm leaving for Sedona in three hours. Come with me."

Why had he asked her that?

His conversation with Bas had ended with the Mountain Faction Leader mentioning that Felipe Hernandez, a former lieutenant in the Cortez Cartel, had clammed up tight and wasn't talking to anyone. Bas and his guards had captured the drug runner while he was overseeing a shipment in New Mexico. Rome and Nick were both sure Hernandez could tell them how their parents had been in contact with Julio Cortez years ago. And if that contact had led to the betrayal of the shifters.

"Maybe you could persuade him to talk," Bas had said after explaining that Hernandez was basically choosing to die of hunger and deprivation instead of telling Bas and his team what they wanted to know.

There was a hint of sarcasm in the man's voice when he'd made the suggestion, and everyone knew sarcasm was Bas's first language. But in the prickly mood X was in he'd taken it as an instant challenge.

"I think I'll do just that."

After a brief hesitation Bas had chuckled. "I'll have a room ready for you."

"Make that a suite. If that bastard Hernandez is staying in luxury, I can, too."

"Whatever, man," Bas said, still chuckling as if he didn't really expect X to fly to Sedona to question the drug dealer.

Even when he'd hung up X wondered why he'd been so eager to get on a plane and go himself. That reason came to him the moment he closed his eyes. Her eyes stared back at him, dark, mysterious, enthralling. In the recesses of his mind he could hear her voice, whispering his name. Just a whisper; she didn't scream it out loud at the moment of her climax as so many women had done before her. No, Caprise wouldn't give in that easily. She'd said it but only so she could hear it. The fact that X picked it up was a testament to the strength of his shifter senses, or a need that he didn't even want to explore.

He'd thought about her from that moment up until the second he stood in front of her bedroom door punching numbers into that stupid keypad. The entry doors to Havenway were all on a computerized lock and also had sensory alarms that tripped if the doors were opened without using the authorized codes. X had programmed them all himself. As for the bedrooms, he'd told Nick that keypads with separate pass codes weren't safe enough. They needed a backup just in case—exactly as he'd done—someone decided to hack the code. All he'd had to do was put in a series of commands that would effectively delete the prior coding; any hackers worth their salt could do it in about five minutes. X did it in two.

When the door swung open and he saw she wasn't in the bedroom, he'd been about to curse. Then he picked up her scent and the cat within calmed. She was still here.

He looked about the room, saw the completely feminine things she possessed, and wondered about this side of her. On the tall dresser that stood between the only two windows in the room there were dozens of small glass bottles, in different shapes and colors. They all contained fragrances that either irritated or incited X's senses. There was an abundance of jewelry, earrings, bracelets, watches. It all appeared very feminine and very unlike the idea he'd had of Caprise.

She was guarded, that was for damn sure. And that didn't really bother X because he had his own shields in place when it came to dealing with females. But there was something else about her he couldn't quite put his finger on, something that made it impossible for him to walk away from her now.

He was still standing there when she came out of the bathroom, surprised to see him. Their exchange had been as was usual for them, except it felt like they weren't alone. There were spectators this time, two very intense and hungry cats, interested in what was unraveling between the humans.

She fought everything he said, everything he tried to do. No matter which way he tried to approach her, it didn't matter. It was as if she lived for moments just like this. When her phone rang, X was instantly on guard. He remembered last night's text and had run the number through reverse lookup before leaving his apartment. Nothing showed. A more advanced search would take twenty-four hours so he wouldn't get the name of the person the phone was registered to until sometime tomorrow. Nobody had spoken when he answered, and that pissed him off. He wanted whoever was on the other end dialing her number to say something, just one word so he could give them the cuss-out of their lifetime. But they didn't afford him the pleasure. Instead he'd issued a threat, one he had every intention of carrying out when he found out whom he was dealing with.

Then out of nowhere the question had tumbled out of his mouth. X, of all people, knew once something was done there was no taking it back. Oddly enough, he really didn't want to take the invite back.

"Why would I go anywhere with you?" she asked, her eyes narrowing skeptically.

He decided to try another approach with her and didn't demand that she do what he asked. Instead, he asked in a lower voice, "What else do you have to do? Rome's not going to allow you to go back to Athena's."

There was no way X was going to allow that, either, but he figured she'd swallow that comment a lot easier if it were coming from the FL.

"He can't keep me from my job," she protested. And in a move he didn't anticipate she reached out, grabbing her cell phone from his hand.

X conceded and didn't use his force to get it back. He could have, but thought it might be best to pick and choose his battles with Caprise from now on. She was hiding something, that much was evident, and until he found out exactly what, X wanted to keep her close. The only way to do that without having to hog-tie and gag her was to be as cordial as he could manage. Which wasn't really his best act, but something told him the end would totally justify the means.

"There's something dangerous going on at Athena's. It's better if you're out of the line of fire."

She looked worried as she turned away from him to put her cell phone on the dresser. "Look, I came back to DC to get my life back on track. If I can't dance, I can't do that."

The last was spoken softly, again, as if she really hadn't meant for him to hear it.

"It's not safe, Caprise. You have to understand we're only trying to protect you."

"I don't need any protection," she said, spinning around to face him once more. "I've done a pretty damn good job of taking care of myself for the past five years. I can handle it now."

"Can you, Caprise?" X took a step closer to her; the distance was beginning to make his cat a little edgy. "Because I've got to tell you, every time your phone rings or beeps you get this look in your eye."

She tried to turn away from him. "You're being ridiculous."

"I'm being straight with you because I figure you can respect that since you're all about facing the truth. I'm not trying to lie to you about what's going on and why you need protection. So you should think long and hard about coming clean with me."

"I don't owe you anything," she replied when her gaze came back to his.

"You don't," he agreed. "But you owe it to your brother to not jump back into his life only to get yourself killed."

She was about to say something else but X held up a hand to stop her. His patience—what little of it he possessed—was quickly growing short. Inside, his cat was making a low growl, insisting on touching, tasting, feeling once more. X, however, did not think that was a good idea.

At that moment Caprise completely disarmed him by sighing so deeply he thought for sure tears would follow. Her right hand went to her right hip, where she rubbed absently. He'd been around a lot of females in his time and while Caprise Delgado was definitely unique even beyond her DNA, he figured he could tell when a female was about to break down.

Of course he was wrong. Caprise would never cry. Not over something like this anyway. But for just a moment she did look completely defeated, as if the right decision just could not be made clear. As if on cue to torment her further that damn cell phone chirped once more.

This time his growl was loud enough that she must have heard him, because she looked from the dresser where the phone was to X. He didn't speak and neither did she.

Chapter 11

"So she's a shadow," Sabar said thoughtfully.

He was sitting at the long spit-shined oak table Bianca had purchased and moved into his dining room. They were in his brownstone in DC, the one he'd been slowly renovating since their first town house was burned to the ground by Rome and his cohorts. After Bianca's arrival a month and a half ago, the decoration of the house had taken on a new urgency. It appeared that after living in a mansion-size dwelling in western Africa, she'd found a new hobby in decorating. Or as Darel would say, she had a knack for spending Sabar's money. Darel needed to learn some respect where Bianca was concerned, and Sabar was just about ready to force-feed him a healthy helping of it. But right now he wanted to know what had gone down last night and why his second-in-charge was in his face telling him things he definitely did not want to hear.

"She's a shadow," Darel replied.

He sat in one of the high-backed chairs that Sabar had forgotten the name of. He wasn't eating, was barely looking at Sabar. The Rogue had been acting weird since they'd fought those shadows on the highway; everything about him seemed a bit different than before. Even his hair seemed longer, more unruly, his facial features rougher, his skin just a shade darker. But that was his issue; Sabar had more important things to occupy his mind with.

"And this shifter that's looking for her, you know more about him?"

"He's definitely not from the Gungi. His accent's different. And he looks weird. I can't say if he's a *Lormenia* or a *Croesteriia*, but he sounds like he's from that region and he's got cat in him."

By *that region* Sabar knew that Darel was referring to the Etinosa, the small but burgeoning village emerging on the outskirts of the Sierra Leone rain forest in western Africa. The assumption could be true, or it could be a clever trick by the newcomer. Sabar would like to believe the latter.

"And he wants her?" he asked trying to remain focused on the here and now.

Darel nodded. "Says she's his *companheiro*."

Sabar scooped a forkful of eggs into his mouth and chewed, even though it was nearing five o'clock in the afternoon. He'd had a late morning in bed and now his hunger had just peaked. The cook had prepared what he'd asked for, no questions asked. Sabar wished everyone around him was that obedient. "Interesting," he mumbled.

"He was pissed she got away, too. I mean, we wanted to get that Faction dude, but he was zapping out about losing the female."

"Where is he now?"

"I gave him the keys to Hanson's place. Figured you'd want to keep a close eye on him until we find out what his real deal is."

Sabar nodded. "Good move. Put him in the club, give him a job, and watch his ass like a hawk."

"In the club? You serious? You want him working with us?"

"I want him under my thumb. So when he makes a move I'll be there to bust his ass."

"That's not the one you need to be watching that way," Darel mumbled.

Sabar was out of his chair in a flash, his face close up to Darel's. "What did you just say?"

To his credit, and this is why Sabar really liked this shifter, Darel didn't flinch, he didn't blink, didn't even breathe out of the way. He simply stared back at Sabar. Which on the one hand was something to be proud of, and on the other . . .

"I think you need to keep an eye on Bianca," Darel told him matter-of-factly.

"Bianca's my female" was Sabar's retort as he backed away from the table. "What's your problem with her?"

"My problem is how she showed up out of the blue. Where's Boden? Did he just let her go? What does she really want, Sabar?" Darel asked, the tension in his voice evident. Hell, his muscles had even bunched at the shoulders like this crazy shifter thought he was going to take a swing at him. Time to remind him who was in charge here.

"She wants me!" he yelled.

Darel nodded.

"And what else?"

Sabar didn't answer, just flexed his fingers, claws already breaking through the skin as his cat was ready for a fight. He didn't want to kill Darel, didn't even want to consider the thought. But knew that if that was what needed to go down, it would. Disrespect was not something he planned to deal with lightly.

Darel seemed oblivious to Sabar's train of thought as he continued. "Think about this: We're trying to build something here. Our product is popular, so our territory is growing. We're working on those fake-ass politicians to get something big set up with the weapons dealing. We're about to be a huge force in this city and across this damn nation. And Bianca shows up just in time to reap the benefits."

"I hear what you're saying," he said, only because Darel had been his trusted confidant for a while now. And Darel never let him down, ever. He knew what to do and he did it without question. Sabar respected him and wanted to keep their working relationship intact. But in this, where Bianca was concerned, there was no middle ground.

Sabar stood from his chair and leaned over the table so that his face was kissing distance away from Darel's, his breath a breeze across the man's ashen face.

"But she's my female. I don't give a damn about what happened across the seas years ago. I don't fucking care where Boden is or if his head's still up his ass. I'm running this shit here and that's all that matters. You," he said, his voice raising slightly as he pointed at Darel, "don't say a fucking word to or against Bianca. Don't even look at her cross-eyed or I'll cut off your balls and feed them to you one by one. These terms are not negotiable."

He sat down then, picking up his fork and eating another bite of eggs.

After a few seconds of silence Darel stood. "I'm going to check on Hanson and the new shipment. I'll take the new guy with me and get him set up for tonight."

"And if that shadow bitch shows up, tie her ass up and bring her to me. I'll decide if Mr. New-Shifter-in-Town gets her or not."

"Whatever you say, boss," was Darel's retort.

If Sabar weren't so busy finishing off his meal and thinking about a hot-ass shifter he could sink his length into, or maybe even enjoy right alongside Bianca, he would have heard the sarcasm in Darel's tone. He would have known that he might just need to watch his back with his second-in-command.

With every breath he took, pain ripped another slither of his heart. After almost five years there should be nothing left. If he keeled over and died right here, on the balcony of this substandard dwelling in this dirty and over-crowded city, they'd cut him open and see an organ the size of a penny no longer thumping, no longer living.

Pathetic, that's exactly what Rolando was. He'd convinced himself of that as he'd finally, after spending end-less days, months, looking for her in the Gungi, dragged his ass back across the country. His home was and would always be India, in the depths of the Lachli village of the rain forest where he'd been born. It wasn't until eight years ago that he'd left the Lachli to join another group of shifters in their exploration of new territory for their kind. That venture had taken him to the Sierra Leone rain for-est in Africa, where a small village of shifters had just begun to live. Then he'd ended up in the Gungi.

And he'd found Caprise.

He'd heard of *companheiros*, as the *Topètenia* called them. His life mate, that's what he knew she was from the moment he'd first laid eyes on her. From that moment on she'd been all he could think about.

Years later, nothing had changed.

Rolando wanted her back. He wanted his mate. No, he needed her, more than he needed to breathe or to live for that matter. The instructions from his commander had been clear in the heavily accented English they both spoke.

"End this mindless search for the female. Get another one to slake your needs. We have bigger, better things to worry about."

That's precisely what he'd said to Rolando, two months ago. That very night Rolando had left the forest heading to the United States, where he'd had a gut feeling his beloved had returned.

And he'd been right. She was here and she was more beautiful than ever.

He had waited the allotted time those other shifters had instructed and still he'd missed her. At first that thought angered him, but now he was calm again. He was close to Caprise and she knew. Oh, yes, now she knew just how close.

His entire body tightened, his cat growling, as his tongue extended to lick his human lips. *Closure* was what the humans called what he sought. The exact name for it didn't matter to Rolando. All that mattered was they would soon be together again. For however long revenge would take.

On his hip the cell phone, the one called Darel had given him last night, rang. He wanted to keep tabs on him; Rolando could relate. And he'd accepted it. For now.

"Yes?"

"Meet me at the club at eight. Don't be late."

"Right" was Rolando's only reply. He didn't want to go to that damn club unless Caprise was going to be there.

But she'd left with someone he'd later learned was another shifter, one with some type of rank here in the States. He wasn't sure she'd come back to the club, not if they suspected danger, which if she left with another shifter through a damn window they probably had.

Still, it wasn't Rolando's goal to piss off anyone here. He just wanted his female. So for now, he'd accept the orders given by the angry-ass shifter they called Darel.

Darel snapped the phone closed and tossed it on the table in his apartment. He walked to the wall in his dining room and removed a picture of some sort of dogs fighting. His walls were painted a dingy green color that had appealed to him on some dismal level. Nothing in Darel's childhood had ever been clean and pure. He embraced that fact and had long ago decided to live his adult life in the same manner.

The house his parents had was a shithole, a two-bedroom jail in the dirtiest part of Brooklyn, New York, they could find. His best friends would have been rats and roaches if he hadn't come into his shift early and scared the bejesus out of those suckers with his sharp fangs and vicious roar. Cats and dogs roaming the neighborhood without a real home or a bath also rubbed him the wrong way, and they met a hellacious end sooner rather than later. His father was a cruel bastard, so it stood to reason Darel would turn out the same way. As for his siblings, he'd never paid too much attention to the younger brother and sister who had been cursed to be born into that household. The one he had paid a lot of attention to was his mother. He'd listened to everything Elora said, hanging on her every word as if it were the gospel, as she'd called it. But year after year, time after time, when she'd preached to him about honesty and integrity paying off in the end, Darel had begun to suspect the untruth.

They never moved up, never had any more than the scraps they'd always had. And his father grew angrier and more violent with each passing moment. Darel never asked what the guy's problem was, never really cared. All he knew was what he saw. And what he saw was the brutality inflicted on his mother, whether verbal or physical. What he knew was the answer, beyond honesty and integrity, was payback. His father had been his first shifter kill, and it had been a glorious one at that. He still remembered the scent of his blood as it ran down his jaws, dripping onto the floor. His teeth still tingled with the thought of sinking into the thinning, putrid flesh of the man's neck. He'd approached him from behind and bit into his neck with enough force that it broke on contact. The other ripping and shredding he'd done was for his mother. He deserved every minute of the torture.

The next day he'd left that awful house, left his father's shredded and bloodied body on the floor in the bedroom while his mother's lay in the kitchen completely bled out after his father's brutal attack on her, and never looked back. Ever.

For more than fifteen years Darel had been working with Sabar. At first it had been here and there, Sabar visiting him on the streets of New York at intervals. Darel had never asked questions. Even when Sabar had come back one time with scabbed-over scars that looked like they'd come from a whip all over his body, Darel had remained silent. He'd respected Sabar because there was an air about the shifter, a total fuck-you attitude that Darel shared. He believed one day they'd be partners in whatever mischief they could come up with. And that dream was coming true.

Except now, that bitch was here.

With the remote in his hand he switched the ON button and spoke clearly through the intercom. "I'm ready."

Through a ten-by-five slit in the wall he watched what was taking place in the bedroom. Yeah, he could just get his ass up out of the chair and go in there to see them, but he preferred to be in his own space during this time. It had taken him a while to figure out what worked best for him, what gave the most satisfaction at the appropriate time, and so far this was it.

The male, a shifter who worked at the club, was just buff enough. His honey-toned skin looked like a succulent piece of candy. Darel's tongue extended of its own accord in an attempt to lift the male's scent from the air

and taste it. He was naked, his buttocks taut and muscled, biceps flexing as he stood over the female. His dick
was long and thick and had the bulk of the pubic hair
shaved down to a neat trim. Darel was meticulous when it
came to body hair.

The female knew this. She wasn't a shifter, but one of
the girls who danced at the club. Her pubic hair was completely shaved off so that her mound looked like a glossed
piece of meat. He could never remember her real name
and hadn't really tried, but her stage name was Raven.
She had long black hair, falling in deep curls down her
back. Her tits were bigger than Darel's fists and heavy as
they hung from her chest like overfilled balloons. Her
skin was an olive complexion that went surprisingly well
with the darkness of her hair and the somber dusky blue
of her eyes. She had an ass that jiggled when touched.
Cheeks that made Darel want to bury his face inside and
never come up for air. She was fine and she knew it,
worked it like a pimp did his whores.

Darel's dick was already rock-hard. He released his
length from his pants and made himself comfortable.

Raven went right to her knees, taking the male's length
so far into her mouth Darel half expected to see it burst
from between her breasts. They'd turned to the side so he
could see everything, from the male's ass cheeks hollow-
ing out as he pumped into her mouth to Raven's cheeks
doing the same in-and-out dance as she held on to that
long rod. The male wrapped Raven's hair around his
wrists then pulled on all that mass until she groaned over
his shaft. Darel's eyes focused on the wet shaft, watched
the bulbous head swell and begin to drip with desire. Raven's masterful tongue scooped the white bead quickly.

"Enough!" Darel yelled through the intercom minutes
later, and they quickly broke apart.

The male bent Raven over the back of a chair, spreading her cheeks wide enough for Darel to see. Still, Darel sat up in his chair, moving his face closer to the slit in the wall. His dick was in his hand, palm moving on the up-and-down stroke that had him gasping for more air.

"More," he spoke again and sighed as the male stretched her butt cheeks open wider.

Darel could see her anal entry clearly, could imagine the feel of that tight passage, and growled.

"Now!" was his next directive.

Without preamble the male positioned himself behind Raven and thrust his length into her anus. She yelled so loud the first wave of release hit Darel and his dick jerked in his hand, spurts of come dripping down to his wrists. As the male pumped hard and fast into her, Raven's knuckles turned white as she held on to the back of that chair while Darel pumped his cock faster, harder.

The shifter came with a roar of his own, a slight shifting of his spinal cord, and a jerk of his taut buttocks. Raven's body convulsed as her release took over and Darel growled, his teeth pressing into his bottom lip until they drew blood. His dick exploded with come.

"Go home" was Darel's final instruction as he stood and walked to his bathroom, where he'd work on the hard-on that was once again emerging.

Chapter 12

"Nick's pissed," Caprise said from her seat across from X as she clicked off her cell phone.

They were aboard the private jet owned now by the Stateside Assembly via Reynolds & Delgado, PA. From what Kalina had told Caprise, they were working to make the Stateside Assembly a corporate infrastructure that would supply aid to all Shadows in the United States and in the Gungi. The shifter democracy was taking shape right before her eyes, and Caprise wondered if her parents were somewhere in their corporeal state doing the happy dance.

"Nick is always pissed about something" was X's droll reply.

She had no idea when she'd changed her mind or when it actually seemed like a good idea to go on this impromptu trip with X, of all people. But Caprise had decided and when she did, she'd quickly packed a bag and had Seth drive her to wherever X was leaving from. He hadn't seemed too surprised to see her, which had almost made her turn back. But that would be running—and wasn't she growing tired of that course of action?

These chairs were beyond comfortable as she sat back, adjusting the seat belt so that it wasn't cutting off circulation at her waist. The smell of leather wafted up her nostrils as she let her head lie back against the comfortable console. Looking around she thought of only one word: *luxury.* And since the jet was originally purchased by Rome, she thought nothing of it. He was the leader of the Stateside Assembly, a *Topètenia* of the highest ranking and a damn good lawyer. He had the looks, the money, and now the phenomenal woman by his side to make him legendary in both the human and the shifter worlds.

Her brother was his best friend and hadn't fallen too far from that same genetic pool of dangerously handsome and a top-notch Shadow warrior. It was no wonder Nick was Rome's right hand. Then Ary had come along and fit like another piece to the amazingly broad puzzle that formed the Shadow Shifters. She was a *curandero*, a healer, and had made herself right at home in Havenway's medical center, which she ran with intelligence and efficiency.

Then there was X. *Gorgeous* didn't quite seem to fit his rugged and lethal persona. Yes, his face, with the skin the delicious color of milk chocolate and eyes as piercing as they were alluring, was a pleasure to look at. But beneath his totally hot body—bulging muscles and a confident stride had always been Caprise's undoing—there was something else lurking. *Danger* probably described it in the most basic of ways, but it wasn't that simple. Whatever it was beneath the surface was what made X the man he was. It had molded and created this fearless leader, this absolutely vicious but methodical killer. Again, Caprise noted she should be afraid of him since she knew what he was capable of. In fact, though, she wasn't afraid, and for that very same reason.

He hadn't grown up with Nick and Rome, not in those very early years. He moved here from someplace— Atlanta, if memory served her correctly. But that was all she knew. Nick hadn't told her anything else, and she'd never thought to ask. Casting a quick glance at him now as he stared out the window, she wondered why it hadn't mattered to her until now. She would be kidding herself if she said that their physical joining hadn't changed anything. It had, and in a big way. Caprise was honest enough to admit that, even if just to herself.

Maybe she should have stayed in DC, she thought fleetingly. But it was a little too late for that now since they were somewhere over Kansas en route to Arizona. She didn't really know why and hadn't thought to ask. It was most likely shifter business, and Caprise figured she didn't want to know the details. For as much strength as it had taken her to return to DC, she still wasn't quite ready to claim the heritage that had been thrust upon her. Should she be? After all that had happened to her?

So many questions roared through her mind at this moment, so many issues she'd thought she had a handle on resurfacing to give her contented state a kick in the ass that had everything tilting on its axis. And wasn't that just how life was: The minute thoughts of safety and completeness engulfed her, everything shifted so that landing on her ass became the norm.

"You're thinking too hard."

His voice was deep and raspy, almost like some maniacal villain in a B-rated sci-fi flick. Come to think of it, X's entire demeanor could easily be mistaken for a villain, rather than a warrior for the good side.

"How do you know what I'm doing?" she asked him. They still had hours to sit on this plane together, so trying to ignore him or having him ignore her was pointless.

"Your scent is full of confusion. It's driving me insane."

On instinct Caprise inhaled deeply and exhaled with a shiver going down her spine. His scent was of pure, unadulterated lust.

"Go ahead, say it," he said, watching her closely.

He had a knack for doing that. Saying things to her that were absolutely true even if she didn't want to accept them. And he was so damn sure of himself, so sure that if he wanted her that meant she wanted him, which wasn't exactly a lie.

"I'm not saying anything," she replied tightly. Then she thought better of her silence and figured if X insisted on tapping into her innermost thoughts and feelings, she could do the same.

"Is sex all you think about?" she asked him.

He shrugged. "What else is there?"

"Work, for one," she said, staring at him incredulously because she couldn't believe he'd just said that.

"My day job has me investigating human traffickers. My second job puts me face-to-face with sadistic killers. What would you suggest I think about in my spare time?"

He was hiding. It was obvious to Caprise, because a year ago she would have probably given the same flippant answer if asked.

"Do you like looking for the bad guy all the time? Don't you ever do anything for fun?"

"Fun is overrated" was his reply.

"I used to think that, too," she answered.

X laughed. And suddenly Caprise was engulfed with warmth, as if those big strong arms of his had wrapped around her, holding her so tightly yet so comfortably she had no choice but to let down her guard.

"You got a problem with sex addicts?"

"Not at all," she conceded. "Just makes me wonder, that's all."

"Don't waste your time."

"Meaning?"

"Don't waste your time wondering about me. I am who I am and proud of it."

And then he seemed to go off into his own world

again. His thoughts were just as deep as hers, she figured, even though she couldn't scent his. Her fingers drummed on the arm of the seat and she began to hum. X was proud of who he was and yet he denied that person the freedom to shine. Why? He was a puzzle, one she was sure she could figure out. That would be a welcome change, she thought. Helping somebody else with his problems instead of trying to sift through her own.

After a few moments she realized what she'd been thinking of doing could backfire on her: Not only could her heart end up broken, but there was a chance that she might not be able to tame the beast lurking inside X. That nobody could.

Sedona, Arizona

Sebastian Perry was a thirty-four-year-old renowned bachelor, six foot one, with butter-toned skin, eyes as gray as a cloudy day, and a mind as sharp as Bill Gates's—if he were in charge of the military instead of being a computer mogul. He dressed better than most of the male models in the country and walked with an air of confidence—some called it swagger—but he'd hold on to confidence because it sounded good, too. An only child to Geneva and Lathan Perry, he was blessed with all the good parts of his parents and loved the fact that all the bad parts had departed along with them after the divorce.

In college he'd majored in hospitality, minored in poetry, and kept a stable of women that still liked to ring his phone even though a good portion of them were now married. Life, and two multimillion-dollar vacation resorts, had landed him in Sedona five years ago. Perryville Resorts were known worldwide, giving their owner even more visibility in the human world. None of them knew he was a lethal beast, his gray eyes turning an eerie shade of red-gold, his teeth growing sharper and longer, his body bulking and covering with fur. It was one of the many secrets he held close to the vest like a seasoned gambler at Caesars.

Perryville Resorts Sedona was located near the secluded Boynton Canyon, sitting on more than eighty acres of natural terrain. Its structure was surrounded by red-rock buttes known for inspiring the mind, body, and spirit. This was the reason Bas stayed here year-round. While he made it a point to spot-check each of his resorts throughout the year, this one was his baby. From the moment he'd opened his first location, he knew he'd end up here. His plan was to expand Perryville until it touched every exotic locale in the world, but here, where he could stand on the balcony to his penthouse suite and look at the magnificent orange and fuchsia swirls in the sky as the sun set over the beautiful red rocks, was where he belonged.

In twenty minutes the jet would land on the private strip of land Bas had designated as shifter airspace. It was completely off the grid, so the FAA had no way of tracking their jets to or from their destination. Just as below the basement floors of Perryville Resorts was yet another twenty-five feet dug into the earth. Here was where the shifter labs and surveillance spaces where kept. The walls of the U-shaped bunker were lined with layer upon layer of reinforced steel and guarded by some of the most high-tech security equipment ever invented. Bas had consulted with Nick on most of the layout and what would be needed to keep the fortress both stable and secure. X had given his input on the technology and the general warfare. Should their security somehow become breached, for whatever reason, this was Bas's territory. He had teams of shifters categorized by their levels of achievement in combat: Lower levels did perimeter checks, while higher levels worked discreetly among the citizens of Sedona. Bas's years as a marine had provided the combat skills required to train hundreds of shifters to protect and safeguard their secret as well as their people. His college years had given him the intelligence and sophistication he needed to rub elbows with the rich and elite of America. The fact that he was a shifter had given him the solid footing he needed to stay sane among everything else.

Comastaz Laboratories, owned and operated by the US government, was studying an unknown species. A human–animal mix was what they thought they had. From the research Bas had confiscated, it looked like they were relying on guesswork, supposition, and the rantings of one man—Julio Cortez.

X wasn't going to be happy when Bas told him what he'd found. He was going to be even less pleased at the prisoner they'd managed to capture but who refused to speak, even after Bas's blue team had exhausted their very best coercion techniques.

"We're land-live."

The voice belonged to Jacques, Bas's Lead Guard, as he reported through the intercom link they all wore tucked discreetly into one ear—it was activated by small chips embedded into the collars of their shirts—that the jet had landed safely.

"Received," Bas responded tightly. "Bring him to my office immediately."

"Received" was Jacques's solemn reply.

Bas's body tensed as his gaze lingered over the rocks, down the base of what looked like a majestic formation of cliffs and caves. They rose hundreds of feet above Perryville, which sat serenely, its reddish brown buildings a complement to the stark blue sky and entrancing multi-hued sunsets. It was serenity served on a platter of the highest quality—royalty within a scenic mountainous region that boasted mind, body, and soul restoration. It was his masterpiece.

And someone or something was threatening to destroy it.

The scents were changing, shifting and eluding as if they were being surrounded. Bas had felt the intrusion days ago. With each moment the sense of being invaded grew, even with the dozen perimeter checks per day. It wasn't the humans who arrived like clockwork according to their reservations and stayed to spend their money in search of something they would most likely leave here without finding—because their minds would only allow them to accept so much of the unknown. No, this presence was different. It was animalistic in all its glory and it was a major threat to all Bas had accomplished. For that reason alone he vowed to hunt to kill, no questions asked, no prisoners taken—despite the mandate of the head of the Stateside Assembly.

X felt it the moment they stepped off the jet.

Eyes were upon him, lots of eyes that saw through his human skin to the beast that lay in waiting.

He scented their stench and growled instinctively, drawing a frown from Caprise, who had stepped down from the steps and stood beside him.

"Easy, big fella, we're out in the open now. Wouldn't want any exposure issues," she reminded him. He looked like he was ready to shift in the next instant.

"Stop," he said, reaching out to touch her arm, to hold her still. "Lift your head to the wind and close your eyes."

"Why?"

"Be quiet and do it," he said with a little more force.

Later, X would marvel at how quickly she'd obeyed him and possibly question it. Right now, however, she did what he'd told her to do.

"It's coming from the west," she said softly, so quiet that the light breeze almost drowned her out. "There." She pointed.

X immediately pulled her arm back to her side. "I know."

"Who—" she began, then cleared her throat. "What?"

"Rogues."

"Great." She sighed. "Everywhere I go now these things are popping up."

She was urged toward the Land Rover that was waiting to take them to the resort. He was beginning to notice that same thing. Not that they hadn't acquired the interest of the Rogues before Caprise had arrived. It still seemed weird that they turned up everywhere she was lately. That couldn't mean anything good, X thought with another low growl. Nothing good at all.

Chapter 13

"I didn't know you were bringing company so this is the only suite available," Bas said, entering the room behind X and Caprise and one of his human staff members, Jewel.

Jewel looked young, probably in her late twenties. She was tall and sure of herself with an awesome body couldn't really be hidden beneath the staff uniform. She went through the unit pulling the drapes back to reveal more scenery through pristine windows.

"You own the joint," X replied gruffly. "You couldn't fix it so I had the best suite in the house?"

Bas smiled genuinely as he joked along. "Not on your life. You're a freebie. The rest are paying customers."

"I'm hurt." X continued the exchange, slapping a hand to his chest and taking a step back.

Caprise watched the friendly banter with interest. Sebastian Perry was one hell of a man, dressed in slacks that weren't fitted, but draped over lean hips and fell to rest with pure style over shined leather tie-ups. His shirt was the color of the rocks that stretched skyward and occupied every view from every window she'd seen so far in the resort. It, too, fit him impeccably well and added sparkle to the gold-and-diamond watch at his wrist, the thick gold bracelet on the opposite side. His hair was wavy, raven black, and about a quarter inch long. The eyes were entrancing, drawing you in completely the moment he set them on you.

But they didn't hold Caprise long. Pretty faces had run their course with her, right alongside smooth words and fancy cars. No, Bas seemed really cool, and he knew everything there was to know about the shifters in the Mountain Faction. He was even very cordial with his staff, as she noticed when he dismissed Jewel, who smiled at Caprise before leaving. But he wasn't X.

The fact that she even cared said a lot.

"All joking aside, if you'd like your own room, I could probably find a vacancy."

Caprise jerked her gaze from the view, aiming it squarely on Bas as she realized he'd been speaking to her. "I can handle it. But thanks," she told him.

If she weren't Nick's sister she doubted the offer would have been extended. She'd seen the look he and X exchanged when she was introduced. No doubt the FL knew she'd been with X intimately. There was a sort of territorial vibe going between them, but she dismissed it.

"I believe you can handle it," Bas commented, rubbing a finger over his clean-shaven jawline.

He was watching her like a cat would its prey, only his hunger was on a totally different level.

"She's staying with me and she'll be just fine," X said, clapping a hand on Bas's shoulder, effectively drawing the man's attention from Caprise.

She only smiled, taking this opportunity to wander through the suite. They would talk about shifter business—some guy named Hernandez and information he wasn't giving them. At this point Caprise was becoming a little curious about what was going on. But she wouldn't tell X that, not just yet.

Even though this was all Bas had available for them to

stay in, it was no minimal arrangement. The living room was huge, with a lovely beehive fireplace occupying its largest wall. Everything was decorated in deep oranges, rustic browns, and soothing beiges, all colors that soaked up the warming rays of the sun and cast a hazy glow about the entire space.

To her left were glass doors that opened to a patio with more cotton-candy clouds and a stunning sunset as its backdrop. To her right was the kitchen and right in front of her, after she'd walked a couple feet from the fireplace, was a small hallway. She moved forward, spying a bathroom to her left just before glimpsing the bedroom ahead. Another spacious room with yet another beehive fireplace and a bed that looked like five people could fit on it. Caprise wasn't nervous. She'd slept with X last night and nothing had happened. She'd had sex with him twice and was almost positive that if—or she should probably say when—the urge hit them they'd have sex again. Unlike many single females she didn't have any hang-ups about sex. It was basic and normal between two healthy adults.

X didn't give the impression of a man who dealt beyond the physical. That worked for Caprise—no strings, no complications, that's what she'd decided to have once she returned. Anything more might test her newfound resolution of her past.

Caprise sat on the bed, rubbing a hand down her back, letting the low muffle of their voices be drowned out by her thoughts. In the next instant her cell phone rang. Dread sifted through the room like tear gas and her heart began to pound. It was him. She knew it as surely as she knew her name. After all these years he'd found her, and he knew exactly what she'd done.

"So how long did it take?" Bas asked X as they stood out on the patio just beyond the living room.

"How long did what take?"

Bas chuckled. "The ass whipping Nick administered when he found out you'd slept with his little sister."

The FL's laughter continued and for a minute X actually considered punching him. But there was that whole ranking thing that held him back. Besides, it wasn't a question he wouldn't have asked if the shoe were on the other foot. So instead of getting physical he simply shrugged. "We talked a bit, then things got in the way."

Bas nodded. "So he really hasn't had the time to dig into your ass yet?"

"Hey, I'm not here for your amusement, Perry. When do I get to talk to Hernandez?"

"Whenever you're ready. But I've got to tell you, the guy's not in any hurry to give up his boss."

"We just want to know the connection," X said. He'd been walking from one end of the patio to the other, looking over the iron railing to the drop of trees and rooftops of the adjoining buildings in this resort that actually looked like a tiny village.

His gaze kept traveling up the red-rock formations, to the tops that looked as if they touched the sky. But X wasn't awed by its beauty or soaking up any of the soul-healing crap. He was looking for someone—or rather, something—that he knew was out there.

"What do you think he knows, other than who's running the cartel?" Bas asked, bringing his attention back to the conversation at hand.

"Raul Cortez is running the cartel now. My questions are about Julio, the father."

"He's in a mental institution now, isn't he?" Bas asked.

"A nursing home," X corrected him, a sarcastic note to his tone. "He's apparently too fragile to talk. But I think somebody's just keeping a clamp on what he's got to say.

Hernandez was his right-hand man. Seems logical he'd know whatever Julio knows."

Bas looked skeptical. "I don't know, man. These families are known for keeping their secrets. Hernandez isn't even Julio's blood, just an employee. Even if he knows something, how is that going to help us?"

X hadn't gone into details with Bas about Rome's and Nick's parents and the possibility that they'd been in cahoots with the infamous drug cartel. What Rome and Nick suspected would be considered nothing less than treason by the Assembly. What that meant for the work they'd both done in advancing the stateside shifters, X had no clue. What he did know for sure was that his brothers needed closure: They needed to know if the men who had raised them had been loyal or not. That was a word X hadn't known until he'd met Rome and Nick. His parents hadn't known what it meant and thus couldn't have taught their only son. Closure wasn't on the horizon for X, and that was just fine. He'd rather hate the ones who enabled that limp-dick bastard Jeremiah to torture him than think any rational thoughts where they were concerned. He didn't even think of them by their names, they were such a distant and disgusting part of his life.

That's what separated him from Rome and Nick. Their parents were important to them; they loved and respected them. Finding out their fathers may not have been all that they believed would be devastating. X wanted to be the one to find out the truth and to break whatever he had to them. As close as all the FLs were, they were no match for the threesome that had begun more than two decades ago.

"Look, I just need about an hour alone with him." X was about to address the quizzical look in Bas's eyes when something stopped him.

He stared inside the suite to the living room, but saw nothing out of the ordinary. Without another word he was heading inside, finding his way back to the bedroom where Caprise was sitting on the bed, her fingers massaging her temples as she rocked back and forth.

"What's the matter? What happened?" he asked immediately, knowing there was something wrong.

From the look she had when she lifted her face to his, she wasn't about to tell him.

"I'm not going to play this game with you, Caprise. I know something's going on with you."

She stood then, slow, graceful. Her arms fell to her sides as she kept his gaze. "You just know everything, don't you? All of you." Her gaze traveled over his shoulder to the doorway where X figured Bas was probably standing. "You think you know everything, can fix anything. Well, you can't! Nobody can!" she yelled before pushing past X and heading to the bathroom, where he knew she'd locked the door tight behind her.

"Relationship problems?" Bas asked.

X whirled around to find the shifter leaning against the doorjamb staring at him with that ridiculous smirk he wore more often than not. "Shut up."

Bas's response was a roar of laughter as X cursed.

Hernandez hadn't had much to say, which X totally expected. What had come as a shock was how frail the man looked—how being out of the spotlight, away from his job and people he most likely considered family, had affected him. He was a fifty-eight-year-old Latino with golden skin that hung on his bones like old leather. Deepset dark eyes had watched X from the moment he entered the room until he sat down across from him. He'd kept his back straight and shoulders squared like a good soldier, his hands folded on the metal table.

"Have you ever heard the name *Loren Reynolds*?" X had asked immediately.

His reply was a shake of the head.

"How about *Henrique Delgado*?"

Another shake of the head.

"Julio Cortez knew both these men. He talked to them almost daily for two years, had meetings with them, even met up with them a couple of times in Brazil. You don't know anything about that?"

He did not shake his head this time, which was a good thing. X was still irritated by Caprise's mood; add that to the fact that he swore he was being followed or watched, or both, and that put him in a pretty foul mood. Another mute-like response and he was bound to reach out and touch the guy.

"Who is Julio Cortez?" Hernandez asked, a slow grin forming across his face.

X sat back in his chair and watched the man carefully. He had no doubt Hernandez had heard of Loren and Henrique. He'd even bet his life the men had all met together. Julio would not have acted alone; he would have needed backup. Hernandez was his lieutenant, aka his backup.

"It's getting late," X started. "And I've been traveling a long time. So here's what I'm going to do. And I want you to understand that I'm being very generous here." He leaned over, resting his elbows on the table as he got closer to Hernandez.

"I'm not generous often so if I were you I'd take advantage of this offer." There was nothing peaceful about X's way of dealing with suspects. Ever.

Rome was the peacekeeper, the negotiator. Nick was the act-now-figure-things-out-later type. And X, he was brute force walking. So when he stood Hernandez should have known to fear for his life. Yet the cocky SOB kept glaring at X as if he were holding all the cards. Wrong.

X lifted one booted foot and pushed the edge of the table until it forced Hernandez back, his chair flipping over. The other side of the table's edge now leveled over the man's neck—he hadn't been quick enough to roll beneath the table when his chair made an abrupt exit from beneath him. He was trapped, his dark eyes bulging as he coughed.

"I've got a pretty little chica named Marianna sitting tight back in DC. She's got the cutest dimples and a body most men dream of," X said. He smiled down at the asshole, but it wasn't a good smile. Not in the least.

Hernandez's beady little eyes perked up. His hands flailed beneath the table as he reached for its edge to attempt to push it away. X only gave him the tiniest bit of space just in case he needed his throat dislodged so he could speak.

"Now I'm gonna go and have me some dinner. You think about those questions and see if you can come up with an answer."

For good measure he pushed the table against Hernandez's throat one more time before pulling back. The table rocked to the floor and hit with a loud bang. Hernandez did have the good sense to roll over then, falling to his stomach on the floor as he gasped for air. X started for the door, then turned back, glaring at Hernandez.

"Try not to think about Marianna and all she's got to offer a man. Especially one who has her locked in his bedroom."

Hernandez came to his knees, one arm extended as he pointed to X.

"¡Bastardo! ¡Te voy a matar si le toca!" he yelled.

"You're in no position to threaten me, Hernandez," X told him, a growl brewing in his chest as his beast prepared for battle. "I'll be back in the morning. Think about

my answers or kiss your daughter good-bye. How's that
for a threat?"

He left then to the sound of Hernandez yelling in Spanish, louder and more fluently. X chuckled as he moved
down the long hallway, shiny steel walls on both sides of
him. There was no danger from Hernandez or his threats.
The man was locked down deep beneath the earth. He
couldn't even imagine daylight, let alone get the opportunity to see it, or to contact one of his henchman to follow
through on the threat. No, Hernandez was locked down
tight and X's threat regarding his daughter was the bait
that would have the man singing everything he knew
come morning. Hell, he could even sing it in Spanish for
all X cared, as long as he gave him the information he
wanted.

Half an hour later X was doing something he'd never in
all his years thought he would do. He was preparing to
have dinner with a woman.

Not just the sit-down-and-eat type of stunt. But a real,
live, I-talk-you-talk sort of gathering. The reason—
Caprise had something on her mind and X was willing to
bet everything he had that something was related to the
phone calls she was getting—the phone calls that had
him outraged.

What X knew about women was mostly between their
legs, or on their chests, or their backsides, or . . . bottom
line, he wasn't real good with actually trying to relate to
them. And if he were being totally honest with himself
he'd have to ask over and over again, why Caprise? She
was stubborn, contrary, moody, bitchy, and usually just a
pain in the ass to be around. On the other hand, X vaguely
remembered her as an intelligent and vivacious teenager.
And presently, she was his best friend's sister and for the

moment, his lover. The fact that he actually cared about her well-being was an added bonus. Finally, she was a female. If there was one thing Shadow Shifters did with all their power and without reservation, it was protect their females.

So he was going to try to get on even ground with Caprise, to calm some of the hostility always brewing between them and talk to her reasonably. And if that didn't work, he was putting her over his knee and paddling her ass until she told him what he wanted to know. The latter thought had his dick hardening as he entered the suite they shared.

X didn't see her when he first entered. That was a good thing, since his arousal wasn't easily hidden; his length rested against his thigh masked only by jeans that weren't the loose-fitting kind. He carried the box of food the woman Jewel had helped him with. She was a timid sort of woman, such a startling contrast with Caprise, but she was very helpful. X figured Bas had assigned the woman to take care of whatever they needed while they were here.

He went into the kitchen and saw the small table with its four chairs. There was a full-size refrigerator, an electric stove, sink, and dishwasher. Unfortunately the space wasn't huge . . . and X was. Or rather he felt like he was when his leg hit the back of a chair then, as soon as he turned, he backed into the sink. Cursing, he figured eating in here would be just as uncomfortable. While Caprise was what he considered a little too thin—except for her bountiful breasts—she was tall, at least five-eight or -nine. Both of them in here together would not be cute, or safe for that matter.

He went back out to the living room and stood there, box of food in both hands. He turned and looked at the couch, the coffee table, the lounging chair. Then he turned in the other direction and looked at the fireplace. They could picnic on the floor. X groaned. This was taking much more thought than he'd anticipated.

"What are you doing?" she asked. X nearly jumped out of his skin because he hadn't heard her approach.

He cursed. Then looked at her and seemed to lose all words, even the bad ones.

It was already after eight in the evening. The sun had set, leaving the sky a brilliant indigo hue that gave an eerie sort of feel to the rocky resort. But none of that was what gave X pause. It was her, the woman he'd been trying to set up this meal for, to talk to, to get answers from. She was the one that had him swallowing hard.

"Do you need help?" she asked, taking a step toward him.

"Dinner," he said and clamped his lips shut tightly. "I brought dinner."

He'd seen women wearing much less—hell he'd seen her completely naked, so this shouldn't have affected him this way. She wore a black nightgown. Actually, it looked like someone had spilled black ink over her, the silky material fit her so snugly. When she walked, one long leg slipped through a split that should have been illegal. There was no way in hell she was wearing anything beneath that getup.

"You want me to take the box?"

He shook his head, reaching once again for his control—the control that only seemed to slip when Caprise was involved. "No. Just trying to figure out where we should eat."

"Come on in here. I've already made myself comfortable," she said, turning to lead him back toward the bedroom.

Here was the thing about Caprise: Even without trying—which he was fairly certain she wasn't doing right now—she was too fucking sexy. Her hair was pulled in a high ponytail, she had no shoes on, and there was no makeup on her face. She was probably getting ready for bed, not sex.

Yet all X could think of as he watched her walking in front of him was holding on to her thin hips, and thrusting deep between the delectable globes of her ass.

She'd climbed onto the bed. The nightgown rose up her thighs unapologetically as she crossed her legs then looked up at him expectantly. "What do you have?"

"Ah." He floundered for a second, his cat scratching at the surface, itching for release. "I don't know. I just told Jewel we needed food. Figured you weren't in the mood to go out."

Caprise shrugged as she reached for the box he lowered to the bed. "I just might be getting used to being locked up all the time."

"I doubt that," X said, sensing the reason she'd stayed in the room had to do with those calls and text messages she was receiving, and not any real attempt at being obedient.

Kicking off his shoes, he joined her on the bed and accepted a container she offered him. He opened it and frowned.

She laughed and his head jerked up. Her smile was genuine, her eyes alight with humor.

"I take it you don't like that," she commented.

"It's got something green in it," he said, still frowning.

She leaned in to take a look. "I think that's spinach."

X shook his head. "Stuff is only good if your name's Popeye. I'll pass."

She was laughing again as she reached into the box. "You mean your mother never made you eat your veggies? Such a brat you are."

X didn't say that his mother never made him do anything, other than visit their neighbor. Inside, his cat roared at that thought, and X shut it out. Something he'd been used to doing for a very long time.

"Is there a sandwich in there?" he asked, knowing there was because he'd specifically asked Jewel for one.

"Yeah, I'm sure you'll hit all the basic food groups with this one," she said, tossing it to him.

Her mood seemed to have shifted, which for Caprise happened frequently. When he'd left her before she'd been angry—no, that wasn't accurate, she'd been upset. The fact that he'd asked what was going on had pissed her off, but that was just a cover-up. Now she would be cheery, or as cheery as Caprise could be, and keep talking as if nothing had ever happened. That's how she'd been when she'd shown up just as the jet was about to take off. She'd bolted out of the SUV Seth drove, marched right across the tarmac, and started up the steps to the jet without so much as looking at him. Once she was seated she'd begun talking about Arizona and how she'd visited here before and was looking forward to the return. Not once did she mention the phone call he'd answered back at Havenway or who had been calling her.

X figured it was a good sign that they'd apparently reached some type of truce. Which was all well and good, but it wasn't going to stop him from trying to find out who was taunting her and why.

Chapter 14

"So where did you go when you left DC?" X asked.

They were lying on the bed, both of them with fluffy pillows stacked behind their heads. He could stretch his arm out between them and wouldn't touch her. Still, the warmth of her presence engulfed the room, the sound of her breathing echoed in his ears, and her scent—a mixture of flowers and a fresh breeze that reminded him of summer—tickled his nostrils.

"I went away" was her quick reply.

"Caprise."

"Don't do that," she said with a huff. "Don't say my name like you're ready to discipline me for not answering every one of your questions, when you do the same thing all the time."

"Okay, where did you go away to?"

She stared at him, wondering just how long it had taken him to become this closed off. He wanted to know everything about her and yet didn't want to share anything about himself. For her that was perplexing. "Why is it important?"

"Because I want to know."

"And do you always get what you want, Xavier?"

It was the way she said his name. It had to be, otherwise X was going to have a hell of a time later trying to figure out why he answered.

"No, Caprise, I don't."

She didn't reply right away.

"Why didn't you contact Nick to let him know you were okay?" He'd rephrased his question because the look on her face was weary. Caprise was no soft and sensitive girl; for all that she looked 100 percent female, X recognized a fighter when he saw one. Wherever she'd gone and whatever had happened while she was away, she'd done her best to defeat it before returning home. She never would have come back if she thought her past would follow her. He was certain of that, but the fact only angered him more.

She inhaled deeply, then said, "I contacted him to let him know I was okay."

"It might help if you talk about it," he said and almost frowned at the thought. He'd never talked about his past and had no plans to. Did that make him a big-ass hypocrite or what?

"We could do something else," she said, rolling over until X could now feel her warm breath on his cheek. "Instead of talk, I mean."

Her tongue traced a line along his neck, moving upward until she was just beneath his earlobe, where she bit him. It was a quick clamping of her teeth over his skin, but the stinging sensation rippled throughout his body, alerting every pleasure–pain instinct he had.

"You have so many tattoos," she was saying, her breath a whisper along his skin as she moved farther down his neck. "Since you like to talk, tell me about this one."

Her tongue flattened over a spot on the bottom of his neck, just before his shoulders began. X sucked in a breath and thought about not responding. Then her tongue

circled the tattoo she'd asked about, and blood rushed
through his body, resting in throbbing persistence at his
dick.

"The moon dripping with blood," he told her in a
voice that had grown gruff. "It's death."

"Hmmm," she mumbled.

Her fingers grabbed the hem of his shirt and she pulled.
The shirt ripped up the center. Caprise continued to tear at
it until she was pulling the remnants down his arms. She
looked satisfied as X peered at her through eyes he'd
known had shifted to his cat. The beast lurked just beneath
his skin, pacing back and forth, wanting nothing more than
to reach out and tear away that godforsaken nightgown of
hers. The man insisted they both wait and see where she
planned to take this new conversation.

One hand flattened over his nipple, her tongue settling
on its twin. As she licked and sucked, her fingers teased
and touched. Only the discipline he'd been spoon-fed by
the military kept him perfectly still. She'd straddled him,
her strong legs bracing his hips. The tips of her breasts
covered in that silky material whispered over his abs as
she moved. He opened his mouth because breathing
calmly though his nostrils was no longer an option. His
hands had been behind his head where he ordered them to
stay, no matter how tempting the idea of touching became.

"This one," she said moving down his side, her hands
and mouth creating a war of sensations all over his body.

"It's the jaguar," he said through clenched teeth.

She looked up at him then, her fingers still tracing the
outline of the large cat that began at his back and wrapped
around to his front. "Your other half?"

"*Our* other half," he said adamantly, holding her gaze
with his own.

Her head dipped slowly, her tongue moving in sweet
circles over his abs.

"So strong," she said. "So powerful. Always in control, aren't you, Xavier?"

He couldn't think of a good answer because as she'd talked she'd moved lower. Her nimble fingers had undone the snap and zipper on his jeans and were pushing them and his boxers down his thighs. When she'd taken them completely off she slinked back upward, her hands instantly going to his rock-hard length.

"I wonder if anybody could ever break your control. If you could ever completely let go with someone," she said, moving her hand from the tip of his dick to the base.

On the down stroke she paused and looked up at him. "What is it?"

X licked his lips and took a deep breath. "Piercings," he told her, knowing instinctively what she was referring to.

When she'd released his dick it still jutted upward as if begging her to touch it once more. Instead she'd leaned down to get a closer look. One tentative finger ran along the underside of his length where the metal piercings were lined.

"Does it hurt?" was her next question.

"It's the best kind of pain there is" came his reply.

She looked up at him again, one elegantly arched eyebrow raised. "Really?"

"Definitely," he confirmed. "It's the kind of pain that makes you feel so fuckin' good you want to scream."

His voice was rough, and his words probably would have been considered crass by anyone other than Caprise. Looking up at her he could tell she wasn't offended, nor was she afraid. There was no intimidation, and the curiosity that had bloomed when she noticed the piercings had now turned to heat. A heat that X prayed would go farther. He wanted her to keep touching him. Better than that, he wanted her to wrap her pretty lips around his thick dick, to take him deep within the heated moisture of her mouth and never let him go. Dammit, he wanted like he'd never wanted before!

As if she'd read his mind, Caprise extended her tongue and licked over the piercings, her wet tongue applying persistent pressure against the skin covering the metal balls. X sucked in a breath. She licked again and again, like he was the best-tasting lollipop ever created. With each stroke of her tongue the metal balls circled, inciting ripples of pleasure throughout his entire body. X spread his thighs wider. Caprise adjusted herself closer, hands on his thighs, tongue on his dick.

"Could I make you lose control, Xavier?" she asked after one long lick.

"You can suck me, Caprise," he told her, his voice raspy with need. "Now!"

There was that smile again. The knowing one that spread slowly across her face, making her eyes shine with yearning—her cat's eyes.

She was beautiful as she looked up at him, hair falling in a wild mass of strands around her face, chest heaving as she licked her lips. She was hellfire all bottled up in one hot-as-hell package, a hungry little cat just feeling her way around. He wondered if his cat could coerce her to come out and play.

"Come on, Caprise. You know you want to."

Her tongue stroked along her lips again and this time X pulled his hands away, extending his hand so one finger touched the tip of her tongue. She licked around the digit, keeping her eyes focused on his.

"Yeah, you want to, babygirl. You want to take all this inside and suck every last drop."

She purred. Yes, purred like one hungry and soon-to-be-satisfied cat.

"You want to take control," he told her as she sucked his finger midway into her mouth. "Take it!"

Caprise pulled back quickly, letting his finger slip past her lips. He was right, she did want it, had wanted the taste of his length in her mouth since last night when he'd thrust so deeply inside her. So why shouldn't she?

Dipping her head, she pulled the tip between her lips and suckled. His gasp was so loud, the rumble of a cat's awakening coming from deep in his chest. Oh yeah, she was definitely going to take control.

Caprise took his length completely, letting the tip rest at the back of her throat as another one of those pesky purrs escaped. He seemed to like that because his shaft throbbed in response. Up and down she worked his length, soaking him with the moisture from her tongue, sucking him hard and deep with the suction of her jaws. His hips lifted off the bed, his fingers burying deep in her hair, pulling until she almost wanted to scream from the prickles of pain. That pain spurred her on, made her take more of him, cupping his heavy balls between her fingers, massaging them until they grew tighter and tighter.

X pumped fast, guiding her head to match the speed. He cursed and he moaned and he wanted to come more than he wanted to take his next breath. Caprise could tell and felt an amazing sense of accomplishment wash over her. In this hotel room, in this moment, she had the biggest and most lethal Shadow Shifter in the palm of her hand, literally and figuratively.

His release came with an explosion that almost knocked her off her game. But Caprise quickly rebounded, accepting all he had with deep swallows and loud moans. When he suddenly jerked her upward by her waist, pushing her nightgown out of the way and positioning her over his still-hot and heavily aroused dick, she could have gasped.

But she didn't. Instead she let out a low growl of her own, felt her incisors lengthen and poke against her lower lip. She'd let her loose. Let the cat inside come out to play, something that had not happened in what seemed like forever.

"There you are," he said with a knowing smirk. "There's my babygirl."

She stretched, lifting her arms, arching her back, letting the wet lips of her vagina rub along the tip of his length. It felt good, it felt long overdue as the cat inside stretched with her.

"Pretty, pretty, pretty," X was saying as he pushed down the straps of her gown to expose her breasts.

He palmed them both, squeezing as if he fully expected milk to shoot through the nipples and into his mouth. Again with that pleasure–pain; his grasp was almost too tight—she was about to scream. But then there came pleasure soaring through her like a tidal wave, hitting smack in the center of her vagina where its reaction incited a creamy release.

When he took one turgid nipple into his mouth, held it between his teeth and moved his head from side to side, Caprise thought she would die from the pain, or the pleasure. She couldn't distinguish anymore. His hands gripped her ass, separated her cheeks, and felt everything in between. She was so slick his fingers just slid from one entrance to another, around her clit, through her plump folds, then sank into her waiting center. She jerked and gyrated with him, only to receive a warning in a voice so deep and so steady she almost trembled.

"Not yet. Not until I say so," he told her.

Ordinarily Caprise wasn't good at taking orders, even those spoken in such a serious tone, but this one kept every muscle in her body still. Biting down on her lower lip was all she could do to keep from yelling out with the intense pleasure that seemed to be strangling her.

"Control doesn't come easy," he told her. "You want it, you've got to take it. So tell me, do you want it?"

She whimpered, hated the sound, then hissed through teeth she tried to keep closed.

"Yes," she said on a ragged release of breath. "I want it!"

"Then take it," he offered, lifting her hips and planting her center over his tip once more.

Caprise slammed down on his length, so hungry to get all of him inside. She undulated her hips, rested with the feel of him so full and deep inside her. Then she pulled up and slammed down until they were both breathless. His upward thrusts were quick and hard but she matched them, loved the magnificent feeling they incited. He grabbed her breasts again, growling with every stroke. After a few moments she couldn't tell who was growling, purring, roaring, whatever. The air was thick with arousal, the scent cascading around them both until release finally came with the force of a hurricane, sweeping them both up in its windy grasp, dumping them like objects—satiated objects—in the center of the bed, where they could do nothing more but collapse.

His nightmare began the moment Caprise's touch was replaced by Jeremiah's—the filthy bastard's. X roared the instant he recognized him. It was the scent at first, stale potato chips and liquor, so much liquor he was always amazed the man could stand up on his own, let alone do the vile things he'd done to him.

"You're my boy," he used to say to him.

X cringed from the memory.

"You're *my boy*."

It sounded sick, the tone, the way he dragged out the

one-syllable word *boy* to make it sound as nasty as X felt inside.

"No!" X roared back.

But the idiot kept coming. He kept walking toward him. X backed against the wall. He didn't want to run, didn't want to be a sissy as his father had called him. He wanted to stand strong like a man.

"You're always gonna be mine," he said, coming closer, taking off his shirt as he approached.

His boxers were dirty and twisted around his waist, his vile body part peeping with disgusting clarity through the slit.

"Stop playing now. You know what to do."

X knew what he didn't want to do. What he wasn't going to let this fucker do to him ever again. Inside him something was shifting, like somebody was moving inside him. His arms trembled, his heart beating so fast he thought it would burst clear through his ribs. He kept breathing, taking in deep breaths, then letting them out quickly. Everything around him seemed like it was spinning—everything but the man who would soon become X's demon.

When he was close enough he reached for X, touching his hand lightly to his shoulder.

"I sure do like you, boy," he told X.

Abruptly the spinning stopped and the rippling inside X intensified. With hands more powerful than he could ever imagine X grabbed the man's wrist, twisting it as he removed it from his arm.

"Don't touch me," X told him through clenched teeth. "Don't. Ever. Touch. Me. Again!"

The man opened his mouth, was about to say something else, but X kept twisting his wrist until he heard the bones cracking beneath his strength.

"Let go, let go," he pleaded, falling to his knees.

But X didn't hear him. He just reached for the other wrist, breaking that one, too. "You don't deserve to touch anyone," he told him as he looked down at him and saw something totally different. It was still the dirty old man who'd lived next door to them, the one who'd asked X's mother if X could come over and do odd tasks for cold cash. The one who'd taught X not to trust anyone . . . ever.

"You don't deserve to live," X said dropping the man's wrists and reaching for his neck. "You sick, dirty, bastard!" he roared over and over again.

And then it was dark, the scent of blood filling the air. X opened his mouth to breathe and choked as liquid filled him. The taste was acidic and made him heave. He tried to stand but sat back quickly as the room swam out of control. His heart pounded, echoes ringing in his ears. *My boy. My boy. My boy.*

"X, it's just a dream. It's just a dream," he heard a female voice whispering.

Hands touched his shoulders, wrapping around his waist as she hugged him from the back. She continued to tell him it was just a dream, rocking slowly back and forth as she held him, comforted him. Nobody had ever comforted X before. Ever.

He opened his eyes slowly to the darkness of the room and remembered where he was, who he was with. Caprise was right. It had been a dream. A stupid fucking dream that he had all the time, one that even with death on his hands did not cease to haunt him. His skin rippled, the cat struggling to break free. It wanted to run, to roar, to kill this ugliness inside once and for all.

But she held him too tight.

"Dreams aren't real. They can't hurt you," she was saying to him. "You wake up and they go away. Everything that happened in the dream goes away."

Her voice sounded distant even though she was right there with him, holding him so close he could feel her heartbeat as if it were his own. X rested his elbows on his knees as he sat on the side of the bed. Just when he was about to turn around to tell her he was fine and make a graceful exit to the other room to get his shit together, she spoke again.

"I have dreams," she said quietly. "I have them all the time. Sometimes they're fine and I don't remember them." She took a deep breath. "And sometimes . . . sometimes, I just can't forget."

A part of X wanted to acknowledge he had the same experience, that they were two of a kind. But that wasn't going to happen. It couldn't. He remained silent and still.

She continued, "I can't forget and remembering hurts. It hurts too much."

Her voice hitched like she might be crying and X shot up off the bed, breaking their contact.

"I'm going to the kitchen to get a drink. You want something?" he asked, the coarse, bitter sound of his voice echoing in the darkness.

He didn't turn, didn't want to see her sitting vulnerably on the bed looking up at him. He just didn't.

After a few silent moments she said in the barest whisper, "No. I'm fine."

"Good," he bit out. "So am I."

But as he stalked out of the bedroom X knew that wasn't true. They were both liars and cowards.

They were two of a kind.

Chapter 15

X had just checked the clock on the microwave, wincing only slightly to learn it was just a little after one in the morning. The roaring sounded a second before there was a light knock at the door. His instincts were momentarily torn. The roaring was coming from outside. There was a cat out there, a big, hungry cat from the sound of its cry.

Caprise was still in the bedroom and someone was at the door. With a curse a he moved to the door, pulling it open, ready to cut loose on whoever the fool was on the other side at this hour of the night.

"You hear it, too?" Bas asked the moment he saw X.

X nodded. "What the fuck is it and how long's it been out there?"

"Just before you arrived," Bas said. "It's a cat no doubt."

"You've never had cats out here before?"

"No," Bas replied as they both headed to the patio. They looked out into the dark, heard the roar again, and knew it was calling for them. This was no ordinary cat; it was a shifter.

"Let's go get the bastard," X said.

"My thoughts exactly," Bas replied.

"I'm coming," Caprise put in.

X spun around at the sound of her voice. "No the hell you're not."

"You don't control me, Xavier," she said with quiet authority. "I can go wherever I want."

"You two are tiring me out," Bas said with a light laugh. "This is serious, Caprise. You could be hurt."

"Or I could help. Now are we going or are we chatting? That cat out there sounds like he's ready to play," she snapped.

Bas shrugged. "She's a *Topètenia* all right," he said, moving past Caprise and back into the living room. "I've got a small group of guards downstairs. If you're coming, let's go."

X looked at her again. Her eyes were already the melted honey orbs of her cat, thin black slits against an almost luminescent background. She'd slipped on some pants and a tank top, hardened nipples pressing through the material. Her sharp teeth were visible when she spoke, clawed fingers at her side.

"Let's go," he said finally and moved past her out the door.

"These buttes drop off dramatically in some spots," Bas said from the head of the group.

X was traveling directly behind him, with Caprise only about two feet to the rear. That's exactly where he wanted her to remain. Close enough for him to protect her at all times. If anything happened to her out here . . .

"The cat's this way," X said, more to refocus his thoughts than to add to the conversation.

"Right" was Bas's reply. "There's two guards ahead of us a couple feet. The minute he's spotted we'll know."

"What the hell's he doing out here is what I want to know," X stated.

"He's a Rogue. What do you think he's doing out here?" Caprise retorted.

X didn't bother to turn back and look at her. She was a shifter, she would know a Rogue when she scented one. He just wondered if she realized how easily she was slipping into their lifestyle, despite her reservations about it.

"We haven't had Rogues in Perryville," Bas said, his anger apparent. "They've been doing some trafficking in New Mexico, but no sightings here."

"Until now," Caprise added once more.

A loud roar, followed by a human scream, stopped their words. Bas shifted first without preamble. He was a golden cat, from his dusky gray eyes that had transformed to look as sparkly as a red-gold coin and his fur that was picture-perfect yellow-gold with the most perfect black-and-brown rosettes. But that was the end of the picturesque jaguar. When he opened his mouth, roaring a message to all in hearing distance, there was no mistaking his lethalness.

X didn't hesitate another second but ripped through his own clothes with a shift that cracked bones and stretched muscle until his six-foot-long almost black cat was running up the rocky terrain behind Bas. His rosettes were black, blending in with his coat without close inspection. His eyes were a muted green, his night vision excellent, instincts on point as he ran the unfamiliar terrain.

Rogues were near, there was no doubt, and blood had been drawn. All bets were officially off.

Caprise watched the two cats in front of her. She witnessed the seamless shift from human to beast and felt a tugging deep in her stomach. All around she sensed activity. From behind there were more guards still traveling in human form, running as fast as they could to catch up to them. Beyond there was Bas and X, sleek jaguars using their clawed paws to grip the hardened red rock that formed the buttes they traveled between. It wasn't easy; this wasn't the jaguars' natural terrain. Then again they weren't natural jaguars.

She continued on foot, feeling the movement inside her but ignoring it. One of the guards had slipped her a gun as they'd left the shelter of Bas's resort. He had no idea if she knew how to use it or not; nobody did really. But Caprise had trained extensively during her time away. She held an eighth dan black belt in tae kwon do, had mastered shooting on an open and enclosed range in her first year's training, and had taken boxing classes for almost a year before returning to her love of dance. She was as limber and detail-oriented on the dance floor as she was agile and deadly in the fighting ring.

This gun was a little heavy in her hands. It was a Sig, and she preferred the lovely Glock 19 she owned and stored in her room at Havenway. If she'd known this trip would be a violent one she would have brought it with her. Instead she was risking twisting her ankle as she ran up and down these rocks with only her brown Coach Bonney Sneakers—even in combat she had the cutest shoes—instead of a pair of sturdy boots.

They were ahead of her by a couple of feet, cats moving much faster than her human legs, but she kept her night vision trained on them, watching their every move. And that's when she saw it, before either of them did.

They were moving along the Boynton Canyon hiking trail. Caprise knew this because she'd spent her day reading the travel brochures in their room. Along the trails was packed dirt with trees splattered here and there, red rock jutting upward as if to break free of the flatland. Bas and X had just circled a butte when another roar sounded. The sound was different than what they'd heard before.

Another cat probably. And it had come from behind the guys, just a few feet in front of Caprise.

It was a cat, a large one with teeth and flanks as long and muscular as Bas's and X's. This was a trap. While Bas and X chased the cats ahead, this cat would corner them. Caprise raised her arm, aimed the gun to shoot, but the cat darted down from the rock. She began to run, cursing as she went. She'd never catch it on foot.

The shift took her completely by surprise. Her human mind was thinking of another plan, her fingers wrapped securely around the gun in her right hand. As she took her next breath the gun hit the ground; so did her arms that were now strong front paws, her legs pulling up the back of her own sleek yellow cat. The chuffing sound came next, a clearing of her throat just before she roared so loud she thought the canyon itself was shaking around her.

Her padded paws hit the dirt, kicking up dust as she went. Strength and training had her going up the side of a butte to where she'd spotted the lone cat. When she saw him he'd stopped again, standing at the very edge of the butte, most likely looking down at Bas and X. Caprise had never battled with a cat before, never had any reason to, until now. Her body moved seamlessly through the night air as she charged the cat, opening her mouth to bite at its back just as she landed on top of it.

The element of surprise propelled them both over the edge of the butte, but Caprise held on, her teeth piercing through the thick fur and tough underlying skin. She tasted blood but would not let go, even when they thumped to the ground. Her flanks ached, jaws were locked as they rolled over, the other cat trying to get a grip on her.

Then it was pulled away, her teeth free of its prey. She growled in protest as two other cats battled the one she'd taken down. It was Bas and X, she knew, and she paced with the anger steadily brewing inside her. When the Rogue cat was still and dead as the night, X turned to look at her, his green gaze piercing and reprimanding through the night's darkness.

Caprise did all she could do at the moment: She growled again, lifting a front paw and swiping it in his direction. His cat lunged forward, stopping directly in front of her, his own teeth bared, a disgusted chuff coming from his mouth. She roared back, then decided he wasn't even worth the time. Her cat turned, running into the canyon without looking back.

Washington, DC

Seth left Athena's at a little after four in the morning. He'd been a part of the last guard shift watching the place for Rogues. Of course they were there, selling their drugs and conducting a strip joint business just as they'd suspected. He, along with a good portion of the guards, wanted to go in and kill, walk out and be done. But the FL had given other orders. They were only to watch, not touch. Something about too much attention swirling around them right now.

That entire statement had struck Seth as BS. They were Shadow Shifters; they moved in the shadows in this city just as they did in the Gungi. Nobody knew of their existence, and nobody ever would. He hated that the FL was tying his hands. Hands that at this very moment itched to shift, his cat all but begging to be let loose to run.

He also missed Caprise. She'd only been gone for two days and he felt like he hadn't seen her in an eternity. That was crazy since she was the commanding officer's sister and as cordial as a Rogue on coke. But she was fine as hell, an older woman that Seth had fallen for the moment he'd laid eyes on her. His hope was to guard her body so well she'd one day want to share it and the rest of her life with him. Others would call him a fool for thinking along those lines; that's why he'd kept those thoughts to himself. However, secrecy didn't make them less relevant.

She was across the country with X, another badass commanding officer whom Seth didn't want to cross in any way. That's why he'd taken Caprise to meet him when she asked. His two goals in life were to move up the ranks in the newly formed Stateside Assembly and to one day become an FL of his own Zone. That goal could be fast-tracked if he and Caprise mated. Or vice versa, he thought with a smug smile as he walked to his jeep.

He was about two steps away when he heard the chuffing sound. Stopping instantly, Seth tuned in to all his senses. There was a cat in this alley with him, a big, strong-ass cat with blood on its mind.

"Its showtime, baby," Seth mumbled with excitement. He'd just grabbed the hem of his shirt, about to rip it over his head so he could shift, when he was knocked down.

His body and face hit the ground with a painful thump. Defenses kicking in, he rolled over instantly to face his assailant but was in no way prepared for what he would see.

This cat was huge, easily weighing more than 250 pounds and probably longer than seven feet, even though he couldn't see beyond the big-ass head full of white fur and crystalline blue eyes glaring down at him. No, the teeth definitely took precedence: All of them were more than two inches long, dripping with spittle down onto him.

Seth's cat reacted instantly, his own teeth elongating, claws emerging from his fingers, body ruffling with fur . . . then the first bite came to his left shoulder. He yelled as pain rippled through his body. The next bite was to his side, and Seth's cat struggled at the halfway point with his human screaming and writhing in pain. Whatever happened after that was a total loss since the world Seth had once known, the dream of becoming FL and mating Caprise Delgado, faded into an abyss of darkness.

Chapter 16

Sedona

"You can slow down now," X said from about three feet behind Caprise.

She was perfectly naked as they moved through the canyons, which made him thankful for the night. Before he'd followed her, Bas had shifted, handing him some extra sweats one of his guards had been carrying. So at least his bottom was covered. He held the top for Caprise, if she'd stop to accept it.

She'd been on the move since leaving the group about twenty minutes ago, and he'd been right behind her. For the first ten minutes he'd decided she needed to come down from the adrenaline rush of shifting. If Caprise didn't want to be lumped in with their shifter community it stood to reason she hadn't taken her shifter form in a while—and most likely she'd never been involved in a battle with another shifter. Yet tonight, she'd done both. Her emotions were liable to be all over the place right now. And even though he was the last person to be on emotion-control duty, X was determined to be the one to see her through this.

The innately sexual look in Bas's eyes as he'd seen her cat in action said the FL was definitely interested in what he saw. A female was fair game until she was mated, and while X and Caprise had enjoyed each other sexually, neither one of them was even considering the mating part. Hell, X didn't even know all the details to shifter mating and all that ceremonial BS Rome and Nick had gone through. And he wasn't rushing to sign up for any type of Shadow Shifter mating class to learn.

At the same time, he didn't want Bas even entertaining thoughts of touching Caprise. Bas was a womanizer, there was no kind way to put that, and it wasn't all just reputation as Rome had endured. It was the cold honest truth. If ever there was a shifter who abhorred even the thought of being tied to one woman for any length of time, it would be Sebastian Perry. Just one more concrete reason why Bas's ogling of Caprise needed to be checked—immediately.

She kept walking right into the dark canyon. A breeze blew by and for the first time, X realized she could actually be chilly. So instead of speaking again he closed the distance quickly, pulling her arm so she'd have no choice but to stop walking and turning her to face him. With his other hand he thrust the shirt at her, an air of déjà vu surfacing. "Put it on," he said forcefully.

Of course since it was Caprise he was speaking to she rolled her eyes before yanking the shirt from his grasp. Another man might have had the decency to turn away while she dressed. But X had never claimed to be like any other man. He watched, with great interest, as her arms stretched upward to slip the impossibly large sweatshirt over her breasts.

"Better now?" he asked when he was certain he could speak without his voice cracking like some punk-ass little boy.

Why the sight of her naked never ceased to arouse him, X had no clue. He'd seen this body a couple of times already. He'd touched her, fucked her, he should be so over it. And yet here he was, standing in the middle of some damn healing canyon after they'd killed three shifters, with a hard-on that was quickly growing painful.

"You're an ass!" was her heated retort.

X chuckled because for one scary-ass moment he thought she might actually cry. Her bottom lip had quivered when she turned back to face him and her forehead looked a little furrowed. And she was a female—whom he'd discovered were prone to emotional fits after battle. But he should have known better.

She was in his face in about two seconds, her bony finger poking—with a little discomfort—into his bare chest.

"You do not fight for me! I can handle my own. And I had that cat. I would have taken him down without your help," she yelled.

After she'd finished and gulped in air for a breath, X grabbed the wrist of the offending finger and pulled. For good measure he grabbed her other wrist and looked her right in the eye.

"I interrupted because I didn't want him to roll over and kill you," he told her.

"I had him!"

X nodded in agreement. "You did." She'd also had a good portion of his self-control as he'd watched both cats tumble over that butte falling about ten feet to the ground. "But I'm not used to watching females take a fall like that. And I'm definitely not used to seeing you in that position."

"I can fight in any form," she told him, yanking at her arms for him to let go. "I can take care of myself, whether it's from a cat or a . . . I . . . I mean . . ." Her voice trailed off.

Then she did look away, her head down, wrists still trapped by his.

"I know you're a fighter, Caprise. But that's not what this is about, is it?"

"No," she said, her head snapping back around at him. "It's about you not trusting me enough to handle myself." She huffed.

Okay, X could accept that. Nothing would stop him from taking down a kill. That's how jaguars operated. And despite her earlier denial, Caprise was a jaguar. And if he wasn't mistaken—which he really didn't believe he was this time—Caprise was about to have some type of breakdown. X still prayed for no appearances by tears, but pulled her close to his chest, kissing the top of her head.

"You did good out there. Even though I told you to stay behind me."

"I don't have to stand behind you or any man."

X waited a long moment, giving her a minute to catch her breath, to clear her mind, which he knew was whirling right about now.

"You want to tell me about the man you did stand behind? The one who hurt you so bad you're throwing stones at me every chance you get."

She remained still. X admitted to himself that he could have been wrong. This could have been about something totally different. But no, he wasn't. From what he did know about females there were only two things that could get them this worked up—family and/or a man. And since Nick was the doting older brother who had been trying his damndest not to even yell at Caprise, X was betting on the latter.

"Why should I tell you anything?" she asked quietly.

"You don't have to," he told her even though right at this very moment he wanted her to tell him more than anything else in this world. "But it might help." Again, hypocrisy almost choked him. But X had good reasons for keeping his trap shut about his past—good goddamn reasons.

"And Caprise, I have to be straight with you about this. I'm going to find out sooner or later. You could save us both some time by just telling me who the guy was that was stupid enough to fuck with you."

Her head shot up at his words. "And what are you going to do? Go shoot him with your big gun? Or show him your teeth and scare him until he pees in his pants?"

She had a sarcastic tone, most of the time. Now was no different, but it kind of made X want to laugh. Was this how she pictured him? The man that handled things with violence. If so, she wasn't exactly wrong. His plan was to find the bastard and snap his neck—okay, no, he wasn't going to snap the guy's neck, but he was going to make sure he'd never mess with Caprise again.

"I'm going to handle the situation, that's all you need to know."

She took a deep breath. "Well, all you need to know is there was a man and now there isn't. It's been over for a really long time."

"But judging from his texts to you, he's not on board with that decision."

"That's not him," she said, and the scent of her lie almost suffocated X.

That alone made him just a little edgier, if that were possible. "Then who is it?"

She shrugged. "Wrong number."

"Wrong answer, Caprise," was his response.

"So what did Hernandez have to say after your overnight ultimatum wore off?" Bas asked several hours later when they were in his office.

X and Caprise still hadn't said more than two words to each other. But he had received an email from his office with the information on the phone number trace he'd done before leaving DC. The results weren't good, but at least they gave X a place to start looking for Caprise's stalker. Unfortunately, it would circle him right back to Athena's.

"He wrote down some dates—I guess for when meetings occurred—and some amounts that he knew were exchanged. I'm going to take all the info back to DC and work on it from there." That wasn't all that Hernandez had told him, but it was all he planned to tell Bas for now.

"Intel from Comastaz came in just before you arrived," Bas said.

He sat back on the chocolate-brown couch that was across the room from his desk. After the early morning they'd all had, coming back to the room to get some food and some rest had been first and foremost. And instead of the cat X had seen a while ago, he was definitely looking at the man now. He wore cream-colored linen pants and a matching shirt; his shoes were some type of loafer, something X would never try to squeeze his feet into. But on Bas it looked right, as if these things were made for this man. Whatever, X shook his head and took a seat in a chair across from him.

"What's going on there? You thought it might be a leak or something," he said, recalling their conversation from a few weeks ago about the government-owned lab in Sedona.

"It's not good. We were able to get a shifter inside, sent him in as a rep from a waste management company. He found some interesting emails on one of the computers."

"The joys of technology," X replied grimly. Bas wasn't looking like his normally suave self; in fact, X noted the guy's brow was just a bit furrowed, his eyes a little shielded.

"Well, that technology has confirmed one of our greatest fears. I'm telling you this before I tell the other FLs because I know you'll report directly to Rome the minute you return to DC."

X sat up, resting his elbows on his knees. "Give it to me," he told Bas.

"Somebody's asking questions about another species. There was talk of some photos and containment. They don't sound like they have specifics, just a hunch. But it's the government, you know where they can go with a hunch."

X let out the breath he'd unwittingly been holding. "I know what the government doesn't do with important hunches and tips. But this, they'll run with this until the end of time."

"You're right," Bas said. "Just like they're still secretly looking for UFOs."

"Great, now we're in the category with UFOs. Fucking perfect. Rome's not going to like this. Do we know who received the emails, who the sender was, all that?"

"I've got a written report in my office."

"On a secure USB, I hope," X said.

Bas nodded. "All our computers are secure. You should know—you installed most of them."

"Right. But we've got to start being real careful about what we say and to whom. Last month at the raid on Rome's place there was a Rogue found on the property. Baxter thinks he came in with the landscape group earlier that week. And then there was the Rogue that was working at the firm with Rome and Nick. They're everywhere now."

"Yeah, I know. But they're masking their scent. We've got to figure out how they're doing it."

X agreed. "As for the chick at the firm, we think she

may have been sleeping with a human. If that's the case he would have carried her scent and she would have been virtually scent-free."

"Damn genetics," Bas swore. "There's still a lot we don't know about our kind. Like I was thinking the other day, what if one of us was to get a human pregnant. What would that be like?"

For a moment X was quiet. Actually, he was stunned because *pregnant* and *human* were not generally words that went together in Bas's vocabulary. For all that he was a womanizer he usually stuck to shifters because he figured they were safer for whatever reasons he may have had. This was different, and the look he was giving X was even stranger.

"You got somebody knocked up?" X asked, trying to keep this conversation as light as possible.

Bas shook his head. "No, nothing like that. I was just thinking. You know with thousands of us here in the United States and spreading out across the country, it's entirely possible that one of us would hook up with a human and a pregnancy could occur."

X shrugged. "I don't know. Nick's mate is pregnant now and that's strange enough. We're all kind of just waiting to see what's going to happen. I mean, shifter births are fairly common now or else we wouldn't be here. But none of us has ever witnessed any."

"Yeah, I don't know what's going on in my head," Bas said rubbing a hand over his face. "So anyway, you and Caprise—where's that going?"

"Nowhere" was X's instant reply. "What I mean is there's no mating or joining on the horizon."

"You sure about that?" Bas asked skeptically.

"Come on, man, you know me."

Bas nodded. "I do."

"You and I are kind of alike. Commitment's not on our agenda," he replied, watching Bas carefully.

"Right. It's not on my agenda. But you're pretty damn protective of her."

"She's a female, Bas. And she's Nick's sister."

"And she's what to you?"

X stood. "She's Nick's sister and she's a shifter. Damn right I'm going to protect her. As a matter of fact I'm going to go see what she's doing and let her know we'll be flying out in the morning."

But as X opened the door Jewel was on the other side. The smile she gave X wavered as he figured he was probably scowling at her instead.

"Sorry, I was just leaving," he told her.

"What is it, Jewel?" Bas asked.

When she spoke her voice was decidedly feminine and very serious. "There's an urgent call for you from a Roman Reynolds."

Chapter 17

Kalina Reynolds was no longer a detective for the Metropolitan Police Department. She was no longer a candidate for employment with the Drug Enforcement Agency. What she was—and most would be absolutely amazed at her transformation—was the First Female of the Stateside Shifter Assembly. She was part woman and part jaguar, and she was absolutely gorgeous in her four-and-a-half-inch-heeled cobalt-blue Jimmy Choo pumps and white sleeveless V-neck Victoria Beckham mini dress.

Never in her life had Kalina imagined she'd be wearing such clothes, walking in these shoes and heading into the DEA satellite office in DC. It almost felt like déjà vu, since about three months ago she'd done this very thing—different clothes, of course. Still, she looked damn good, felt spectacular, and let her cat purr just slightly as she knocked on the door of Agent Dorian Wilson's office.

It took only seconds for him to beckon her in, and she moved with the slow, sleekness of a cat. Her lips spread into a friendly smile, while her hazel eyes found his glare and locked into place. Gentleman that he was, Dorian stood, extending a hand across the desk toward her immediately. Kalina accepted his hand graciously while surreptitiously glancing around his office.

The space consisted of a cluttered desk, a high-backed faux-leather chair for him, two hard need-to-be-reupholstered chairs for guests, a file cabinet that looked to be on its last leg of life, and no windows. Four walls surrounded the closet-like space, effectively boxing its occupants in for the duration they stayed. Kalina felt claustrophobic already.

"Nice to see you again, Kalina," Dorian said as she let her hand slide from his grasp.

He had a nice, firm handshake and was dressed in dark brown slacks and a beige dress shirt. He'd forgone the tie but from the haphazard way the top button of his shirt was undone she knew it was most likely somewhere in this office. Probably beneath the suit jacket that hung on the back of the door Jax had just closed. Her guard with his six-plus-foot, 285-pound body looked like he was being stuffed in this Cracker Jack box of an office. But he wasn't leaving Kalina's side, not for one instant.

"Hello, Dorian. It's been a while" was her cordial response as she took a seat.

Dorian's gaze went to Jax, who'd fitted himself in a corner, crossing his beefy arms over his massive chest.

"Jax is my guard," she said nonchalantly. "He goes where I go."

Dorian nodded, giving Jax no more than another quick stare before returning to Kalina.

"So you need a guard now?" he asked, taking his seat again and coming forward to rest his elbows on his desk. "Somebody after you?"

Kalina shrugged. "You never know. My husband would rather be safe than sorry."

"That's right." Dorian nodded as he spoke. "You

married Roman Reynolds. The subject of your previous investigation. How's that going?"

"It's going very well, thank you" was her quick reply. She was sure to keep a smile on her face and her gaze on Dorian. He looked at her as if he could see things that weren't there. A few months ago this might have made Kalina nervous, as she was just getting used to the feline side of her gene pool. Now, as comfortable in human form as she was on four legs, she simply watched him in return.

There was something about the agent that he didn't want people to know, a part of him that wasn't quite the norm. She recognized that as a trait she'd carried for most of her life and wondered briefly where Dorian's secret door would lead. But that wasn't why she'd come.

"I understand you're investigating murders now? Has the illegal drug trade dried up?"

Her words were only a mild surprise, which Dorian masked with a tentative smile. "You know how it is, Kalina. You find a clue that seems to connect the dots and you follow the trail. That's what I'm doing, following the trail."

"And it's led you to Xavier Santos-Markland?"

"It's led me to a suspect."

"He's not a killer," she said, knowing in her mind that was only half true. "He couldn't have done that to that girl."

"How do you know what was done to her? And what are you, his character witness?"

"I'm his friend. And I know what was done to her because I've seen the autopsy report. And before you even bother to ask, I probably got ahold of it the same way you did so don't get all dignified about your precious confidential information."

"You're no longer with the MPD," he told her. "You shouldn't have access to any of their records for any reason."

"And you should? This is a local crime. You're a federal drug enforcement agent. *Out of your jurisdiction* seems to be appropriately pinned on your collar."

"Like I said, the murder connects to my active drug investigation. But I must say this is a pleasant surprise—to have you here defending one of my top suspects."

"If he's a top suspect, your case isn't worth crap. All you have on him is his business card. How many strippers or prostitutes have your number, Agent?"

He looked startled for a brief second, then sat back in his chair. His hair was like ebony, cut low and smoothed in thick waves; his eyes were dark and pensive in a face that was handsome but definitely stressed. He wasn't married and had never been, had two sisters and his parents were still alive. Dorian Wilson was the average male, overworked, underpaid, and unhappy. But there was something else. Kalina couldn't quite put her finger on it, but she knew instinctively that there was more to this man than what the eye could see.

"I'm not the one being investigated. Markland is. What happened to you, Kalina?" he asked her seriously. He didn't look to Jax again, but she knew he was asking specifically about her union with Rome and subsequently her departure from the police force.

"I grew up" was her simple reply. "I opened my eyes and realized that no matter how hard we try to convince ourselves otherwise, this world we live in is not black and white. There are always shades of gray that we overlook because we're too afraid to accept or to not be accepted. That's how I know Xavier is innocent and why I came here to tell you to step back and take a hard look at this situation. You might just see the things I've seen."

Not that she wanted him to see the Shadow Shifters—no, that was absolutely not what Kalina wanted. She only asked that Dorian take a deeper look into this murder to see that X wasn't capable of doing those horrific things to Diamond Turner. The girl's primary cause of death was an overdose of an unnamed drug. Only she knew the name; they'd begun calling it the savior drug, as evidenced by the shield on its package. It was Sabar's greatest creation—a deadly mix of an herb called damiana and acids used to base cocaine. It was imperative that the shadows put a stop to him before any more people died because of it. If Dorian directed his energy toward getting the drug off the streets, that would be a tremendous help for the shadows. If he continued to look at X, Kalina was afraid it would end in his demise, because neither Rome nor Nick was going to allow X to be put away for murder. And knowing X, he'd kill anyone who even thought about throwing him in jail.

"Sounds like you're writing a book," Dorian quipped with a shake of his head. "But I'm living in the real world. I didn't drop my job and all my responsibilities because some rich playboy decided to look my way. You breached one of the department's most profound rules: You slept with a suspect. Hell, you married him when you know there's a possibility he could be as dirty as his friend. So I have to ask you again, why are you here? Why come to me about Markland? You have to know that your character is just as tainted as his now. What makes you think I'd take anything you say seriously?"

His voice sounded incredulous, as if he really didn't take stock in anything she'd said. Kalina knew this would be a possibility. To the human eye she had done the unthinkable. But to herself, for her own peace of mind, she'd done the only thing she could have. She'd chosen to be who she was and to live the life she was destined for. Unfortunately, Dorian would never know that.

She came to her feet slowly, clutching her purse under her left arm and staring down at Dorian.

"If you don't take what I say seriously you'll keep running in endless circles trying to pin this murder on Xavier. He's not a killer. And the longer you keep looking in his direction the longer the real killer circulates the streets, being ingested by innocent victims and making a mad race up the charts for the world's number one drug killer." Then she shrugged. "But what do I know, I'm the traitor on the force. The one who wouldn't be handled like a puppet in your game of politics versus justice any longer. It was my fault to think you, of all people, might be above that. My fault indeed."

As she turned to leave, Dorian got up from his chair, racing around the desk to grab her by the arm and turn her back to face him.

"Kalina, wait," he was saying only about a split second before Jax pushed between them.

He held a palm to Dorian's chest while his bulky frame blocked Kalina from further assault.

"Don't touch her again," he told Dorian.

Dorian looked down at Jax's hand, then reached for the gun in his holster, pulling it out and clicking off the safety right in Jax's face.

"You do realize you're assaulting a federal agent. I can either kill you or arrest you. Take your pick." Dorian's brow wrinkled, his lips going to a thin line.

Kalina put a hand on Jax's bicep but looked directly at Dorian. "You won't do either if you know what's best for you," she said as calmly as she'd come into his office and spoken ten minutes ago. "We're finished here, Jax."

The shifter gave Dorian a slight push as he moved his

hand from his chest. He backed away from Dorian, keeping Kalina protected by his body. Dorian continued to hold the gun outstretched. He continued to stare at both Kalina and Jax. He did not pull the trigger and he did not call for backup to have them arrested.

Later, Dorian would wonder why.

It was just after five in the afternoon when Kalina walked into Havenway—or into what she considered complete chaos.

Jax always brought her in through the underground entrance. So after she'd taken the elevator up to the main level she came out at a side door in the front hall of the building. The original dwelling had a T shape, but Rome had ordered new construction to start on the remaining side so there would be two very long hallways with rooms and a connecting wing that would house their main briefing room, the kitchen, dining hall, and medical center. Normally, this hallway was quiet; everybody liked to use the side entrances. But today, it was brimming with shifters, guards all wearing their com links, some in small groups, others lining up and heading to the temporary briefing room. All of them were spitting mad.

Her nostrils flared at the scent of anger and rage wafting through the air. It was a strong, potent, and very distinctive smell that reminded her of the ammonia her foster mother made her use to clean the bathrooms. Something was definitely going on.

An alarm blared and she startled, putting a hand to her chest. That was the signal that Rome was ready for them in the briefing room. She had just taken a step to join them when Jax grabbed her arm. He'd been right behind her when she entered; then she lost track of him because of her concern for what was going on in the place she called home. He was whispering something in his com link but wouldn't let her go.

"FL wants you with him, now," was all Jax said before guiding her through the mass of guards heading in the same direction.

Her heart beat frantically in her chest as so many different scenarios raced through her mind. At least Rome was safe; she could breathe easily about that. But this, everything going on around her, was definitely a sign of something big.

The briefing room was roughly the size of a gymnasium, which wouldn't be able to house all the active shifter guards in DC much longer. There was a stage toward one end, and a podium with a sound system had been set up there. Behind the stage the wall was draped in black, the *Topètenia* insignia in a vibrant green color that reminded her of the foliage in the Gungi poking through the intense black, growing and dominating just about every part of the rain forest. The floor was a dark laminate with cushioned chairs lined in rows of twenty across, ten upward, on each side with a three-foot-wide aisle in between.

Jax escorted her down as guards filed inside, taking whatever seats were available. The stage was still empty, so she looked around for Rome and let out a breath of release when he and Nick followed by Eli and Ezra came through a side door. Everyone took the stage except Rome, who stood there looking at her like he'd lost his best friend. The fact that his slacks and suit jacket were black added to his somber facade. His shoes were shined as always, the dark-chocolate hue of his skin and deep brown eyes lending its own air of resignation to his stance.

"Oh God, X," she said rushing toward him, falling into his open arms.

He shook his head, enfolding her against his chest, holding her there tightly. "No. It was Seth."

The strangled cry that came from her then was heartfelt and cut through her with a ruthless intensity that had tears stinging her eyes. "What happened?" she asked, pulling back just enough to look into her husband's somber brown eyes.

"Rogues" was all he said.

Kalina could tell this was hard for him. His teeth clenched so tight a muscle ticked in his jaw.

"They're all here," Eli whispered to Rome.

Rome nodded and kept his arm around Kalina. She took the stairs to the stage before him, but felt comforted by his hand at her back. Eli and Jax followed them both just like shadows. She could literally hear them breathing behind her, they were so close.

When Rome approached the podium it took only a few seconds for silence to fall over the room like a drape. His presence beckoned obedience throughout. Maybe it was because of the pure power his six-foot-two-and-a-half-inch stature exuded, or it could have been the calm that emanated from him regardless of the situation. Whatever the cause, the guards sat straight in their chairs or stood with legs partially gaped, hands clasped in front of them, eyes focused on their leader, waiting for his command. He stood strong, Kalina standing right beside him. She'd been clasping and unclasping her hands until he reached down and laced his fingers through hers.

"We've just been alerted that Seth Jamison is dead. As many of you may already know, Seth was attacked earlier this morning. The attack was not by a human."

Collective sighs, curses, and gasps sounded immediately. Rome lifted a hand to silence them.

"His vehicle was recovered. We're reviewing the video that was picked up from his dashboard camera.

Preliminarily I will say that it was a shifter of unknown variety."

More comments and some slamming and stomping filled the room. Jax stepped even closer to Kalina.

"For now, we will stand down," Rome continued.

The crowd did not like those words.

Rome spoke even louder, so that it sounded like his voice would break every speaker in the place.

"I said for now," he reiterated, taking a slow, deep breath before continuing. "But we will find out who did this and when we do, he and whoever he's connected to will pay."

Now there was applause. From her peripheral vision she could see that even Nick clapped. At that Rome stepped to the side and nodded to Nick.

The butter-toned shifter who stood about an inch above Rome was dressed in a navy-blue suit, crisp white shirt and sky-blue tie. On his left hand he wore a diamond-encrusted wedding band. On his right wrist was a Tag Heuer, its face glistening in the spotlight that had been lit on the podium. And when he spoke, as with Rome, there was complete silence, absolute obedience. This could be attributed as much to Nick's volatile nature as his sculptured good looks and lethal candor.

"We will increase the patrols around Havenway. Jamison's parents will be brought here to stay for the burial ritual. Five troops will head into the city and form a perimeter around Athena's. Reports are to come in hourly on who goes in and who comes out. If we get a visual of Seth's attacker from the video we'll email it securely to all the guards on duty." Nick paused for a minute, both his hands gripping the sides of the podium as if he were holding on to the last bit of his control. "We will not immediately attack to kill. If at all possible we want this bastard alive . . . at least for a while longer," he said.

There were murmurs, disagreements, of course.

But Nick continued. "This is the mandate of our Assembly leader. No one, and I mean absolutely no one, is to deviate from these orders." There was no mistaking the seriousness to Nick's tone. While he may disagree with the way Rome decided to handle certain things, he had nothing but respect for the man as their leader and would gladly dish out a tremendous beat-down to anyone who dared go against him.

Kalina stood back, watching the crowd, listening to the words being spoken, but it didn't seem real. Just last night she'd seen Seth and Lucas, the teenage *Topètenia* who'd come back to the States with them after they'd visited the Gungi to find Ary. Seth had been training Lucas, giving him kickboxing lessons and teaching him how to handle different weapons. He'd said Lucas was a fast learner, and Kalina could tell the man had received much joy from sharing his knowledge with the teen. Seth would lead one day, Kalina remembered thinking. He'd definitely have his own guard team very soon; both Rome and Nick had noticed the young's man abilities, which was why they'd entrusted him to guard Caprise.

And now he was gone.

Her heart ached at the thought of how his parents must feel, how any parent would feel at such a loss. And for a moment she wondered if her parents—her real parents, the ones who'd been born and lived in the Gungi—had felt the same loss when they'd sent her away.

As the meeting ended she was once again escorted by Rome, with Jax and Eli pulling up the rear.

"I didn't see Lucas," she said when they walked out of the gymnasium heading toward their rooms.

"He's probably still in the medical center. Once he heard Seth had been hurt he raced there and wouldn't leave Ary's side as she and Papplin worked on him."

Dr. Frank Papplin was a shadow who had obtained his medical degree from a human college. He worked at a human hospital, when he wasn't here at Havenway assisting Ary in the medical center and teaching her all he knew about Western medicine. Ary, in turn, was teaching Papplin about healing shifters as a *curandero*. Together with the small staff Ary had acquired, they were both making Havenway's medical center a safe and knowledgeable place for the shifters to receive treatment.

"I want to see him," she said insistently the moment they stopped in front of the door to their rooms.

Rome shook his head. "Not right now, Kalina. We need to get X back here. Somebody has to tell Caprise. Nick and I have to coordinate the teams to go out tonight. And I need you to find out what the cops know about the incident."

She was torn, once again, between her duty as the wife of a shifter leader and the instincts of a woman who'd lived her entire life trying to belong. Kalina didn't know why, but she'd gotten the impression that Lucas was a loner, even though he was born and raised with the tribe. No one had claimed him, no one had argued when Rome said he was coming with them. She wondered why.

"Rome, he's new here. Baxter's been teaching him English but he barely understands what we're saying, let alone watching the man he'd come to adore as a trainer die. He doesn't need to be alone."

Rome was opening the door to their room when he looked over his shoulder. "I hear what you're saying, baby. But this is the priority. Once we're finished here you can go to him."

Kalina knew what he was saying was right, she just didn't like it. "Tell Baxter to get him some food and let Lucas know I'll be there shortly," she said to Jax as she followed her husband into their room.

The suite of the Assembly leader and the First Female were of course the grandest in Havenway. They actually consisted of five rooms adjoined by computer- and sensor-locked doors. There was the bedroom, which was the largest of all the rooms; their private bath; a small kitchenette that connected to the living room; Rome's private office; and on the far end a small conference room. That's where they were headed now. Only seconds later Nick and Ezra joined them.

"Call X," Rome said. Eli immediately went to the phone, which sat on a side table in the room.

Kalina took a seat next to the chair at the head of the table. She always sat on Rome's right. Nick would take the seat on his left. If X were here he'd sit next to Kalina. Their guards would normally sit at the table with them. Today Ezra stood right behind Nick's chair. When Eli finished initiating the call he would move to stand behind Rome and Jax would return to take his stance near Kalina. They were now officially on high alert.

The room was quiet, everyone lost in their own thoughts as they faced what would be called their first shifter loss since the battle with the Rogues began.

"He's not picking up his cell," Eli said.

Nick frowned. "Call Bas," he told him.

Caprise was with X. She'd had sex with him and now they were both in Sedona, thousands of miles away from where Nick could either punch X or shake Caprise for what he believed was their madness. Kalina was silently grateful for the distance. The last thing they needed right now was fighting within the ranks. Even though she was almost positive Nick and X would put the Assembly and the shifters before their personal rift, the tension would still be a huge weight for them all to carry.

"Sebastian Perry." The voice sounded throughout the

space as Eli initiated the speaker that sat in the middle of the conference room table.

"Bas, we've got a situation. Is X with you?" Rome said immediately.

"I'm here," the heavy male voice said. "What's going on?"

Despite the urgent nature of this call both Nick and Rome grew quiet, but only momentarily.

"Seth was killed this morning. Some type of attack by another shifter."

Both X and Bas cursed, with X rebounding first.

"What the hell happened? Where was he?" X asked.

"He was on watch at Athena's. He'd already called in to say he was on his way back when he was attacked. We've got footage from video in the truck but—" Rome paused and looked at Nick.

"But what? Who the hell did this to him? Was it a Rogue?" From the sound of X's voice he was ready to come through the phone line to get to Seth's killer. This situation was so not good.

Kalina clasped her hands and tried to take slow breaths. Her eyes stung each time she thought of Seth and his young face but manly build. But she wouldn't cry. She was a leader now, she had to set the example. Instead she sat with her shoulders squared and let her husband do his job.

"It wasn't a Rogue," Rome said slowly.

"It wasn't *Topètenia*," Nick added.

Complete silence filled the room and the phone line.

"Where is Caprise?" Kalina asked finally. "She has to be told. I can talk to her on a separate line."

"No!" X yelled through the connection.

Then they could hear a throat being cleared, and Kalina suspected it was his. Interesting.

"I'll tell her," he said.

"Kalina's going to see what the cops know about this, and Nick and I are organizing teams to go back to Athena's tonight. I need you back here to analyze this video. I know you've trained some guards to do computer work, but I'd feel better if it was you," Rome said sitting back in his chair.

He looked tired, as if the boulder he'd been carrying on his back had finally tipped over the edge. Kalina reached for his hand, then gave him a small tense smile when he took it and held on tight.

"Did you get what you needed from Hernandez?" Rome asked quietly.

"Yeah, I did. I'll tell you all about it when I get back. Send the jet, we'll be ready to fly when it arrives," X said.

"Where's Caprise?" Nick asked.

"She's in our room," X said.

There was an awkward sort of pause in the conversation. Bas spoke up, saying, "We had some action here this morning as well."

Nick leaned forward as if that would somehow get him closer to X or his sister. "What kind of action?"

"Rogues. Three of them taunting at the perimeter of Perryville. We took them out but it's not a good sign," Bas told them.

"We? Please don't tell me my sister was hurt," Nick said, a tortured look on his face.

"She's fine," X said. "I don't think she's ever fought another cat and—"

"Caprise was fighting? She shifted and she was fighting? What the hell, don't you have enough guards for that, Perry?" Nick's calm was quickly shattered.

"The important thing is that she's all right," Rome interrupted. "Eli's already called the pilot. You two get back here as soon as possible. Bas, do you need help following up with your Rogue problem?"

"No. I've got teams out searching now. We'll handle it. Keep me posted on what you find out about this new attacker," Bas told Rome.

"Will do. Let's plan to talk to all the FLs later this week. I've got a feeling whatever we uncover now will soon affect us all," Rome said.

"I agree" were Bas's final words before the line was disconnected.

When the room was silent again Rome looked to Nick. "You have to get a grip on this thing with X and Caprise. She doesn't need you two butting heads when she comes back to find out her guard is dead."

"You don't understand," Nick started to say.

Rome continued to look brutally serious. His compassion, even though Kalina was sure it was there, was carefully masked by the serious nature of their current situation. "Look, X is our friend. He's our brother."

"And she's my sister, Rome. Tell me you wouldn't feel pissed the fuck off if it were your sister he was with. You know how he is." And in return Nick's frustration filled the room like a huge gray cloud.

"I know what and who X is and I trust him with my life. With Kalina's life," Rome stated finally.

Nick shook his head. "This is different, Rome. It's so different."

"It's life, Nick," Kalina chimed in. "We don't get to pick and choose who we mate. It just happens."

"That's the problem. They're not going to mate. That's not the type of man X is. Rome knows this and I know this. And that's why I have such a problem with this whole situation," Nick said only a fraction calmer than he'd just been. Worry was clearly etched in the shifter's eyes, in the slump of his shoulders. This wasn't easy for him—especially so soon after his ordeal with Ary. It was a lot for anyone to withstand, but if anyone could get over it and move on, Kalina was sure Nick Delgado could. He simply had to want to move forward. That was the hard part. She was quickly learning how stubborn these male shifters could actually be.

Still, Kalina wasn't 100 percent sure of what Nick was talking about. There seemed to be a lot left unsaid between him and Rome. But what she did know without a doubt was that the sound in X's voice when Caprise was mentioned was not that of a man who had no feelings for that woman. X probably hadn't figured that out yet—and if she knew Caprise, as she was sure she did, Kalina was certain she didn't know it, either.

The two of them were in for a stark surprise.

Chapter 18

Her limber body moved in ways X had never seen before. She bent at the waist, flattened her hands on the planks of the patio floor. Her knees did not bend and she rested there for what looked like an uncomfortable amount of time. When she returned to a complete standing position, she leaned to the side, her entire torso bending like a flower in the wind. She circled and arched her back. Then she came up on her toes and did some sort of spin that left him breathless. She lifted a long leg, planted her ankle on the railing of the patio, and leaned over so that her head touched her knee, her hand cupping her foot.

His dick was hard, his body alert to every sexual tendril sifting its way slowly down his spine. His chest constricted when she stood straight and turned, her gaze immediately finding his.

Caprise had sensed his presence. From the doorway, he could see her nostrils flaring, her eyes darkening, and her nipples growing to ready peaks beneath the thin white T-shirt she wore. She'd scented him.

X inhaled deeply, picking up a warm musky scent himself, one he'd never smelled before. Then, because this was the only way he knew how to do this, he took a step toward her and said, "Seth's been killed. He was attacked by another shifter. Not a *Topètenia*."

Of all the things X accepted himself as being, a psychic was not one of them. So there was no way for him to predict that Caprise—of all the women he knew, on legs he'd admired when she'd danced on that pole and when they were wrapped securely around his waist—would crumple to the ground.

With a curse he took another step, caught her before her head hit the railing, and lifted her into his arms. Her eyes remained closed as X held her there, like a baby in his arms. He didn't sit down, didn't have to because he doubted she weighed more than 130 pounds. He made a mental note to see that she ate more. With her head resting against his shoulder, the scent he'd smelled upon entering the room was even stronger. It was intense and played with his senses as if he were a kid in a candy store. He wanted so much and then that didn't even seem like enough. This shit was making him angry.

"Caprise." He said her name because he needed her conscious. Needed her to talk to him, argue with him, whatever to keep his mind off what the hell was going on with his senses.

"He's dead because of me," he heard her say in the barest whisper. "It's my fault."

"You weren't even there" was his reply. "We need to get packed so we can go back."

She shook her head then. "I don't want to go back. I should never have come back."

"Why do you say that?" X asked, thinking of what had made her run away in the first place. "Why shouldn't you have come back to your home?"

"It's not my home. It's Nick's home and my parents' home. I don't have a home."

She sounded like a teenage girl, and when X looked down into her face he almost thought she was one. Her eyes were open, barely, teardrops teasing her long lashes, as if waiting for permission to fall. And as X surveyed the rest of her face his gaze lingered on her lips. He'd kissed those lips that morning when they were in the elevator. The significance of this act—X had never kissed another female before. It was too intimate, a word he had long since dissociated himself with. And yet he'd kissed Caprise without a second thought. Why he was thinking of that right at this moment, he had no clue.

"Your home is Havenway," he heard himself saying even though X would swear his mind was taking a walk down the carnal hall of fame. He wanted her again, his entire body ached for her. And yet he stood perfectly still, holding her like a baby, talking to her in a calm, solid tone he didn't even know he possessed.

She shook her head, still not willing to believe him. And as if that were a cue, X did something else that was so not in his repertoire. He kissed her forehead—just a light brush of his lips over her forehead where wispy tendrils of hair lay quietly.

"He was only twenty-five," she said. "And he was assigned to protect me. I should have protected him."

"That's not how male shifters work. Seth was doing his job."

"And it got him killed. So what's the point in all this shifter crap if all you're going to do is end up dead?" With that she began to squirm in his arms, trying to break free.

X put her down. Reluctantly. He stood back as she pulled on the hem of her shirt. She rubbed her palms over her face, down her head along the ponytail she wore.

"I'll go back but I'm not staying at Havenway anymore. I'm not staying in DC," she told him.

Inside, X's cat roared, pushing at every inch of him to growl loudly and stake his claim. But X ignored it. Sort of.

"Get your stuff and meet me downstairs in an hour."

"Fine" was her tight reply.

"Fine" was his in return.

X left the room. He had no other choice. It was either leave or throw her over his shoulder and carry her straight to the bedroom. Words would not get through Caprise's thick skull, but X was sure he could reach her on a more physical level. And then what? That was the million-dollar question.

Why was it so important Caprise stay at Havenway, and why did he give a flying fuck about how sad she looked when she said she didn't have a home? It didn't matter. None of it did. He was just fine before she'd returned. Just fucking fine!

Now? Now he was pacing up and down the hallway in the resort like an expectant father. His fists were clenching and unclenching at his sides while his teeth gritted so hard he figured they'd all fall out the minute he opened his mouth. But if he opened his mouth, the first thing coming out would be a roar that would likely tear this whole place down. Bas would not be happy about that.

Once more X found himself with a shitload of questions and not enough answers to buy himself a get-out-of-jail-free card. The one answer he did have without a shadow of a doubt was that Caprise Delgado was never leaving him again.

Blood pooled in a pothole that DC's Department of Public Works would most likely say didn't exist in the alley right behind Athena's. The MPD had been called when a dozen larger-than-normal, bouncer-like guys—their words, not Dorian's—had showed up.

"What else did the witness see?" Dorian asked Detective Eric McCoy, his brother-in-law.

"Between twelve and fifteen big dudes surrounding an

SUV. Maybe a jeep, he couldn't really tell since it was still dark and the SUV was black."

"Were they all males?"

Eric nodded. "All males."

"All black?" Dorian asked as he walked around the spot of blood. He'd been looking down on the ground, then looked up to Eric.

Eric shook his head. "No. It was a mixture, some black, some white. Then he said one or two looked Hispanic."

"So he was close enough to see they were Hispanic but not close enough to make the vehicle?"

"Come on, Dorian. He's an addict. He was probably high."

"But you believed his word enough to call me to have a look?"

"I believed his word because he's a good informant. You've been looking into those weird killings. I thought this was connected," Eric told him seriously. He'd been on the force for more than fifteen years and married to Dorian's older sister Miranda for half that time. As far as family went, Eric was a part of Dorian's and he was to be trusted.

Dorian saw a plastic bag near the wall. He'd guessed at the size of the vehicle and tried to configure where it would have been parked. Right up against this brick wall would have been the passenger-side door. If somebody fell out of the truck, shot maybe, or stabbed and cut like the other victims, they could have fallen right where that pothole was and bled out. Kneeling, he picked up the plastic bag and turned it over between his fingers. There was a symbol printed on one side, like a shield, and below it was the word SAVIOR. Back at his office, in the accordion folder where he'd been storing all his information about these killings, was another bag just like this one. It had been found with the body of Diamond Turner.

"So where's the truck and where's the body?"

"That's why I really called you. MPD's not even looking into this. Said without a vehicle or a body we don't have a case."

"Which is true," Dorian said.

"Somebody lost a hell of a lot of blood out here. It's at least worth finding out who," Eric implored.

"The blood's on the ground, man. We can take a sample and have it tested, but I'm sure it's been compromised. Besides, if it's not from a criminal whose DNA is already on file, we're never going to find out who it belongs to."

"Right. So we let it go?" Eric asked, nodding.

"No," Dorian said, clenching the plastic bag in his palm. "We're not letting it go."

"They got a report about a truck and some strange-looking guys standing around it. A unit was sent to investigate, came back with nothing," Kalina told Rome and Nick first thing the next morning.

"Are they asking around?" Nick asked, taking a sip from the mug in front of him.

It would be tea and not coffee; Kalina knew that after living here with Nick for weeks and having breakfast in the dining hall most mornings with him and Ary. As volatile as Nick's personality was, she'd half expected him to drink cold hard liquor every morning when he awoke. But that just went to show how you never really knew a person until you lived with them.

"No. The caller was an addict, so they're not putting too much credence in what he had to say. He did mention that the men didn't look human."

"Shit." Nick cursed quietly, putting his mug down and scrubbing his hands over his face.

"But they're not looking into it so it's fine," Rome commented.

"How'd the team do last night?" she asked.

"Sabar's not showing his ugly face. His second, Darel, is there every night. He's got two big-ass cats that walk every step with him. And there's a new guy," Nick said.

"What new guy?" Rome asked.

Nick sat back in his chair, pinched the bridge of his nose. "Jax went in last night, since you were here with Rome," he said to Kalina, then looked at Rome. "He reported this new guy who wasn't mentioned in any of the previous reports on who's been seen at the club. He's tall, looks foreign, blue eyes."

"Foreign like a *Lormenia* or a *Croesteriia*?" Rome asked.

"Either or," Nick said with a shrug.

"A tiger or a cheetah," Kalina said incredulously. She'd learned of the different types of shifters and their origins when she'd been joined in the Gungi. "Here in DC?"

"It looks like it. Problem is, we don't usually run in mixed groups," Rome said seriously.

"Remember that first Rogue we caught and killed? The one that had been after Kalina, he was *Croesteriia*. And he'd been with Sabar's clan," Nick reminded him.

Rome nodded. "But none of them had bothered to come for him when we caught him. That shows no real loyalty to him. Probably because he wasn't *Topètenia*."

Nick was shaking his head. "Rome, these cats have no loyalty to anyone but themselves. Right now they're all doing Sabar's bidding, but that's most likely because they have something to gain by it."

"He's right. They don't seem like the let's-stay-together

types," Kalina added. "And without the shaman to perform that ceremony again creating his band of totally crazy Rogues, Sabar's depending on them continuing to follow him blind."

Rome sat back in his chair, taking in everything that was being said. "What if this new guy's not playing by Sabar's rules? What if he's got his own agenda?"

"Then we're all fucked," X said, making his entrance into the conversation by pulling out a chair and dropping his large body into it.

He looked tired, was the first thing Kalina noticed. Like he hadn't been getting a lot of sleep. Which could mean one of two things: He and Caprise were really enjoying each other sexually, or X was spending every waking moment trying to figure out how he really felt about Caprise. Either one, Kalina thought, was very interesting. In fact, she thought it was so interesting that she was going to go find Ary in the medical center because it was time the three female *Topètenia* had a heart-to-heart chat.

She rose from her seat then and kissed her husband longingly on the lips. "I have something to take care of," she told him, keeping her eyes leveled with his. Rome most likely didn't know exactly what she was intending to do, but he knew enough to trust her instincts.

When he nodded she moved around him, touching a hand on Nick's shoulder as she passed him to get to X. With him, you never really could tell. He was like the big bear of the threesome, always brooding, usually quiet, like something was crawling around inside him, something that ran alongside his cat but that X definitely did not agree with. She'd never spoken her assumptions about this shifter, never wanted to invade the camaraderie the three of them obviously shared. Now, she figured, was time she made herself and her position known to Xavier Santos-Markland.

With a hand on his right shoulder, she leaned forward and kissed his cheek. "Glad to have you back," she said, giving him a warm smile.

His body tensed beneath her touch, his dark eyes finding hers and holding even though he wasn't totally sure how to react to what she'd just done. Kalina chuckled because he looked like a lost boy. One she prayed Caprise was sent back to rescue.

"Eat some breakfast before you get to work," she said, then left them alone at the table.

"You picked a good mate," X said to Rome about ten seconds after he'd watched the leader's wife walk away.

"I think so," Rome replied.

He looked a little perplexed at X's random statement—which, if he admitted it, X was, too. Shaking his head to get his thoughts together, he went back to the matter at hand.

"I think the new guy's here for Caprise," he said solemnly. "If that's the case, he's mine and mine alone. Is that understood?"

X looked down the table at his two closest friends and waited for their reply. In his inbox this morning he'd received information on the number he'd traced. Not only did it go back to Athena's but it was officially linked to a corporate account that traced back to Slakeman Enterprises. He planned to give them all this information, after they understood his position.

"That depends," Rome said slowly. He was watching X carefully, trying to figure out what was going on in his head.

X wished him lots of luck in that area.

"What is it you're not telling us? How do you know about this outsider?" Rome asked.

Nick was remarkably quiet but X knew that wouldn't last long.

"Caprise has been getting some hang-ups on her cell," he started, making sure he remained as obscure as he possibly could without lying to them. "I traced the number and it went back to Athena's."

Nick looked like he was about to break his silence, but X held up a hand to stop him. If he was going to go off, he'd rather he get all the information and do it all at once.

"Athena's Entertainment, LLC, which falls under the umbrella of Robert Slakeman Incorporated and Slakeman Enterprises," X finished.

"Shit," Rome grumbled, leaning forward and putting his elbows on the table.

"Wait a minute, you're telling me that Slakeman, one of the largest weapons providers for the US government and who knows how many others, has subsidiary companies that filter down to a strip joint in DC?" Nick asked.

"Sounds straight out of a tabloid, I know. I was thinking the same thing when I read the report," X said. "But then I thought about it. Remember that rumor about Slakeman selling those banned guns?"

"Yeah, Senator-elect Ralph Kensington supposedly found him a buyer. But where's the connection?" Rome asked.

"We know Sabar's running his drug through Athena's, which tells me that he's probably running the whole damn club. And if that's true, then he knows Slakeman," X said.

Nick was nodding. "And if he knows Slakeman, odds are he's the buyer. Fucking bastard! Now he's arming his bunch of delinquent cats."

Rome did not look happy about this, but he didn't look like he was in disbelief, either. X knew that Rome trusted his gut when it came to these matters. He also knew that the FL would want to take the time to think things through, to make sure whatever solution he came up with was the best one for the shadows first and foremost, then for the humans who had unknowingly gotten themselves involved in this war.

"Tell me what you know about the stranger," Rome requested quietly while Nick frowned beside him.

"I think he's been stalking Caprise. And that's why—" X raised his hand when Nick looked like he was about to say something else. "—that's why I said he's mine. I answered the phone once when the gutless bastard called. I made him a promise that I have no intention of reneging on."

"So she's being stalked? Is that what all her secrecy has been about? Is that why she came back?" Nick asked.

X shook his head. "I don't know any of that."

"You don't know or you're not telling us?" Nick asked.

X took immediate offense, but refrained from jumping up to punch Nick in the mouth. He understood where he was coming from, but Nick needed to understand that X had this situation under control. "You think I would sit here and withhold information from you guys? Look, Nick, I know she's your sister. I get how you feel about her. And despite what you might think you know about me, I'm not out to hurt her. In fact, I'm just trying to protect her."

"What or who do you think she needs protection from?" Rome asked before Nick could speak again.

"My guess, from the look on her face every time the bastard calls, is a man from her past. Someone she was involved with maybe. The calls are definitely freaking her out, but she won't tell me who he is."

Rome nodded. "So you took it upon yourself to find out?"

"Fucking right" was X's immediate reply.

"Which tells me that not only do you want to protect her, but that you care about her."

Rome was slick, X thought. And he was a lawyer so X should have known to be careful with this little question-and-answer session they were having. Rome made that a statement and not a question so X couldn't deny it. But it didn't matter. X was used to doing what he wanted when he wanted; he wasn't about to stop now.

"Don't go dressing this up like some sort of mate connection. I care about her because she's Nick's sister. I'm protecting her because right now she's my lover. End of story," he said with a definitive look at Nick.

"How can you be so sure she's not your mate? She's a *Topètenia* and you're undoubtedly attracted to each other. Your protectiveness rivals mine and Nick's put together, and we're already joined. So how can you sit there and say you haven't even considered her to be your mate?" Rome asked him.

There was only one reason X knew Caprise wasn't his mate—one absolute and undeniable reason that no rule in the *Ética* would change.

"I'm not cut out for that mating crap. Too much has happened for me to reach for a happy fuckin' ever after. So I don't waste time kidding myself."

Nick smirked. "But you'll waste my sister's time gladly."

"Your sister's an adult, man. She could have said no and you know I would have walked away. I don't force any female, shifter or human."

"And you don't know how to let go of the past," Rome said, which X thought was more than hypocritical since Rome was still chasing the truth about his parents.

"Whatever happened back in Atlanta—look, I'm not asking you to tell us. You know I'd never do that. That's completely your deal. But whatever it was happened a long time ago. You obviously survived for a reason. Sentencing yourself to a lifetime of suffering is childish and pointless," Rome said.

"It's what I feel is the right thing to do, for all involved. Now can we please let this shit go? We've got bigger things to worry about." X gave Rome a look that said, *Hey, I respect you, man, but I'm not telling you jack*.

Rome thankfully nodded as he stood from the table, dropping his napkin onto his half-empty plate. "I'm going to the office. Find out who the stranger is and what he's doing here, *before* you do anything, X. I want to know what you're walking into to see how we'll coordinate backup."

"I don't need backup," X said defiantly.

"Humor me, okay? Get the information, give me a call and we'll go from there. Got it?" Rome asked.

X only nodded, not sure he could trust himself to answer Rome. Because he knew the answer Rome wanted to hear would be a blatant lie.

In the next second they were alone at the table. X and Nick—a confrontation that had been coming for the last few days.

"She's my only blood," Nick said slowly as he stared down at the table. "I'd give my life to protect her from any more hurt."

"That makes you a good shifter and a great brother. But I'm not the one, Nick. I'm not the one trying to hurt her and I'm unfortunately not the one she'll spend her future with," X told him. And it was the absolute truth. If inside, his cat was bristling, that was its problem, not X's.

"For all that she is or that she may have done while she was gone, Caprise has always been smart. She wouldn't sleep with you just to pass the time."

X shook his head. "She doesn't want anything to do

with shifter life, Nick. Mating is the farthest thing from her mind, trust me."

"I just don't see how this can end well" was Nick's final tortured reply.

"I'm not guaranteeing that. I just know that at some point, it will end."

And how the hell he was going to deal with that, X had no clue.

Chapter 19

"You've had a busy week, huh?" Kalina asked the moment Caprise let her and Ary into her room.

All she'd had a chance to do when she arrived late last night was unpack her bag, grab a shower, and get into bed. It was too late to go and speak to Seth's family and she didn't want to speak to her family, so she'd chosen sleep. The pesky little pastime hadn't come easily, though. Her mind wandered over things better left alone for longer than she cared to admit.

That's probably why she was up so early this morning, already dressed and ready for the day. Only she had no idea what the day would entail. She had no real job, which was still a bit bothersome since she had qualifications to work at the school. No, she hadn't had formal dance training since her tween and teenage years, but she was good and the school had accepted her ten years prior as a student.

She'd thought she was content dancing at the club, but something told her that was going to be a little more difficult to pull off this time around. So here she was in her room, all dressed up with no place to go and memories that were more than ready to haunt her.

"How was Sedona?" Ary asked, totally ignoring the fact that Caprise hadn't said a word since they'd entered.

"It was pretty, as usual" was her reply after another second of futile hesitation.

Caprise had taken a seat on her bed and for lack of something better to do with her hands, picked up a pillow, pulling on the decorative fringes at its edge.

"And how's X?" Kalina asked.

Caprise looked at her. She was a pretty woman with a natural golden tan. That was reason enough for a woman to hate her, never mind the fact that she'd married Roman Reynolds. Her eyes were pretty, a warm hazel color. And her hair, which Caprise could tell she was trying to let grow out, cupped her chin neatly in a fiercely cut bob.

"X is the same as usual" was her reply. She found herself wanting to say more, needing to say more. Her chest had actually begun to hurt with all that she'd been holding in. Still, because she wasn't used to behaving any other way, Caprise waited to see if they would ask her first, which they probably would: This was definitely a tag-team interrogation no matter how they masked it with smiles and soft tones.

"Are you still sleeping together?" Ary asked, coming to sit on the bed beside Caprise.

She was about an arm's length away. Caprise figured that was why she could smell her perfume so clearly. Something floral and soft, it fit Ary perfectly.

"We did in Sedona. I mean, we shared a suite." She tossed the pillow. The damn thing was making her more edgy.

Kalina watched, from her perch on the chair next to the dresser, as the pillow tumbled and fell off the other side of the bed. "Hmmm" was all she said.

"What does that mean?" Caprise asked, her defenses all ready to go up. But the pounding in her chest continued and she took a deflating breath.

"I was going to ask you the same thing," Kalina said.

"Caprise, you can trust us you know. Whatever you tell Ary and I won't go beyond this room. We're family, we want to help."

Family? They weren't her blood. She'd walked away from the only blood she had to find—what? She still didn't know. Leaving after her parents' funeral and traveling the world did nothing to still the restless feeling she carried like luggage. Each time she'd thought she was someplace where she could be happy, where she could be safe, that feeling reared its ugly head and she ran again. She was so damn tired of running.

"He's just a guy, right?" she asked quietly. Her pride wouldn't let her hold her head down in shame at the weakness she heard in her voice. Instead she looked from Ary to Kalina and back again, waiting for their reply.

Both of them stared back at her with compassionate looks on their faces. Like pity—*No,* she told herself before her mouth started going again. It wasn't pity, but understanding. But how could they possibly understand what she was going through? They had no idea what had happened to her in the Gungi all those years ago. Nobody did.

"He's just a guy that acts like he's my father. And does everything else like he's some kind of perfect god," she said with exasperation.

"He's a powerful shifter," Ary said slowly. "He's one of the commanding officers in the Stateside Assembly."

"And he's your brother's best friend," Kalina added. "And you knew all this when you slept with him. So what did you think was going to happen?"

Caprise ran a hand over the loose braid she'd put in her hair. "I thought it was just sex," she answered finally.

Ary seemed to let out a breath before shaking her head. "And now what do you think it is?" she asked.

"I think we're both too screwed up to think beyond

sex. I mean, he's like got all this stuff going on in his head and it makes him almost crazy. And I've got my crap. We're just a mess." And when she'd finally said that out loud it didn't seem totally true.

Kalina nodded. "Wouldn't it be better if the two of you sorted out your mess together?"

That sounded too logical for it to make sense. Or Caprise simply wasn't trying to hear the logical explanation and resolution for what was going on between her and X. Besides, there were other important things going on.

"Look, we'll figure it out. I mean, I guess we'll do what we need to when the time comes."

"You'll have a joining ceremony?" Ary asked.

Caprise was already shaking her head. "I was talking about when it's time to part ways. I enjoy sex with Xavier but I don't know about all these shifter rituals."

"How about the *companheiro calor*?" Kalina asked. "You don't know about that one?"

"I know about it, but I'm not trying to get caught up in it. I live in a different world than the two of you," Caprise told them with a sigh.

Ary reached for Caprise's hand then. "You'd be surprised how quickly you get caught up, Caprise. Almost even before you realize it you're mated and then there's nothing you can do—nothing you want to do—besides have a joining ceremony. Because to be apart from your mate would surely be like dying."

Been there, done that, Caprise thought with an inward push at her cat, which was slinking along the surface as if it, too, belonged in this conversation.

"It's not like that with me and X," she said but wasn't totally sure that was the truth. Her head was throbbing, matching the rhythmic beat of pain in her chest. "We're too different."

It was Kalina's turn to shake her head. "On the con-

trary, I think you're too much alike. He's just as stubborn
as you are. But eventually you're both going to have no
choice but to face the facts."

Caprise took a deep breath. "The fact is that a young
man is dead because of me."

"You're talking about Seth?" Kalina asked. "No,
honey, he was killed by another shifter. You had nothing
to do with that."

"But I did," she said. "That shifter is looking for me
and he found Seth because Seth was my guard. It's my
fault." One tear slid free, falling to leave a dark spot on
the comforter.

Nick only wanted what was best for his sister. That was
all. When his parents died he'd wanted to take care of her
because he knew that was what they'd expect of him. But
she'd disappeared. And truth be told, he'd harbored a
shitload of guilt over not carrying out his parents' wishes.

When he first found out about her and X, he was livid.
He'd wanted to kill Xavier Santos-Markland and shake
some sense into his little sister. But then he'd realized two
things: Xavier was one of his best friends, and Caprise
wasn't little any longer. She was an adult and so was X, a
healthy male shifter and a beautiful female shifter. Logi-
cally it made sense they'd come together. But logic had
been clouded by emotion—in Nick's world, nothing new.

So it had taken him some time to decide confronting
his sister was the right thing to do. X wasn't backing
down where Caprise was concerned. Nick didn't blame
him; if someone had tried to take Ary away from him
after he'd found her in the Gungi, he would have been
ready to do bodily harm. This morning at breakfast, X
looked like he was at that point, like he would get physical without a doubt should Nick take a firm stance about
him seeing Caprise. Nick wasn't a fool, he knew that at

the end of the day Caprise was going to do what the hell she wanted. She always had. And X, that crazy shifter, hardly ever did what he was told.

He was just about to knock on Caprise's door when she came out. She looked the same, her dark eyes flanked by long lashes and thick arched eyebrows. She looked like their father.

"Hey," he said, clearing his throat. "I was just coming to talk to you."

She sighed as if he was the last person in the world she wanted to talk to. "Nick, I don't have time for this right now. I have to go see Seth's parents. Then I'm going into the city."

Nick took her by the arm, leading her down the hallway and into one of the meeting rooms on this floor.

"Look, give me a minute, Caprise. I'm trying to get some things off my chest."

"When will you learn everything isn't about you, Nick? You called me a couple of days ago yelling and screaming about who you thought I should be with and what I should be doing with my life. Now you want to tell me what's been on your chest. Did it ever occur to you that I have my own life, my own problems?"

She was absolutely right. Nick didn't mind eating crow if it meant the women in his life would eventually end up happy. He'd watched X this morning, listened to his reaction to Rome's questioning about him and Caprise being joined. Standing here, in this close proximity to his sister, he could see that even though she looked the same, she'd definitely changed. His first clue was the heavy musky scent that circled her like a cloud. It was the *companheiro calor*, he knew that without a doubt. What he wondered now was if Caprise and X knew it.

"I apologize," he said instantly. "You're right, I've

been a selfish goof. But here's the thing: I'm your brother and I just want what's best for you."

"What's best for me is to live the way I want. If I want to dance on a pole I should be able to dance on a pole without anybody giving me the stink eye. And if I want to sleep with your cranky-ass friend, then I'll do just that."

Her saying she was sleeping with X still didn't melt like butter over Nick, but he was trying to accept the facts. "You're an adult. You sleep with who you want and work where you want. I get it."

He could tell his easy acceptance of what she'd just said shocked her. She'd actually opened her mouth, prepared to argue with him some more, then snapped it shut.

"Well, I'm glad you came to your senses."

He smiled. "Yeah, well my wife has a way of bringing me around."

"She told you to back off, didn't she?" Caprise asked with a smile of her own.

Nick shrugged. "Yeah, something like that."

They shared a laugh together. It felt really good, like old times. And for a minute, just this small snatch of time, Caprise looked happy.

"What if he's your mate?" he asked, because he didn't want his sister disillusioned about X or the man he was. No matter how loyal to his friend Nick was, he knew there was a darkness to X, a place he went where neither he nor Rome had ever been with him. He wondered if Caprise knew this.

"You know I don't live by those Gungi laws," she said flippantly. A little too flippantly for Nick to believe she was sincere.

"There arc signs you cannot ignore, Caprise. Telltale signs that a couple has mated."

"We did not mate, dammit! We had sex!"

"Please," Nick said, shaking his head. "Don't keep saying that. I'm getting a visual and its making me nauseous."

"Then stop bringing it up," she snapped.

"If it's true, you can't hide from it. Mating is a natural part of being a shifter." Nick held up a hand when she tried to say something else. "I know you want to believe you're not a shifter, but you are. You can't run away from that any more than I can get away from what you and X have done. So I'm telling you to be careful. Because once you've crossed that line there's no going back. No running away, because he'll find you. He'll track you to the ends of the earth once he's mated you. And I don't want to lose my sister and my best friend."

"You don't have to worry about that. X and I cannot mate. It's impossible according to those laws of the *Ètica* you like to live by."

Nick wanted to ask her why she thought it was impossible but Caprise—true to form—had already left the room. She was finished talking and way beyond her quota for listening.

He thought about going after her but axed the idea in favor of thinking harder on what she'd just said. The laws of the *Ètica* said Shadow Shifters would find their mates, and they would be joined for their entire life span. It also said that there was only one mate for every shadow, one true love, one life's connection. He frowned with his next thought. Had Caprise already been mated?

It had taken too long for night to fall, too long for X to wait for Athena's to open.

But he'd waited, and he'd used the time sitting in the front seat of his truck to research Slakeman Enterprises and all its connections a little deeper. Robert Slakeman was one corrupt individual, the trail of illegal dealings he'd made following him like a bad stench. Miraculously, he'd never been caught, never prosecuted. Which said pretty damn clearly to X that somebody with lots of money and even more clout was protecting him. First thought was Ralph Kensington, but he'd only become senator-elect on the death of Senator Baines a few months back. However, Kensington had also known Baines personally.

X tapped a finger on the steering wheel as he looked over at the laptop he'd positioned on his passenger seat.

Kensington, Baines, and now Athena's. Baines and his daughter were mauled to death. Two strippers were killed in the same fashion just weeks after that. Diamond Turner was, too.

It was starting to add up, but X wasn't happy about what the math was proving. The connection between these men and Sabar wasn't coincidental.

X stopped, all thoughts of the connection and the connotations paused. His entire body went still, his senses prickling, his cat ready.

Someone was coming.

Hitting the ESCAPE button on his computer to instantly lock the machine and shut it down automatically after three idle minutes, X moved only his hands as he reached for the door handle. He was out of the car in a flash, standing with his booted feet planted firmly on the ground, legs spread, fists ready at his sides.

"Trespassers will be prosecuted," the man now standing in front of him said.

It took about two seconds for X to figure him for a shifter. His scent was dull, as if something was muting it. But it was there, the scent of the cat. Only this was no *Topètenia*. His eyes were too blue, his hair too black, his stance cockier, as if he had a right to be that way. He was no cheetah, either.

"Stalkers will be beaten to death" was X's response, finally.

The man had the audacity to feign innocence. "Excuse me?"

X was in his face in the next instant. "Don't jerk me around, cat. I'm not in the mood. You're the one who's been calling Caprise."

It was a hunch. But X's hunches were never wrong. Ever. And this time was no different.

The corner of the guy's mouth lifted slightly, his eyes alight not with humor, or with disinterest—either of which would have garnered a more acceptable reaction from X. No, it was lust, pure and simple lust at the mention of her name. X wanted blood. Right here, right now, he wanted to rip this motherfucker's throat out.

"Why would I need to call the woman who belongs to me?" he asked.

Again, wrong words, wrong time, wrong fucking shifter.

The fist that plowed into the man's jaw was powerful, knocking him back a good couple of steps before he was able to shake it off. Almost. His next step was a little wobbly. But X didn't care; he moved in for more.

"I told you not to call her again. Now you can take this as your final warning." X punched him again.

The man's head snapped back. The next hit had his head jerking, then falling forward as he spit out a mouthful of blood. X could have finished him off right then. He could have completed the human ass kicking and broken a few of his bones. Or he could shift and crack his skull. He did neither, only because he wanted the bastard looking right at him when he died.

Instead the man came to his full height, which was a couple of inches shorter than X. His eyes had changed, the blue even brighter, almost to the point of being iridescent. X didn't need to look down at his hands to know that his claws had sprouted. The white Bengal tiger was about to emerge.

But the man held it back.

"She belongs to me. I own every inch of her magnificent body," he told X.

"You don't own shit! This is my town and she's my female. We can stop with the talk and settle this once and for all if you're still liable to believe otherwise."

"You have no idea who she is or what she's done," he said clearly.

The alley was dark, the back sides of three buildings caging them in. An urban jungle prepared to host a feral battle.

"I know what I need to know" was X's heated retort.

"Did you know she was a killer?"

The pause in X was minute. Nothing about his outward demeanor changed. The word *killer* rubbed him the wrong way, especially since it was referring to Caprise. But this shifter would never know that.

"You're a dead man," X said and made another move forward.

The tiger wasn't about to take more hits without dishing some out. It lifted its head, blue eyes sparkling in the dark of night.

"Stop!"

The female voice had both males halting. Then X inhaled. His body paused. His cat stiffened.

What the hell was she doing here?

He was about to tell X.

Caprise hadn't wanted to see him. She actually thought she could come down here and bring X back to Havenway without any altercation at all. She was dead wrong.

From the moment she'd admitted to Kalina and Ary that the shifter who'd killed Seth was really after her, she'd known she'd end up here. X was determined to find out who was calling her; it was logical that he'd want to come to Athena's to see if that person worked here, since this was the only place Caprise went outside of Havenway. He would also want to look for the shifter who'd killed Seth. No matter what the FL had ordered, X would want to take care of that situation sooner, rather than later. Knowing all this did not mean she cared for this man or felt connected to him in any way. It just meant she was perceptive. She'd known him before she went away and had been forced to spend time with him in close confines these last couple of days. That was all.

So she'd waited until it was night to slip out of Havenway, which was not easy. And she hadn't gotten far before she was caught. Luckily for her, the newest shifter captor was a female by the name of Nivea Cannon. She was a guard but she was a female first and recognized the rebellion in Caprise's eyes. Instead of taking her back or even calling Nick or Rome to tell them where she'd gone, she'd accompanied Caprise to Athena's.

The minute she heard Rolando's voice, Caprise reverted to that young girl, in that foreign land, in a foreign body, doing things when she had no idea what their repercussions would be. Her body had shaken all over. All she wanted to do was run. But she was through with that; she reminded herself and the cat that lurked beneath that running was no longer an option. It was time for her to stand.

So on shaky legs she'd come around the corner, watched as X's large form was about to pounce on Rolando's. It would be a fight guaranteed to make the front page of the tabloids: a jaguar and a white Bengal tiger battling to the death in the alley behind a strip joint. She couldn't let that happen. The shadows couldn't risk the exposure, not because of her.

X found her gaze the moment he turned around and for

a split second Caprise felt like there was no one else in that alley. It was just her and this man, and the restlessness that had plagued her for years dissipated.

"Shit!" she heard Nivea say from behind her.

That was about two seconds before the alley was filled with flashes of light. Nivea charged past Caprise, jumping up to kick the Dumpster that was about ten feet away from where Caprise was standing. From behind, a female and a male holding a camera emerged.

"Hey, it's a free country," the female quipped.

"If you don't get your ass out of here you're going to get a lesson in just how free this country really is," Nivea replied. Her small frame didn't look as if it carried a punch, but Caprise figured the way she'd kicked that Dumpster a good distance—it had almost knocked the woman and man on their asses—was a pretty accurate judgment of the damage she could do.

The twosome raced out of the alley, passing Caprise in a blur as they went.

"Go home," X said, his voice feral as he gazed at her.

"She is home," Rolando stated, coming from out of the shadows where he'd gone while Nivea did the kicking-trash-can thing.

Her heart tripped at the sound of his voice, and when his hot blue gaze settled on her, Caprise thought she would actually pass out. It had been years since she'd seen him, since she'd left him asleep in the forest.

"You shut the fuck up!" X yelled, pointing at Rolando then turning back to Caprise.

Caprise shook her head. "No, he's right. I am home. I was born and raised here in DC. This is where I belong." The words sounded strong and concise. She heard them and wanted to clap for herself, for this step ahead in life she'd taken. But now was certainly not the time.

"I want you out of here," X said again.

His voice was lethal, his cat's eyes glaring at her. The body she'd grown so familiar with was bunched with tension, muscles bulging, claws already released.

"She won't leave, will you, Caprise?" Rolando moved closer. X stood between them.

"You will stay because you know you owe me at least that. You owe me your life," he told her precisely.

"I owe you nothing," Caprise told him.

She stood just behind X, could feel and scent his anger building.

"You lied to me and used me. In return, I left your conniving ass in the forest. I'd say that makes us even," she told Rolando.

Rolando's head tilted just slightly, his incisors showing as he grinned a malicious smile that almost stopped Caprise's heart. This was the real Rolando. This was who and what she'd realized he was, only that realization had come too late. And it had come at a great cost.

"You lied to me. Then you ran like a coward. You went to those humans and together you killed my child. Buried him beneath the earth like he was nothing. For that," he said with a chuckle, "you, my *companheiro,* must pay."

The next actions happened in a blur but Caprise knew she'd never forget them. The sounds, the scents, the death. She would store this memory alongside that of her son, Henrique, for the rest of her life.

Rolando's shift was quick, his cat's heavy paws hitting the pavement with a thump that rocked the entire alley. It lunged right over X's shoulders, pushing Caprise back onto the ground. She didn't have a second to think, to reconsider, or to retreat. Her cat ripped free of her human body with a roar that echoed. Leaning back on its hind legs, it threw its front paws up just in time to catch the first blows from Rolando.

Behind her she heard another cat's growl. Then Ro-

lando's head reared back, its mouth opened wide, teeth
bared. Another ferocious roar and the tiger was out of her
reach. Through her cat's eyes she watched as X, now in cat
form, sank his teeth deep into Rolando's neck. The tiger
roared and tried to swipe back, but X was on its back, jaws
locked, eyes focused . . . on her.

The tiger writhed and roared, tumbling along the ground
of the alley with the jaguar fiercely hanging on to it. It was
dying. X was killing Rolando. Caprise's cat roared so loud
she thought she might actually go deaf from the sound. She
stumbled back, heart thumping wildly.

When X shook his cat's head, jerking with all his
strength, the tiger went down on its front legs. Its blue
eyes rolled back and forth then locked on Caprise's
cat. Her flanks heaved with the effort it took for her to
watch. There were two big cats fighting in an alley. Both
she'd shared herself with. One was dying. The other was
killing.

And suddenly the bravado the human had was being
chased by the sight of the cats. She backed away, on four
legs, slowly moved until the sight of X and Rolando grew
blurred. Coolness pelted her fur and she realized it was
raining. It came down in sheets as heavy and disfiguring
as those in the rain forest. The scent permeated her senses
and flashbacks ran rapidly through her mind.

Running through the forest with Rolando, making love
beneath the misty canopy, lying beside him in the long
night hours, listening to him breathe, wondering if he
were her mate.

Realizing he was not who he said, seeing the differences in his eyes, his stance, his claws when retracted. He
was no *Topètenia*. Everything between them was a lie.

She'd run that night, her paws clamping to the bark of
trees as she went higher and higher into the canopy then
moved fluidly from branch to branch until she was a safe

distance away. The cat ran as far as it could before the human had to take over the journey.

Months later there was the pain of labor. The death of a child. Tears and pain she thought would kill her. The eyes of her dead child staring back at her—one brown like hers, the other blue like Rolando's.

Caprise turned from the alley then, her cat running through the rainy streets of downtown Washington, DC, at full speed.

Chapter 20

"You were seen," Rome said as calmly as he could manage when X and Nivea returned to Havenway. It was almost dawn. They'd spent hours looking for Caprise before deciding to come back here.

"There were two humans, one with a camera," Nivea added in a slow, quiet voice.

"What the fuck? Are both of you insane?" Nick asked. "Pictures? There are pictures of cats out there?"

X shook his head. "I hadn't shifted. Nobody had shifted at that time. Nivea chased them off before any of that happened."

"So we should be glad they didn't see you kill a fucking tiger? Is that what you're saying?" Nick was not in a good mood.

And X was sick of Nick's bad moods. He was in the other man's face in a split second, grabbing his shirt and pushing him back a step as he spoke right in his face. "Look, I'm not in the mood for this shit. It happened and I couldn't stop it. So be it. Let's move on."

"Get the hell off me," Nick said, pushing back at X. "You need to think first, idiot. You were in a public place."

"I need to think first?" X asked. "You don't even want to go there with me, Delgado."

"Enough!" Rome yelled. "I'm sick of you two bickering like two little girls. Now is not the time for your pissing match. Like X said, what's done is done. Now we need to do damage control. But you can bet we'll talk about you disobeying my direct order later."

"Where's Caprise?" Nick asked when he stepped away from X and had gone to stand near Rome.

X rubbed his hand down his face and walked away, too. Nick wasn't his immediate concern. As for Rome's comment, he'd deal with the FL's wrath later. What he needed to do right now, before he took his next breath, was to see Caprise.

"I'm going to get her now," he said, heading for the door.

"I'll come with you," Nick said.

X turned slowly. "Stay. The. Hell. Back."

Rome put a hand on Nick's shoulder when the shifter acted as if he were going to ignore X's command.

X didn't speak again, just walked out, not giving a damn what any of them said when he was gone. Out in the hall he moved quickly toward Caprise's rooms. She had to be here.

Instinct had finally led him here. He'd been trying to scent her on the streets but he couldn't. Focusing was definitely an issue right about now. He and Nivea had burned the body of the tiger and left its ashes right there in the alley to be washed away by the rain. He'd known Caprise had run off and had considered giving her some space before he went to her demanding to be told everything.

Because make no mistake about it, Caprise would not walk away from him again without telling him. Something happened between her and that tiger, something that tore her apart. No, it hadn't torn her apart, it had stolen her innocence. Not the way his had been stolen, but just as traumatizing. A part of her had been missing ever since, a part that had been replaced with the cold candor of the female that had returned to Washington, DC. The chip on her shoulder was more like a boulder that she carried because she thought she had to. He was going to set her straight once and for all.

X lifted a hand to knock on her door. But he couldn't knock. He stared at his own hand, dark skin he'd been used to seeing all his life, bruised knuckles on the same four fingers as he'd always had. The difference now was how those fingers and that hand shook. With a curse he yanked his arm down to his side. He was shaking. Xavier Santos-Markland was never shaken. Ever.

Except now, he was.

Inhaling slowly, he let out the breath and closed his eyes, trying desperately to calm himself before going in. She didn't need the angry X. If he went in yelling and demanding the way he wanted to, and normally would have, she'd no doubt fight back and keep everything that was already bottled inside her to herself. That's not how he wanted this to end, not this time.

So he was a lot steadier when he finally knocked on the door. She didn't answer. He knocked again because X knew she was in there. Her scent was strong now, his nostrils flaring with the sweet musky smell. There was no doubt in his mind she was standing on the other side of that door. So when he knocked once more and still received no answer, X punched in the code and waited until the lock clicked before pushing his way in. Being the one to reprogram her lock after he'd broken it had come in handy. That's exactly the way he'd planned it.

She sat on the side of the bed, her back facing him. X pushed the door closed and waited until he heard the locks click back in place before walking quietly across the floor. Then he stopped, his teeth clenching, fists balling at his side.

It smelled like raindrops. The scent broke X down to a level he'd never experienced before. She didn't move, didn't even lift her head to see him. But X knew she was crying.

"Caprise," he said. She still didn't look up.

X went to his knees in front of her, pulling her hands from her lap and holding them tightly.

"Tell me what happened, babygirl. Tell me what he did to you."

For endless moments she was quiet. So quiet X wanted to grab her shoulders and shake her. Hair curtained her face but tears fell steadily, staining the shorts she wore.

"I thought he was like us," she said so softly X almost didn't hear her. "But he was so angry one day, like he wanted to kill somebody. He kept talking about traitors and sabotage. He said he wanted to go back home but that choice had been taken from him. I didn't know what he meant, didn't realize he wasn't talking about the Gungi, until it was too late." She shook her head but still did not look at him. "Then I tried to calm him down. He wasn't trying to listen to me. He walked off and was gone for a while. I followed his scent and I saw him. I saw his claws and his eyes and then he shifted and I saw the tiger." She let out a deep sigh as if the admission itself had been a tremendous task.

Her fingers were limp in his hand, warm, but still. Without thought X saw his thumbs moving over the back of her hand, rubbing the soft skin in soothing circles.

"I was afraid and I was angry. He never said he wasn't *Topètenia*. I didn't know why a tiger would be in the Gungi but I couldn't think of any good reason. I wanted to run to the village to warn them. Then I just wanted to run away period. Forever." Her breath came in slow waves, guiding her along in this long-overdue release.

"I thought he was someone I could count on—that this was who I was meant to be with. But after he lied I knew that was wrong. I wasn't meant to be with a liar, man nor cat. My parents had already left me because they were cats and wanted more than they should have. I hated everything about shifters, their scent, their looks, their lives. Everything. I wanted to go so far away nobody would ever think I was a shifter again."

Because he remembered how it felt to be confused and angry, X dropped one of her hands and lifted it to brush her hair back. He cupped her cheek and moved his hand gently so that her head lifted to look at him.

"Where did you go?" he asked.

He swallowed hard after asking her because when he looked into her eyes he didn't want to talk. All X wanted to do at that point was hold her. He wanted to wrap his arms around her and allow her to cry until she was completely diffused. If he had to watch those tears fall from her eyes, he wanted all her pain and hurt washed away with them.

"There was a village a couple of miles from the forest. I was so tired and hungry and I felt sick. Some missionaries saw that I was American and took me in."

She looked away from him then and took a deep breath. "I was pregnant by Rolando," she said finally.

"I stayed with the missionaries until he was born."

He couldn't ask her what happened next; his mouth just wouldn't form the words. So for endless seconds they just sat there, neither of them speaking or moving.

"I gave birth and he looked normal," she started again, her voice a little shakier.

Tears flowed faster, so fast her eyes didn't even look like they blinked, just leaked incessantly.

"He looked just like my dad." She took a deep breath. "I named him Henrique because he looked like my dad."

The hand he was still holding she pulled back. When she stood and walked across the room, stopping at the window, X could only stare at her. Inside, his cat wanted out; he wanted to rip free and find any and everyone who'd ever hurt this woman and break their necks, the way he had Rolando's. Instead he stood, folding his arms across his chest.

"He died because he wasn't normal. He wasn't human," she said quietly.

Her back had been facing him but she whirled around so fast she was looking at him in the next instant.

"He wasn't even part human. He was parts of two different shifters and that killed him!" she screamed.

"Did a doctor tell you that's why he died?" X asked still trying desperately to remain calm.

"There was a midwife and a shaman. They both looked at him and knew he wasn't normal."

"But you said he looked like your father."

She nodded her head vehemently. "He did. Just like my dad. But his eyes were different. That's how they knew."

"They knew what?"

"That he was a shifter. The shaman kept saying "shadow" over and over again. But the midwife shook her head. She said something else: *abomanción*. She repeated that several times before she began wrapping him tightly in a blanket. They buried him that night after the sun had gone down at the border to the forest because they were afraid to go any farther."

"This midwife, was she an American human?"

"No, she was Portuguese, but she was human. Just like the shaman. When they came back they prayed with me and they . . ." She hesitated, then took another steadying breath. "They gave me this."

Caprise pulled down the band of her shorts and pushed the shirt away so that the tattoo on her right hip was visible. X had seen the tattoo before. He remembered the swirling lines that circled into the shape of a heart, something intricately written in the center. He just assumed it was a personal choice to be inked, as his had been.

"It's his name in Portuguese so that I would never forget. The shaman said to use it as a warning so I'd never mix with another breed or procreate again."

"You should have told his fake ass to take a hike," X grumbled, remembering the shaman Yuri who'd actually turned against Ary and the shadows for the American money that Sabar offered him. That had gotten the spiritual medicine man killed. X promised that the next of these bullshit healers to cross his path was getting a bullet through his skull.

She was shaking her head again. "He was mixed with the blood of two different types of shifters. There was no way he could have survived."

"You don't know that," X heard himself saying. This was really Ary's area of expertise. She and Papplin were doing some research on the shifters and their unique DNA, so they would know the probability of a mixed-breed shifter's mortality. What X did know was that this was a new scenario for the shifters to deal with. As of now it had only been known that shifters mated with like shifters. Occasionally there was a human shifter mating, but those were usually in the Gungi where the humans were more likely to believe and to keep quiet about the existence of the shadows.

"He may have had other problems and that's why he didn't live. Without an autopsy you can't be sure why he died."

"It doesn't matter," she said with a sigh. "None of it matters anymore. I don't know how Rolando found out about the baby. He must have thought I'd killed him, for whatever reason. I guess he never really knew me at all, either."

He was tired of holding back, tired of restraining himself where she was concerned. Up until this point he'd never had to treat her with kid gloves and he was sick of doing it now. This wasn't the Carprise he knew. Gone was the fight in her, the flash of anger in her eyes. Now she was standing there feeling sorry for herself because of circumstances that were beyond her control. And X had had enough of it.

He moved to her then, grabbed her by the shoulders, and pulled her closer to him.

"Stop it! Shit happens all the time, Caprise. It happens to the best of us. You do what you have to do to get through the situation, to survive. And that's what you did."

"I should never have run. If I'd stayed with him—"

X cut her off. "If you'd stayed with him you don't know if he would have killed you or not. You said yourself you had no idea what a tiger would be doing in the Gungi. He was too far away from home for it to be for any good reason."

"I was far away from home," she said sullenly.

"No. The Gungi is a part of you, Caprise. It's time you start to accept that."

"Every time I turn around somebody's telling me to accept something. This is my life—why can't I live it the way I want?"

"Because the way you want isn't the right path. I used to think the same way, Caprise. I used to feel like the whole world was against me. That if there were something bad in the grand plan, it was scheduled to happen to me."

X remembered those thoughts with a certain irritation of his own. While his running away had been in the form of moving from Atlanta to DC with his parents, it had still been running. He'd wanted to stay, to stand up to any more of the Jeremiahs of the world, but his parents were too afraid of the repercussions.

"What did happen to you?" she asked when his eyes had taken on a distant look.

He was still holding her close, but she could move enough to press her palms against his chest. "What happened to make you the hard-ass you are?"

Because really, a lot of this advice X was tossing at her could be hurled right back in his direction.

As she'd expected, X took a step back from her. "This isn't about me. What happened tonight was about you and that tiger. He shouldn't have been in the Gungi when you were and he shouldn't have been here in the city. But that's all over now. We can finally move on."

"And how will we do that?" Caprise asked. She wiped her eyes, feeling a lot stronger than she had just a few minutes ago.

What X had said to her was right. A part of her had known all along what happened with little Henrique wasn't her fault. She had been half delirious with pain, so whatever that shaman and midwife told her, she would have believed. Then it seemed as if she'd traded one type of pain for another as realization dawned on her—she'd had a son and now he was dead. Her parents were dead also. Everyone she loved left her in some form or another. Everyone except Nick; he'd always stood strong.

"How will we move on, Xavier? You've killed Rolando, that's all well and good. I've told you what you so desperately wanted to know about me. Now what?"

"Now we continue to work to get rid of these Rogues. I

have to clear my name since I'm now suspected of murder, and you have to find yourself a real dancing job because I really will become a cold-blooded murderer if I have to sit back and watch men gawking at your half-naked ass one more night."

He'd said a lot, Caprise thought with a nod of her head. But he hadn't answered her question.

"And what about us? What do we do, Xavier?"

He took another retreating step. Caprise thought about following him, about crowding him the way he always seemed to do with her, but she suspected X needed to be handled differently.

"We do whatever we want," he told her. "Isn't that what you said, that you want to live your life the way you please?"

She nodded. "I did say that." She'd said a lot of things and, if she remembered correctly, so had Nick just before she'd left Havenway to go find X. He'd said that once things were set in motion there was no turning back. Caprise remembered how it felt when X had looked at her in that alley, like no one else existed but them. And when she'd gotten closer to him, even amid the scent of anger, rage, and humans, she'd picked up something else. It had been subtle, surrounded by the other scents, but right at this moment it was burning her nostrils, sending licks of desire through her body. *Companheiro calor* was the term that came instantly to her mind.

"So that's what we'll do. I've got some other things to talk to Nick and Rome about," X said, moving toward the door. "You, ah, get some rest, or something."

Caprise nodded. There was more she could have said; she could have pushed a little harder. But she didn't. That wasn't how these cards were going to play out. So she stood there looking at X as if she were listening to his every word, obeying his commands. When truth be told, Caprise was planning, getting her strategy in order. And as he closed the door behind him she shook her head. "Xavier Santos-Markland, you have no clue."

Chapter 21

Darel closed the door to his apartment and walked straight to the bar. He picked up a glass, poured himself a healthy helping of vodka, and emptied it within seconds. He hadn't bothered to turn on any lights because he knew his way around his own apartment. In a couple of hours it would be full daylight. Police would no doubt be combing the alley behind Athena's once more. He'd seen those two cops there the night before, the night Rolando had killed that Shadow.

Darel had seen that coming a mile away. That shadow had been with Caprise each time she'd come to the club; he'd stuck to her like glue. Once Darel mentioned that to Rolando and pointed the shadow out to the shifter when he'd come into the club that night, he'd known how it would end. Rolando was a loose cannon, just as Darel had tried to tell Sabar. And he wasn't to be trusted. That was something else he'd found out. He was still trying to decide how he was going to deal with that little fact.

"Busy night?"

The female voice startled him, but Darel didn't show it. He'd thought he was alone and even now when he inhaled deeply he did not pick up a scent. A second later the lights came on and what Darel saw standing in the middle of his living room made him pour another glass of vodka and take another deep gulp.

"I thought it was time we talked," she said.

Like hell. When someone wanted to talk they were usually fully dressed, not standing there wearing what was the equivalent of underwear.

Bianca Adani was in his apartment. She was Sabar's girl. She was also the ex-girlfriend of Boden Estevez, the crazy-ass *Topètenia* shifter who had kidnapped and abused Sabar and other young shifter boys for years. Sabar had warned him to stay away from her, and Darel was more than happy to keep that promise. He hadn't invited her here and didn't really want to talk to her. But damn if he didn't like looking at her sexy-ass body since she'd put on display.

"Why don't you come over here and take a seat. We've got a lot to talk about."

Darel shook his head. "No we don't."

Bianca walked toward the bar. Guess she figured he wasn't coming to her. As she did, Darel looked his fill at her long gorgeous legs. A patch of white satin covered her mound; matching satin hid only the shape and color of her puckered nipples. She wore heels like the girls at the club, and her auburn hair was left loose, hanging past her shoulders. Stunning blue eyes watched him as she came to stand right in front of him.

"I know you saw us talking. Rolando and I," she said, lifting a finger to run along Darel's chin.

He wanted to be repulsed, to push this whore away from him and kick her out of his apartment. But he didn't. His dick was hard as nails, pressing painfully against the zipper of his pants. He hadn't wanted to fuck a female since the crazy gray-eyed bitch had gone ballistic on him. Watching had been his mode of getting off as of late.

Now, though, his body itched to rub against hers, to dive deep inside the pussy of the magnificent Bianca and make her forget both Boden and Sabar.

But he waited.

"I take it you two knew each other," he said instead.

"He worked for Boden. It's a good thing that shadow killed him. I'm sure Boden had no idea he was here. He doesn't want his shifters in the States."

So she'd witnessed that little episode tonight as well. Darel had seen it on the security monitor in his office. He'd watched with satisfaction as the shadow did him a huge favor.

"Why not? They can't stay hidden forever," Darel told her.

Bianca shrugged. "Boden has his own plan for what his shifters will do. It's nothing like what Sabar has in mind for his Rogues."

Darel nodded. "And what's your plan, Bianca? Why are you here?"

She took a step closer, rubbed her palms up his chest, wrapping her arms around his neck. "I came for you."

"Why?" he asked even though her words could not be trusted.

She was a good liar. "Because I wanted to."

"And Sabar?"

"Only has to know what we tell him."

Which Darel figured would be whatever Bianca constructed when she felt the time was right. He didn't trust this bitch as far as he could toss her. She was up to something, he was positive of that fact.

"You're a liar," he said, reaching up to grab a handful of her hair and tugging with a good amount of strength. "Boden sent you here to find out what Sabar was up to. You're fucking him because Boden told you to."

She hissed when he pulled on her hair once more, her tongue coming out to swipe quickly over her bottom lip.

"I'm here because I want to be with you," she said pressing her breasts to his chest.

"You don't want me any more than I want you," he told her, disgust lining his voice. "You want to do Boden's bidding and you're trying to get me on your side."

"You're wrong."

"Prove it," he told her.

Bianca yanked away from him. Or rather, he loosened his grip so she could get away. She backed up only a little, her hands going to the thin band of her panties, pushing them down her long legs. Reaching behind her back she unhooked her bra, let it fall to the floor.

Her nipples were a beautiful blush color, thick and puckered against heavy breasts. She picked up the bottle of vodka he'd been pouring then backed up until she had to hike herself up on the bar. She scooted backward, knocking over glasses and other bottles without a care. When her ass was far enough on the bar she lifted a leg, planted her foot against the edge. Her pussy opened like a blossoming flower before his eyes. Plump folds already damp with desire, tightened clit ready for licking.

Darel stood perfectly still.

She lifted the bottle and tilted it until the clear liquid began dripping over her chest. Rivulets of liquor ran over her breasts, down her flat stomach, washing over her cleanly shaved mound, drenching the succulent folds of her vagina.

Darel growled.

"Come and get it," she said, tossing her head back and thrusting her chest forward.

He knew exactly who and what she was. Knew this was some kind of cheap setup. But what Darel also knew was that he had the power to kill whatever plans Bianca had come up with. He could snap her in two right this moment. Ot he could take what she was so eagerly offering . . . then snap her in two.

Unbuckling his pants and pushing them over his hips Darel moved closer to the bar. He leaned forward and licked the vodka from her center, lap after delicious lap. When she bucked beneath him, he pulled back immediately, denying her the release she'd been about to experience. He thrust his thick length into her without reserve. Pounding into her with all the strength he had. If Bianca wanted him, she was going to get him, and then some.

"The shipment will be in Friday at midnight," Ralph Kensington told Sabar at their lunch meeting. They sat at a corner table in Zaytinya, a sleek and modern Mediterranean restaurant in DC.

Ralph wanted an open setting when meeting with this character again. The last time they'd met in his office, things had gotten a little . . . choppy, for lack of a better word. This was the leader, Ralph noted as he sat back in his chair, sipping on his glass of red wine. He had a band of followers and they were preparing for some kind of takeover.

But Ralph was one step ahead of them.

Born in Staten Island, New York, to London-born parents who became US citizens in their teen years, Ralph Edward Kensington was the poster boy for the American Dream . . . if the American Dream ended in corruption and deceit, which Ralph convinced himself was just his form of taking advantage of every opportunity offered. He'd worked in a bakery when he was fifteen, swept flour off the floors for four hours after school every day. He'd gone to NYU to study political science, with a minor in information technology. His third job out of college landed him at Slakeman Enterprises, where he met Robert Slakeman. And from there his life had taken a dramatic upswing. Now the senator-elect filling the shoes of the late Mark Baines, he had more power than he'd ever imagined possessing.

And with power came great sacrifice.

His wife was a delusional drunk, his two college-aged children barely spoke to him, and his parents had long since ceased communicating with him. None of that mattered to Ralph. He was on the path that was set for him. He believed that and worked harder every day to get exactly what he thought he deserved. For a while the lovely Melanie had provided him with all the physical attention he needed to balance what work took away from his life. Now she was gone. He blamed the man sitting across from him for that.

"That's five days from now," Sabar said.

His eyes seemed larger today, as if they were dilated. They were a somber brown tone, but Ralph had seen them change to a golden-yellow that was both eerie and scary as hell. He wasn't human, this man sitting across from him. Melanie hadn't been, either.

And that fact, Ralph thought, was his new claim to fame.

"In five days you'll meet him at the warehouse. You give him the money—one million cash—and he'll give you the weapons." Ralph outlined the deal once more for him. They'd been over this a couple of times, but this lunatic liked to hear it over and over again.

"The UK79865. That's the weapon I want."

Ralph nodded. "That's the one."

The UK79865 was a highly sensitive heat-tracking semi-automatic rifle. It came with a built-in silencer and scope with range of accuracy of more than one hundred feet. The bullets for this weapon were what set it apart from others used in the military—hollow-point lead-only bullets designed to expand immediately upon impact. This feature was prohibited by the military but used in some law enforcement weapons. Slakeman had created a special alloy-and-lead solution that would create the effect of an explosion once the bullet pierced its target.

Sitting across from him was some type of creature, a non-human. Ralph knew there had to be others—and given how adamant this one had been about the weapons he wanted and the number he was willing to buy, Ralph thought there had to be some kind of war either brewing or already beginning. A war that this one planned to win.

"What time?" Sabar asked him

"Midnight. I'll give you the address."

Ralph pushed a card across the crisp white linen tablecloth. "I know you've got your little setup going down at Athena's. Heard money has been pouring in pretty good for you. But this is the real deal." He leaned his hefty elbows on the table. "This guy doesn't fuck around so I'd suggest you keep your end of the bargain or this transaction will go to shit faster than you can blink those funny-looking eyes of yours."

He knew the moment the words were out they were a mistake.

"Don't threaten me," Sabar said slowly, using his large dark-skinned hands to pull back the locks of his hair, so that they now fell down his back.

He looked feral, this one. Like at any moment he would jump over the table and rip Ralph's throat out. That was a genuine fear, because Ralph sensed that even being in a public place didn't mean much to this guy. They'd robbed that bank a month ago not giving a damn who saw their faces and their claws. Ralph had confiscated all the tapes—paid a pretty penny for them, too. They were sitting now in a safe at his house, his insurance policy for when these animals decided they wanted to change the rules.

"I'll be there and I'll have the money. You make sure this guy has my shit or both of you are gonna wish you never met me."

Ralph was kind of wishing that right now.

Tonight was like a flashback of old times. X hadn't realized how much he'd missed being with Nick and Rome like this until just now.

At Rome's old place they had a room that had been specially designed for them. There was comfortable leather furniture big enough to accommodate all of their six-plus-foot heights, a pool table, plasma television with an entertainment system that would rival any department store, and a full-service bar. At Havenway, Baxter, Rome's longtime butler and confidant, had seen to it that they had a comparable space.

It was almost midnight when they'd finally finished the conference call with the other Faction Leaders. Neither Nick nor Rome had been ready to return to their females after that enlightening conversation. And if truth be told, X wasn't really in the mood for the solitude of his own place. In fact, he was dreading going back there alone, dreading lying in his bed and facing the dreams he knew would come. The nightmare that continued to haunt him.

This room was actually bigger than the one they'd had back at Rome's. It was on the first level of the compound, with gleaming hardwood floors, because cats had a tendency to rip through carpet in the heat of their shift. Instead of the glass patio doors that had opened out to the running space Rome had constructed at his mansion, there was a control panel hidden beneath the regular light

switch that opened two heavy steel doors at the far side of
the room. Those doors opened right into the dense foliage
of Great Falls National Park. Of course it wasn't the
Gungi, but it was open space where the cats could get out
and stretch their bodies without too much fear of being
noticed. It seemed the chance that the shadows might be
revealed to their human counterparts was ever growing.

"It sounds like they've got some pretty in-depth notes
on this mystery species they're researching," Rome said
as he sat at one end of the wheat-toned leather sofa.

Nick was in a recliner, leaning all the way back with
his hands folded behind his head. He stared up at the ceiling as he nodded. "A government lab looking into an un-
identified species—sounds awfully familiar," he said.

"They have to have some concrete evidence to launch
this type of investigation," X told them from the spot
where he stood looking out one of the small windows. It
was dark outside, and to anyone but a shifter nothing
could be seen. But in his night vision he saw the sway of
trees in a pre-fall breeze. Every now and then he'd see the
eyes of an owl staring out into the darkness to see if there
was anybody or anything staring back.

"You think they have a shifter in their custody?"
Rome asked.

X didn't immediately answer, as if to do so would
somehow validate his thoughts.

"It would not be the first time this government has
possessed another being and held it for investigation,"
Baxter said, coming to stand in front of Rome with a tray
holding three filled glasses.

Rome took his glass and stared quizzically at his
friend. "What are you saying, Baxter?"

The tall thin man, with his weather-beaten brown skin
and watery rimmed eyes, walked with quiet footsteps
over to the chair where Nick sat offering him a glass.

Well, not necessarily offering. With Baxter you took what he was giving you or dealt with his silent reprimand. Most times all he had to do was give a knowing look and his will was obeyed. There was a quiet authority about the guy, a sort of allegiance they paid to him even though none of them really knew why.

Baxter knew everything there was to know about the shadows, and some stuff they didn't even know. He'd been with the Reynolds family for longer than any of them could remember. He was also on speaking terms with the Assembly, which meant that he was accepted by them in some way. But he wasn't a *Topètenia*. That fact had always perplexed X.

"I am saying, Mr. Roman—" He spoke as he came up behind X, stood, and waited. "—that they must have some proof in order to investigate. What you should be trying to figure out is where that proof originated."

X turned to take the drink even though he didn't really want it. Baxter's impending scolding was even less welcome, X thought as he took an absent sip.

"Bas said he was planning an operation where he'd send in a team to check things out more thoroughly," he said.

"And that is a good idea. Mr. Sebastian has a good head for planning operations. He will no doubt come out with knowledge. The remaining question is, what will you do with the knowledge he obtains?" Baxter left the question hanging in the air as he moved back to the bar to place the tray he'd handled there.

"I'd say bust in and kill the nosy bastards, but I think what's happening was inevitable," Nick said with a sigh, coming to sit upright in the recliner. "The exposure of the shadows wasn't something we could expect to have avoided forever."

"We've done a damn good job of it so far," Rome said.

"That was before Sabar and the Rogues," X chimed in. "Shadows live by the *Ètica*, we care about the threat of exposure. Rogues don't give a damn what they do or how they do it. You saw that when they robbed that bank and when they started a battle with us right in the middle of a public street."

Rome took a swallow from his glass. His skin was darker than X's, and so was his cat. He looked menacing even though he rarely scowled and usually had a mild-mannered demeanor.

"So somebody else might know about us as well," he said, then cursed.

X figured Rome was feeling this was his fault as the Faction Leader. He was supposed to protect the secret of the shadows.

"You can't control what others do," X told him. "Rogues don't give a shit; they're out there for all to see. There's no way we can contain that type of blatant attack."

"I hate to say it but he's right, Rome," Nick added. "Even if we kill Sabar tomorrow, we need to accept that the damage may have already been done."

Rome was shaking his head. "The damage was done when our parents started working with Cortez. That's where the door opened to our exposure."

X had already told him what he'd learned from Hernandez. They'd decided that the immediate issue was still Sabar. But now it all seemed to be coming together to make it all relevant.

"Kalina found some journal entries," Rome offered. "The dates match those same dates Hernandez gave you."

"So your father took notes after meeting up with Cortez?" X asked.

"Yeah, brilliant man that he was," Rome quipped.

Nick shook his head. "At least your father left you

something to follow his trail. If my parents had anything I guess it went up in that car fire with them."

"Either way, the evidence shows that your parents weren't traitors. They were doing what was necessary to keep the tribe viable. We probably would have died out there in the forest without any outside help." X had been thinking about this since returning from Sedona.

Yes, Loren Reynolds and Henrique Delgado went to Cortez and took his drug money to supply the needs of a tribe that shouldn't exist. A wrong deed to support a good cause. X couldn't hate them for that. Hell, at least their parents had cared enough about their own children and the families of others just like them—whether they knew them personally or not—to take such a risk. If you asked him, they should be commended.

"I think you guys need to lay off your parents about this. They did what they thought was best at the time," he told them.

Both Nick and Rome looked at him as if he'd spoken in another language. X shrugged. It wasn't often that he talked about their parents like this; usually he just went along with what they said because he didn't want to offend them or because he just didn't know. How was he supposed to know how good parents acted when his were at the bottom of—no, they were beneath—the totem pole?

"They put us all in danger," Rome said, staring down into his glass.

Nick shrugged. "They probably thought it was the only route to take."

"You do what's best for that moment. Sometimes you can't think about the long term," X said.

"And what about your parents—you forgive them for not thinking about the long term?" Nick asked.

X's already weird mood took a turn for the worse. "We're not talking about my parents," he said.

"We never do," Nick rebutted. "But it's obviously affected who you are now, who you're trying to be."

"And why is that your business?"

"Because who you are now is tied to my sister."

X cursed. "Dammit, Nick. We've been over this already. What Caprise and I do is none of your damn business."

"But what happens to all of us as a result of what you and Caprise do is relevant, X." Rome put his drink down and took a deep breath. "Look, you know we've never pried into your past. Even when we could have looked back to see exactly what happened in Atlanta, we didn't, because you're our friend and we respected your privacy. But you've got to respect where we're coming from now."

X walked across the room, leaving the window yet keeping his back to them. They were supposed to be his friends, but right at this moment he wasn't so sure. He wasn't sure about a lot of things, especially after talking to Caprise earlier.

"That has nothing to do with the here and now," he told them.

"You sure about that, X? I mean, I've watched you over the last few years with women. I know the stuff you're into and I don't pry because what goes on in one man's bedroom has nothing to do with me. You're a good agent and a loyal shifter, but you're haunted by something and it seems like it's taking its toll on you now," Nick said.

He wasn't yelling, wasn't accusing as he had been in the last few days. He was just telling him something, as he'd done many times in the past.

"I think that's part of the reason that agent is looking at you for this Diamond Turner thing. He had to see something in you to make him think you could do a thing like this."

X whirled on Rome so fast, his entire body shaking with rage. "I did not kill that girl! And FL or not, I should kick your ass for having the balls to stand there and accuse me."

Rome stood up, went toe-to-toe with X. "I'm saying what that agent is thinking. From his point of view you've got the rage, the strength, and since he has that business card he figures the opportunity to do this."

"He said as much when he called me yesterday," Nick added.

"He called you and you didn't tell me?"

"I'm your attorney, but I don't have to tell you about every call I take."

"When it concerns me and my life you do."

"X, he's not charging you. He doesn't have enough evidence for that. But you standing in an alley killing that tiger wasn't helpful."

"Oh, like you killing Ary's father in a fucking parking garage? Nick, give me a break with your psychoanalysis bullshit! You're just as volatile as I am and you would have done the same thing if you'd seen the fear he put in Caprise. Shit, half the shifters in this building would have done it. It's who and what we are."

"We're not disputing that, X. We just think maybe there's something else bothering you," Rome said.

"No. There's nothing bothering me," X said before storming out of the room.

After he'd slammed the door Nick and Rome exchanged knowing glances.

"Do not worry, Mr. Rome," Baxter said from the spot he'd been standing beside the bar.

He had been trained in the art of being there but not being noticed. It was part of his heritage. But he'd seen and heard everything. In fact, he'd known this was coming. Mr. Xavier had been like the proverbial pot of boiling water, only someone had set the flame very low with him years ago. Now the water had just begun to boil, the rage just ready to explode. Unfortunately, the remedy was not going to lie in this friendship.

"He will survive this," Baxter finished. "He will survive and be much better because of it."

"How do you know this?" Nick asked. "You always know everything, even before things happen. How is that, Baxter? Who are you really?"

Rome did not object to any of those questions, even though they may have been better coming from him. But he looked at Baxter waiting, hoping, he would deem it appropriate to answer at least some of them.

He did not.

"I am who I am, Mr. Dominick. And I am doing my job. Watching the three of you grow up has been a privilege. You are very good friends to Mr. Xavier. But you are not who or what he needs to make it over this hurdle. That is for his mate alone."

To that Nick cursed and Rome shook his head. It seemed neither of them had much faith in their friend or the true strength of a *companheiro*.

Chapter 22

"Took you long enough," Caprise said the moment X came out of what they called the "boys' room."

The room was at the far end of the north corridor, and was always locked. She'd figured out long before she'd overheard them talking about meeting there that it was expressly for Rome and his two commanding officers.

Thanks to Lucas, the shifter from the Gungi, she'd known exactly when they finished their official meeting in Rome's private conference room. Lucas didn't speak much English, and Caprise had only gotten to know him because he'd clung to Seth like a wet T-shirt. He was tall and gangly, still trying to figure out how his sixteen-year-old body was going to suddenly morph into the bodies he saw every day of full-grown shifters. He had intelligent eyes and an inner strength that some of the shifters around here would envy. She could see it in the way he held his head high, how he was determined to speak English, to learn to fight, and to prove to Rome he hadn't made a mistake bringing him here.

Tonight he'd been in Rome's rooms, as Kalina had summoned him there. He'd asked Caprise to come along because her Portuguese was a lot better than Kalina's and he was hoping she could translate. She really hadn't felt like being bothered with a lot of people, but it had actually worked out for the better.

"So you've seen X already tonight?" Kalina had asked when they were in her sitting room. Lucas was eating dinner because Kalina swore if he missed one meal he was going to shrivel up or possibly pass out. Caprise thought it was a little much. He was a growing boy; he'd eventually get hungry, at which time he'd eat. She understood all too well the starvation that came with grief. How many days had she gone without eating after her parents died? Double that after little Henrique had passed.

"Saw him, talked too much, moved on," she said quietly.

"Talked too much, huh? I know that feeling. When I told Rome about my past as an orphan I felt like I'd talked too much, too."

"He didn't talk at all" was her reply.

Kalina simply shook her head. "They're like that."

"He's not playing fair. He wanted me to tell him everything and I did," she said, absently rubbing the mark at her side, her son's name surrounded by floral swirls. "He should have reciprocated."

"Is it important to you to know what he's holding back?" Kalina had asked.

Caprise thought about that for a long moment, then sighed. Before last night, hell, about two weeks ago, it wouldn't have mattered to her one way or another. Today she couldn't say that. "Yes, it is."

Kalina's response was a genuine smile. "I knew it."

"You did not know anything," Caprise said, only slightly agitated. It was different having someone she could confide in. Kalina had said she and Ary were there for Caprise, that she could share things with them and they wouldn't tell a soul. Caprise believed them and she appreciated their offer.

"So how are you going to get him?" Kalina asked after she'd cleared Lucas's plate from the table and come back to sit on the couch next to Caprise.

"I don't know yet."

"My advice—and I know you've known X a lot longer than I have—I would smother him. Don't give him a moment to think of why the two of you joining is not a good idea. Don't let him find refuge."

Caprise let her words sink in. "Like in battle you'd never let your opponent get a catnap," she said slowly.

"Precisely. Stay on his back until he has no other choice but to face you, to face what's going on between you two."

"Or run and hide," she followed up with. There was the possibility that X really didn't want this mating thing with her. *Maybe he wanted to mate with someone else. Maybe . . . stop it!* she berated herself. Xavier Santos-Markland wanted her, she knew he did. The *companheiro calor* was so strong, if it were a drug she'd be high as a kite right now. No, whatever was standing in their way had nothing to do with her, but with him.

"You won't run and hide, it's not in your nature. You'll bide your time to figure out a strategy, then you'll strike." Kalina picked up her mug of hot chocolate, blew on it, and smiled before taking a sip. "And when you do Xavier won't know what hit him."

Lucas had interrupted then, attempting to tell Caprise that X and the others were on their way out of the conference room. To avoid seeing him right at that moment and any awkwardness between the two of them and her brother, she'd slipped out the door before they made their way to this part of the First Female's suite.

Now she was back, and she was ready.

"What are you doing here? Shouldn't you be in bed?" X asked, his brows drawn in a tight line.

He looked like he was about to explode, he was so angry. Any other woman would have run screaming. Caprise wasn't any other woman and she wasn't running anymore.

"I don't have a curfew," she said, taking a step closer to him.

His body was tense, anger rolling off him in heavy rivulets that assaulted her like huge waves. She didn't falter, simply took another step closer.

"Do you have a time to be home, or someone you have to go home to?" she asked him.

He closed his eyes, took a deep breath, and let it out slowly. She watched his muscled chest, beneath the fitted material of his black T-shirt, move up and down. Her mouth watered and at the same time her heart melted. He was trying so hard to keep a lid on whatever was inside of him. It was almost painful for her to watch.

"There's no one else, Caprise," he said finally, his eyes opening slowly as if he'd been drugged. "And don't tell me you're going to play the jealous girlfriend now."

Caprise chuckled because of all the human and shifter traits she possessed and would inevitably claim, jealousy was not one of them.

"Just clearing the air about where we stand."

He looked tired as he spoke.

"We're currently standing in the hallway in the middle of the night discussing whether or not I'm sleeping with someone else."

She nodded. "Well, are you?"

He didn't speak right away but stepped toward her. She probably should have backed up, his height combined with his thick build could be intimidating—*very* intimidating. But she stayed still until her breasts brushed against his torso.

"When I touch you, nobody else touches you. Got it?" was his terse reply.

Caprise shook her head. "We weren't talking about me, buddy." She lifted a palm, placed it right over his left pectoral, and let the beat of his heart vibrate through her fingers, up her arm, until it seemed like their rhythms matched . . . finally.

"For the time you're in my bed, no one else is," he said finally. "Does that satisfy you?"

Caprise licked her lips. "Not quite."

"You don't want to do this right now, Caprise. Just go back to your room and go to bed," X told her solemnly.

His eyes were already shifting, the dark brown going to intense green in a matter of seconds. And that wasn't the only change. A heady scent filled the air around them, circling them both and holding tight until Caprise felt like she was breathing the exact same air he was. She was smelling what he was; they were sharing something so acute and so intimate when they were both fully dressed and standing upright. It was an intense feeling, so much so that she swayed a bit and damn if her big brooding hero didn't reach out and wrap a muscled arm securely around her waist.

"I know what I'm doing. And I'm not going to bed without you."

"You don't want this right now," X said when they were closed in her room.

His mind was dark, fathomless, and void of anything real. Or at least that's how he felt. It was that strange feeling that overcame him sometimes, the one that left him uncontrollable. His palms itched, fingers clenching and unclenching. Even the cat inside him was looming like it was ready to pounce at any moment. He could do anything right now, absolutely anything. Fuck, drink, run, or even kill. Nothing seemed to matter.

And then there was her scent. It had changed somehow, was stronger than the floral aroma that had originally drawn him to her. Heavier, more intense, this new scent clogged his lungs until he felt like he wanted to choke—to cough it up and finally be rid of it. Even his normally excellent vision seemed a little blurry around the edges.

Caprise stood at the end of her bed. She wore shorts that were too fucking short and a shirt that hugged her breasts too goddamn tight. His dick took the hint and perked the hell up instantly. X growled.

"I want you right now," she said, her voice settling over him just like a full glass of Hennessy.

Hell, his mouth even watered the way it did just after the Hennessy slid down his throat. He licked his lips. She licked hers in response, keeping her eyes on his as she did.

He yanked at his shirt until it ripped and fell from his body. "This isn't going to be pretty," he told her as his hands went to his belt.

Her eyes grew darker and she pulled her shirt over her head. "I didn't ask for pretty."

"I mean it, Caprise. I don't do soft whispers, cuddling, and all that shit." His zipper down, he was about to push at his jeans but he remembered his boots.

Bending over, he untied them with record speed, probably broke the damn laces but didn't care one way or the other. When he stood again he kicked them off, pushed his pants and boxers off, and looked back to Caprise to see if she was still interested.

She was naked. Like fucking Christmas morning the best damn gift sitting under a perfectly decorated tree, naked as the day she was born.

"I want you," she repeated. "Just as you are."

X didn't believe in forcing females, had never done that a day in his life, no matter how out of control he felt. At the same time, no other female had said the words she'd just spoken to him. They rendered him still for about ten seconds. Then the darkness pressing firmly against his skull pushed him forward.

He grabbed her at the waist, his fingers pressing tightly into soft skin. She gasped, her hands moving to his biceps to hold on. She needed to hold on because he wasn't going to be able to stop once he started. He knew this without a doubt and sighed, dropping his head so that his gaze fell solidly on the tattoo at her side.

The tattoo of her dead son's name. She'd borne another man's child and that child had died. She'd lost her parents and her son and she was still standing, ready and willing to take him with this darkness engulfing him inside her. The knowledge almost broke him. Almost.

"I don't want to hurt you," he said in a voice that didn't sound like his own.

The next thing X felt was her hands at his cheeks, pulling upward until his gaze met hers.

"You won't hurt me," she told him in a strong and clear voice. "I trust you, Xavier."

She didn't. She couldn't. She had no idea who or what he was, what he'd been through, how he came to be this beast that barely held on. He opened his mouth, determined to tell her, to warn her. But when he did she came up on tiptoe and covered his lips with hers, thrusting her tongue inside his mouth, rendering him totally speechless.

The kiss was like liquid fire moving through him. He gripped her tighter—if that were even possible without breaking her in two—his mouth sucking at hers hungrily. His teeth scraped along her bottom lip, clamped down and tugged until his tongue wanted to taste her once more. Her arms had gone around his neck and she pulled him closer, hugged him tighter.

Admittedly, kissing wasn't X's favorite pastime. The act never appeared during his sexual escapades because he didn't allow it. Now, despite his past misgivings, X was drowning in this kiss. With his eyes wide open he watched her and she watched him. But he was falling, felt the weightlessness as their tongues touched and dueled. Inside, his cat growled and paced, wanting him to take more, take faster. He lifted her off the floor, dropping her onto the bed and breaking their kiss. She landed on her elbows, shook back her hair, and glared at him. Her cat's eyes glowing, her teeth bared and sharp. "I'm okay," she told him.

He hadn't asked; in fact, the question was so far back in the recesses of his dark, addled mind, he wondered how she knew. With a shake of his head, a futile attempt to gain some clarity, X lowered himself until his face hovered just above her tattoo.

"I saw this that first night you were in Rome's house. I wanted to lick you all over the second I knew you had been inked."

He didn't give her a chance to respond, but flattened his tongue over the tattoo and licked. Her hand went to the back of his head as he licked again and again, some small part of him wishing it had been his child. The thought led him to her stomach, where his tongue delved into her navel. Beneath him she spread her legs and it was like a beckoning. His hands slid down her thighs until he clasped her just behind the knees and pushed upward. The action opened her wide for his perusal and peruse he did, gladly.

With feral hunger gnawing at him, he looked down at the plump folds of her vagina, already glistening with her arousal. Her center opening creamed, and X's cat growled. Lowering his head he caught the juices on the tip of his tongue, savored them for a moment, then licked her until he would swear she'd be bone-dry. But when he pulled back, she still glistened with wetness, her woman-hood as beautiful as everything else about her. Waiting wasn't an option . . . no, this time it had to be. X pushed back against the urgings, rising above her to cup her breasts. His dick hurt, the skin pulled so tightly over the bulbous head he feared a really bad result. But he didn't care, as his palms worked over her breasts, his eyes closed, and that weightless feeling comforted him. It lulled him against the darkness like a huge pillow. He swore the scent had intensified like a pillowcase rubbing softly against his skin.

"Xavier." She called his name and X heard her clearly. Not like before when it could have been a whisper on the wind.

This time it was loud, or at least loud to his ears. "Say it again," he urged her.

"Xavier" was her quick reply.

He still stood over her, hands on her breasts, eyes closed.

"Again."

"Xavier."

His hands moved quickly from her breasts to her wrists. Opening his eyes, he watched her closely as he pulled her arms up over her head. "Don't move," he told her.

Cursing, he wished like hell he was at his place where his things were. As it stood he'd have to make do. Climbing off the bed he found his jeans, pulled the belt from the hoops. He went to the headboard and grabbed Caprise's wrists, tying them tightly to the heavy wood. To her credit she didn't even wince.

X leaned down to her then, licked over her lips, then

thrust deep into her mouth, kissing her until she was breathless. "Stop," he told her. "All you have to say is *stop* and this is over."

She nodded, licking her trembling lips. "I won't."

"Listen to me," he said louder. "It's all you have to say."

"I understand" was her next reply even though her eyes still said she planned to be defiant. X almost smiled at that. It was like a little ray of light spearing through the darkness.

His mouth covered one delectable breast, sucking the nipple in deeply as his hand grasped the other. He didn't lay on top of her, so only his mouth and his hands touched her. She hissed loudly, her legs parting, lifting up off the bed then slamming back down as his ministrations grew stronger, harder. Her skin was such a perfectly creamy hue, he hated to bruise her, but knew that was probably going to be impossible.

She tasted like heaven, a place he'd never dreamed of, never even dared to mention. Yet here it was right in front of him. Switching to the other breast, he sucked his fill until he was intoxicated with the taste of her. When he pulled away it was because all his nerves were on end, every part of his body begging for something more. He straddled her at the shoulders then, lifting his length to guide it to her lips. She was so eager her lips were already parted, ready to accept him. Before she did X held his dick upward and she smiled. Her tongue lapped along the line of his piercings over and over until he was now saying her name through gritted teeth.

When she raised her head higher and scraped her teeth over the metal balls X roared, loud and long, with the pleasurable sensations ripping through his body. Pressing a finger on his shaft he aimed the tip at her moistened lips, watched as she took him in slowly. When he pumped his hips he wondered if she'd gag or try to turn her head. He should have known better.

Caprise sighed over his length, sucking him to the rhythm his hips moved. Moisture dripped from her lips onto his shaft until they were both glistening.

"Enough!" he finally yelled, pulling out of her mouth and reaching for her legs.

He pushed them back so far she could probably kiss her kneecaps. When he thrust his throbbing length inside her waiting pussy they both yelled. The room seemed to capture the sound so that it bounced back at them like an echo.

X didn't care. Nothing and he meant absolutely nothing mattered at this moment but this pleasure. This woman. This shifter that had pushed her way into his space. His dick sank deeper and deeper with each stroke, her body sucking him in graciously. He wasn't gentle and he knew he wasn't small, but she rotated her hips, giving as well as she was receiving.

Spasms of light speared the darkness in his mind. His cat stood on hind legs, growling and hissing its pleasure. More and more was what he wanted from her. Everything and then some. Her legs trembled and shook in his hands. His name streaming from her lips over and over as her release took a strong hold.

His followed with a tightening at the base of his spine, the stiffening of his thighs and buttocks as he emptied himself completely inside of her.

When he was completely depleted, and only then, X closed his eyes once more.

The darkness was gone.

He opened them.

Caprise was still here.

Chapter 23

"Two more girls are dead," Darel said with no more emotion than it took to announce there was a leak in one of the bathroom toilets. Even though one of the girls had been Raven, who had provided him with tremendous entertainment last week, he couldn't muster a lot of sympathy for the pathetic strippers who would rather get free drugs than cold cash.

Sabar stood at the glass window that overlooked the main room of Athena's. He wore a gray suit and black collarless dress shirt. His dreads had been pulled back from his face to fall like limp snakes down his back. His stance said he was pissed off without him even speaking.

"Sales are up," he said with a low growl afterward.

"They died here in the club. Yandy found them when she went to get them to go out on stage," he finished.

Sabar kept staring down at the floor. "Production's still on schedule," he said. "The warehouse is full of product that's ready to go."

"Did you hear what I said?" Darel asked, raising his voice slightly. He didn't want an altercation right here, right now, with Sabar, but damn if he was going to keep his mouth shut this time. Especially not with all the leverage he now had against his so-called leader.

"I don't give a damn about some fucking strippers.

So they snorted too much and died. Fuck them! You need to get your mind off that petty stuff and start planning the expansion. I want to have locales like this in every state by the end of the year. You can start interviewing for the managers but I get the last say. I want to know who's working with the money at all times."

Sabar hadn't even turned to look at Darel as he talked. He was only the second-in-command, no need to give him any goddamn respect. Exactly the type of treatment Darel had grown sick of.

"Cops are all over the place now," he continued. "They're coming back with a search warrant because one of those dick-ass detectives found some blood out back. I'm telling you, this enhanced drug is bringing on too much attention. I think we should scale back and just peddle the normal shit for a while."

Sabar did turn around then, in enough time to get right in Darel's face.

"I don't pay you to think. I tell you what to do and you do it!" he yelled, then took a step back, rubbing a hand over his face.

If Darel weren't so pissed off and tired of bullshit he would have noticed that Sabar's eyes looked a little red-rimmed and his shoulders slumped a bit.

"Everybody wants to be the boss. Bianca's right about one thing: I've got to get a handle on you guys. Keep everyone in line all the time."

Her name caught Darel's attention and he opened his mouth to say something. What? Was he really going to tell Sabar that he'd fucked Bianca? No. Not yet. He'd tried to warn him but he hadn't listened. Bianca wasn't worth the time it took to say her name. She was a pretty good fuck, but nothing to write home about. Another fact that confused him about Sabar's obsession with the conniving bitch.

Darel had a plan for her, though it wasn't time to implement it yet. She was meeting him later tonight; he was sure for another round of what she considered her mind-blowing sex. Or maybe he should say *mind altering* after watching the unraveling of Sabar, the shifter he'd dedicated his life to working beside, following without qualm. All that had changed. It had to. Nobody controlled Darel now. They all thought they did, but that's only because he allowed them to think it.

"We're getting a big shipment on Friday. I need you and those two clowns out front there to go with me. I don't want too many so that these suits get scared right off the bat. But I want to be covered and covered good by someone I trust."

If Darel had feelings he might feel guilty for planning what he was and hearing Sabar say he trusted him.

"Where and what time?"

"I'll text you later. Ears in here may not all be on our side. Like you said, there are cops every goddamn where."

He was looking out the window once more. "That one's FBI," he said, pointing.

Darel went to the window and looked down at the African American man who had just taken a seat at one of the back tables. He was clean-shaven, dressed in slacks and a button-down shirt. He looked out of place here even though he was trying to fit in.

"I've seen him here before," Darel said. "Like four or five times this week."

Sabar nodded. "Put one of your shifters on him. Find out why he's become a return customer."

"Sure thing," Darel said. Then because he just couldn't resist he asked, "Where's Bianca tonight?"

Sabar's neck could have snapped for how fast he turned to glare at Darel. "I told you not to even utter her name."

Darel shrugged. "Just looking out for you. Fine woman

like Bianca can get herself in a mess of trouble if she's not kept on a tight leash."

The sting of Sabar's fist crashing into his jaw wasn't a surprise. The fact that he held his stance, only allowing his head to jerk back slightly, fists at his sides, ready but not jumping just yet, was.

"That's your last warning," Sabar said, his sharp teeth cutting into his bottom lip as he stared at Darel for another second before walking out of the room.

"Likewise," Darel said, rubbing along his jaw with one clawed hand. "That was your last warning, boss."

X walked into Nick's office with a ready frown. The message on his phone when he'd stepped out of the shower in Caprise's room was not the kind of news a man wanted to hear after a night of phenomenal sex.

What it did was offer him a quick route out of Caprise's room, before she could expound on the weird-ass scent that still lingered in there and the way said scent was making X feel. He'd left her a quick note since she was still in the bathroom and made a getaway in the style he hadn't employed in ages.

Now he was in downtown DC about to visit his lawyer and most likely that jackass Dorian Wilson from the DEA.

Nick's assistant was an attractive enough middle-aged woman with enough photos and plants on her desk to make the small space before Nick's office look more like a person's living room than an office.

"Hi, Kerry," he said with a smile. "Nick's expecting me."

She nodded, her eyes alight with the sincere smile she offered in return. "I know, Mr. Markland. Go right in."

He did and wasn't surprised to see Nick wasn't alone.

"Good afternoon," he muttered as he closed the door behind him because by the time he'd made it to his place to change clothes, then downtown, it was well after noon.

Following a nod from Nick, X sat in the guest chair closest to Nick's side of the desk while Wilson and another man he hadn't met yet sat across from them. X figured the new guy for a cop, probably local and most likely homicide since Wilson really had nothing to do with Diamond's murder.

Nick made the official introduction: "This is Detective Eric McCoy. Detective McCoy, this is my client Xavier Santos-Markland."

"Where were you two nights ago between the hours of midnight and five AM?" Detective McCoy asked immediately.

Nick looked at X and nodded again.

"In Sedona," he said simply.

"Doing what?" Agent Wilson asked.

"Was anyone with you?" McCoy asked simultaneously.

"His alibi is Sedona and we'll provide you with a list of corroborating witnesses," Nick interjected. "Is that all, gentleman?"

"No," Wilson stated. "When was the last time you visited Athena's?"

"Last week" was X's reply.

Wilson didn't believe him. X didn't give a rat's ass. McCoy looked like he had more questions, but when he went to speak again Nick held up a hand.

"As I already stated, if you don't have a warrant for my client's arrest, we don't have anything to talk about," Nick told them.

"So are you saying your client doesn't plan to be cooperative in this investigation?" Wilson asked.

"In what investigation, Agent Wilson? Because here's what's confusing to me. You work for the DEA, correct?" Nick didn't wait for Wilson's response. "So you really have no claim to the Diamond Turner case."

"I'm investigating the Diamond Turner murder," Mc-Coy put in.

Nick nodded. "Fine. When you get enough evidence to arrest my client, give me a call and we'll gladly head on down to the station. But until that time, you"—he pointed at Wilson—"stay out of his face or you'll be slapped with a harassment charge so fast Detective McCoy's head will spin."

"I didn't kill Diamond Turner," X stated seriously. "If you want to find her killer, you need to take a closer look at what's going on down at Athena's."

McCoy nodded, tapping the pencil he'd been using to write in his notepad against his chin. "Funny you should say that. We picked up two more bodies from Athena's last night. Both females that worked there, just like Diamond."

X was instantly alert. "How did they die?"

"You tell us," Wilson interjected.

"You're dangerously close to a formal suit being filed against you and your department, Agent Wilson," Nick said, shaking his head with a smug smile.

McCoy shared a glance with Wilson, who didn't look terribly intimidated by Nick's threat.

With a shrug McCoy said, "Coroner thinks it may be a drug overdose, but there's still some traces of foul play. One's name was Raven, the other Icy. Those are their stage names, of course. Sound familiar?"

"I'm not a regular at the strip club so no, I don't know either of those ladies," X told them.

"You sure?" Wilson asked. "Because here's where it gets really interesting. Raven was the one who told us about you giving her and a couple of other girls a hard time one night a few months back. And one of those girls was Diamond Turner."

Inwardly X cursed as he replayed that night in the

alley when he'd first met Diamond Turner. Raven had to be the tall one with all that dark curly hair and smart-ass mouth.

"This meeting is over," Nick said, standing. "You two can see yourselves out. Remember what I said about that warrant."

McCoy and Wilson both stood, Wilson eyeing X as he rose slowly.

"Just so you know, these new developments officially make you a suspect in not one, but three murders. In light of these circumstances I have no choice but to alert the director of the Bureau immediately."

X stood as well, rage simmering slowly inside him. It wasn't just that the man thought he was a murderer, but that now he would attempt to threaten X's job. He wanted to prove Agent Wilson right and leap across that desk to take a chunk out of his throat. But he remained calm, or as calm as could be expected for a *Topètenia*.

"You do what you have to do," he said coolly.

"I'll caution you, Agent, don't dig your ass a hole you can't climb out of," Nick said.

Wilson cocked his head at Nick. "Is that another threat, counselor?"

Nick shrugged. "Take it as advice from someone who's not real used to losing in the courtroom. Build your case and find the real killer. In the meantime, leave my client the hell alone. We clear?"

"Get your house in order" was Wilson's response to X as they moved to leave the office. "I'm coming for your ass."

"Then you better come correct," X said, unable to contain another ounce of restraint.

When they were gone and the door to the office was closed, Nick sat down with a huff. "Fuck!"

X echoed that sentiment as he turned to stare out the

window. When he awakened this morning it had been after a night with no nightmares, a night when he'd thought light was penetrating the dark that had stalked him for so long. Now, as clouds moved slowly over the sky, he felt as gloomy and dour as the weather. This was his fate; he should have known better than to believe otherwise.

Chapter 24

Nivea Cannon was a twenty-eight-year-old shifter whose parents owned a nonprofit organization that provided aid to underprivileged children——with a good deal of those children being shifters. She was the younger of two sisters and the only sibling to leave New York in search of her own life.

Those were the specifics as Nick had read them from a data file he kept on his laptop. In addition to his duties as a commanding officer, Nick was also head of security for the Eastern Zone. More often than not his security upgrades reached out to the remaining Zones as well. About an hour ago Eli had met with Ezra, Rome, Nick, and X. The topic of discussion was of course Sabar and what they were now calling his gang of Rogues down at Athena's. It had been decided that at the moment the shadows could not take a more active role in ridding the world of these cretins without bringing more heat on the investigation against X.

"They're building a circumstantial case against him," Nick had said from his seat beside Rome. "I can blow holes in every theory they have right now, but more dead bodies will only give them more ammunition."

To that announcement X had growled, his fists pounding on the table. Eli understood the man's frustration.

There was nothing worse than being wrongly accused—he could so relate to that.

"Agent Wilson seems to be really gunning for you," Rome said to X. "Any ideas why?"

X shook his head. "Never dealt with the man until I came across his name in Kalina's files. I think his fixation is with the three of us since he was behind the initial investigation into the firm."

Rome nodded. "You're probably right. He couldn't find anything on me so now he's connecting the dots." Rubbing a hand over his chin, smoothing the neatly trimmed goatee, the FL looked like he was in deep concentration. "I want to know what he knows before he tosses it in our faces again," he said solemnly.

Nick picked right up where Rome left off, which was normally the case between these two.

"We need twenty-four-hour surveillance on him. Two guards, not males. The way he was eyeing me and X, I sensed him putting together similarities. In light of all the suspicions and investigating of our kind, I don't want this guy piecing anything together. Females will work better because he won't suspect them," Nick said.

"Nivea Cannon's good," Ezra said immediately. "She's been in battle with us twice now and holds her own."

"I agree," X commented. "She escorted Caprise down to Athena's the other night and gave those nosy-ass peeps a fright when she almost toppled them with the Dumpster."

"Did you find out who they were?" Rome asked with what seemed like an afterthought.

"Nivea found a card on the street right outside the alley. A reporter named Priya Blake," X said with a frown.

Eli hadn't been terribly surprised by that revelation. These stripper murders were making headlines. Assumptions were being made about the possible connection to

the females who'd died in that apartment building and to
Senator Baines and his daughter. It was no wonder the
sharks were out with all the blood that had been spilled
so far.

"That's just what we need," Ezra stated.

"Who else? I don't want Nivea tailing this guy alone,"
Nick said. "Find another female, give them rotating
shifts. They'll report directly to you, Eli."

Eli nodded, not totally thrilled with the assignment but
resigned to take it anyway. He and Nivea had history. Of
course that meant it wasn't good history; that would be
too much like right.

"As for the reporter, Ezra, you get somebody to research her. I want to know where she works, eats, and
sleeps. And I definitely want to know which paper she's
writing for," Rome told the guard.

"No problem" was Ezra's quick and smooth response.

Eli had wanted to elbow his twin. Nothing bothered
Ezra, ever. He was the easygoing twin, the suave and
totally-in-control one. Eli was the one with the rough
edges, the youngest by two and a half minutes, and the
one who was always trying to find his place. Lead Guard
for the Eastern Zone wasn't a bad place to be. Personally
guarding a commanding officer was just as prestigious
but sometimes Eli wanted something that was just about
him, based solely on the man he was, not the shifter he
became.

He was thinking like that and hating himself for doing
so as he walked into Havenway's gym where he knew he
would find Nivea.

And sure enough there she was, tearing up the track on
the treadmill, her small feet eating away at the rubber belt
as if she was on a mission. Nivea was always on the move,
always volunteering for training sessions, always ready to

go into battle. She was like the shifter GI Jane with better breasts.

Straight coal-black hair streaked with bronze strands was pulled back into a tight knot. For a moment Eli stood and simply watched. She was dressed in spandex shorts and sports bra, with a significant amount of her pecan-toned skin visible. Eli stared, enjoying the sight, because first and foremost he was a Shadow Shifter and that package came complete with a ferocious sexual appetite. Said appetite never failed to go into overdrive when Nivea Cannon was around.

"You gonna just stand and watch or are you planning to do a little work yourself?"

It took him a second to realize she was not only looking directly at him, but asking him a question.

"I kind of like watching," he told her with a shrug.

"I'm sure you have better things to do," she retorted, her arms moving in stride with her feet.

She wasn't even winded, although the treadmill had to be on the highest speed because Eli had never seen it moving that fast. Admittedly, he didn't do the treadmill when he came to the gym, stayed pretty much to free weights. He preferred to get his deeper workouts by running. Moving out here to the park had been a godsend, giving him more than enough room to get his daily exercise outside.

"Actually, you're on my list of things to do."

The way her head snapped in his direction and the shocked look on her face had him backtracking fast.

"I mean the commanding officer sent me to find you," he corrected.

She was visibly relieved and he felt only mildly deflated. It brought back memories, ones they both swore never to speak of again.

"Arggghh," she groaned. "Nick or X? They probably want to chew me out for not trying to stop Caprise from leaving the other night."

He shrugged. "Caprise is not easy to stop," he said. "X actually backed you up in that regard."

She looked surprised. "So it's Nick that wants to lecture me." She sighed. "I swear I've heard enough lectures to last me a lifetime."

"People are trying to guide you in the right direction," he said simply.

"I know what the right direction is for me, thank you very much." She switched off the machine and did a running step to climb off. "I'll get a shower. Where does he want to meet?"

"Actually, you're meeting with me, and it's not about the whole Caprise thing. You stay dressed and I'll change, meet you by the back entrance in fifteen."

He was batting a thousand with her today because she looked as if what he'd just said was not what she expected from him. When she opened her mouth like she was going to question him he shook his head.

"In fifteen, Nivea."

She nodded in agreement. When Eli walked out of the gym it was with the feeling that this assignment wasn't going to go as smoothly as he planned.

Two days later the headline in the news was the raid on Athena's, with Priya Blake reporting.

In addition to the raid, two guard jeeps had been found on the outskirts of the city, deserted. Things were changing and not for the better.

Rome called a meeting of all Faction Leaders, and this time Elder Umberto Alamar had also been included. The conference room table in Rome's suite was almost full with Kalina, Nick, X, Ary, and Caprise. Each of their guards was also in attendance—Eli, Jax, Ezra, Zach, and Leo. X had assumed responsibility as Caprise's guard for the moment. Nick wanted to assign her someone else but X had been adamant that Caprise stay with him at all times. Nick, wisely, hadn't argued the matter further.

Out of the corner of his eye X saw Baxter standing off to one corner. He'd already set glasses of water in front of everyone seated. He'd pulled the small shutters down on the slim windows in the room and rechecked the locks on the door. Baxter had also been the one to get Alamar on the phone, as if Rome wasn't privy to the Elder's telephone number. Again, X wondered about the older man and his protectiveness of Rome and the *Topètenia* as a whole. There was definitely something there, something he doubted any of them knew about specifically.

"There were a lot of drugs found on the premises," Cole Linden, Central Zone Faction Leader, said through the speakers centered on the conference room table. "Enough that CNN picked up the story; that's how I knew what happened before you called."

Rome sat at the head of the table, his face grim.

"There were pictures of the plastic bags with the symbol on it. So we can breathe a sigh of relief that some of the savior drug is off the streets," he said.

"What if there's more?" Ezra asked. "I can't see that Sabar would be stupid enough to keep all his drugs in one place."

Nick nodded. "He's right. There's got to be a stash house somewhere."

"Most likely outside the city," Eli added.

"The more pressing question is, were any Rogues arrested in the raid?" X asked.

"Right. That would not be good if they were being jailed. Who knows how they'd act under those circumstances," Kalina said.

"They would have scented the cops coming," Rome said with quiet authority.

It still amazed X how easily his friend had migrated into the role of leading all the stateside shadows. As he sat with squared shoulders, nondescript facial expression, hands clasped in front of him in all seriousness, he oozed power and control.

"I doubt anyone of importance was still in there by the time the raid was executed. Which means our guy is still out there."

"What are you going to do about it?" Bas asked. "My team has killed a total of twelve Rogues in the last week. They seem to be growing in the trees here, making their appearance known throughout the night, pacing around the resort like they're planning a feast. We shut them down quick and without question because I'm not willing to risk one of my guests being hurt."

"You're all but secluded out there," X told him. "We can't make kills like that in the city."

"X is right," Nick said, sending a closed look at X. "We're already under a microscope here. We can't afford any slipups."

"They are settling in," Elder Alamar said in his quiet, raspy voice. "We knew this time would come."

From the corner, Baxter took a step forward as if the Elder was speaking specifically to him. "Yes, we knew."

Everyone else in the room and on the extended lines went absolutely quiet. Until finally Rome spoke.

"There seems to be an outside conversation going on here. You two want to tell us what's going on?" he told them.

Baxter looked at Rome with somber eyes, his usual glare.

"Now or later, it will eventually come out," Baxter said.

"As we knew it would" was Alamar's reply.

"Are you fucking kidding me?" Nick roared. "If you two have something to say—"

His words were cut off by Rome, who raised a hand and gave Nick a level look.

"Now is the time to tell us everything. Humans are dying. Shadows are dying. Rogues are multiplying. If either of you gives a damn about this tribe you will tell me what we're dealing with so I can counteract."

Again with that cold power, that ominous tone Rome possessed naturally that fell like a thousand boulders in the center of the room.

"We were all as one hundreds of years ago. Our existence remained a secret because we remained together in the forest, in solitude. There were five tribes, all living as one because there was no choice," Alamar said clearly.

"After a while there became turmoil. Lions wanted to lead. Cheetahs wanted to run. Tigers wanted to feast. Cougars and jaguars wanted to kill. The peace once harbored came apart. The separation would come *tarde o temprano.*"

Baxter continued when Alamar grew silent. "He speaks of the different tribes—the *Topètenia,* the *Lormenia,* the *Croesteriia,* the *Bosinia,* and the *Serfins.* We were all once a community of shifters, a group of those that were different. It was those differences that kept us together but ultimately pulled us apart."

X sat up, leaning his arms on the table as he watched Baxter coming closer. Everything about the man was still the same, and yet it was different. X wasn't looking at a devoted employee of the Reynolds family any longer. No, what he was seeing right here, right now, was a revelation. One that was going to either make or break Rome, judging from the wary look on his friend's face.

"You're saying that cougars, cheetahs, lions, tigers, and jaguars once lived together," Kalina clarified.

"Somewhere in a South American rain forest there was a legion of shape shifters that eventually separated and migrated to other parts of the world."

Baxter nodded. "The ones who saw this as an inevitability made a plan: Within each tribe a different shifter was placed. Overseers is what we are called."

"Sonofabitch!" Nick roared. "You're a goddamn shifter?"

Baxter showed absolutely no reaction to Nick's outburst. "My father lived in a village near the Gungi. He was a shaman and helped the *curanderos* from time to time. I grew up with your parents, Mr. Roman. When they moved to the States I asked to come with them. That is when the Elders made me an Overseer," Baxter stated simply.

As simply as if all that he'd said, all they'd both said would be swallowed and this meeting would go on without pause.

X was already shaking his head. "What about the other Overseers—are they shifters or humans?"

"I am the only human Overseer. It is so because of my father's abilities and his dedication to the tribe. Others are shifters but they will not shift. Our job is to watch, to teach, to preserve," Baxter continued.

"To lie and betray," Nick said. "You've been lying to Rome and his family for years."

"No!" Alamar's voice echoed throughout the room. "What we do is not an untruth. We have been watching and waiting for the division in our tribes to stretch wider and it has finally begun. No longer are we even fighting on our own grounds. We have moved to these places that are highly populated with humans. We are endangering yet another species and it must stop before there are no more," the Elder said with vehemence. "No more of any species."

The room grew silent. Absolutely no one spoke. Kalina had reached for Rome's hand, clasping it within hers. Ary's hand rubbed her protruding belly as Nick's larger hand soon covered hers to make the same comforting gesture. Beside him X could hear Caprise's slow intake of breath, even slower release. She was absorbing all this information. Taking it in as slowly as she could so as not to become overwhelmed. This had to be even harder for her, the one who did not want to be a shifter. When he turned to her, to do what he wasn't quite sure, X was a little startled to see her watching Baxter.

She gave the man a close look, a careful scrutiny that couldn't be easy to undergo. But when X turned his gaze to Baxter, he saw the man leveling his stare at her just as evenly. Almost as if they were communicating on some eerie level.

"So what's going on now, the drug war this Sabar character is orchestrating, the death and cruelty being left in his path, it was all pre-ordained," Caprise said to Baxter.

"There was no way to tell in what variation the battle would come. But yes, we knew it would happen someday," he replied.

She continued to stare at him as if there were some sort of recognition. Until finally she shook her head and cleared her throat. "So what now? How do we stop them?" was Caprise's next question.

It caught X off guard because last time he checked Caprise wasn't into the shifter thing and didn't want to hear about the Assembly at all. Sure, she'd come to this meeting, but he figured that was more out of curiosity than anything else. Now he was sensing something different.

"We find Sabar and kill him," Rome said with finality. "I'm not about to let this escalate. We take their leader and they'll scramble, hopefully back to whichever region they've come from. But they will not invade our Zones without a fight."

Nick nodded his approval.

X's phone rang at that moment. He looked down to see the number was a familiar one. "I've got to take this," he announced, pushing his chair back and leaving the room.

All eyes seemed to fall to Caprise in his absence. She knew what they were thinking: that she was his mate and that all was well with them. They didn't have a clue. She'd begun to accept the mating thing, since the *companheiro calor* was so strong she almost couldn't scent anything else when X was near. But there was still a distance between them, one she thought she'd been close to closing only to be slapped in the face with a note and his disappearance.

Of course he'd returned later that day in a foul mood, giving out orders as if everyone within hearing distance were under his command. That was sort of true, but she didn't have to like it. One of his orders was that she remain with him at all times. She wasn't receiving a new guard because X was taking the job. It was crazy even though Zach was big and strong enough to guard them both. Kalina and Ary had advised her to let X have his lead for a while. They all knew he was going through something. But Caprise was getting damn tired of waiting to figure out what.

The Baxter issue seemed to be tabled, for now. Rome had announced that he would speak to Baxter and Alamar privately. He didn't look at all pleased with these new developments but moved on because he had no other choice.

When the FLs began talking about training and Nick added his opinions about assigning teams and strategies, Caprise excused herself and left the meeting as well. She hadn't really expected X to be right in the next room. He'd left at least fifteen minutes ago; surely he would have gone farther. But here he was, sitting on one of the dark cherrywood chairs at the table Kalina used for her work area. His elbows were propped on the table, his head lowered, cradled in his hands.

Rage circled him like a storm cloud, its scent clogging Caprise's throat as she closed the door to the conference room behind her. She went to him immediately but didn't touch him. She just stood behind the chair watching as his muscled back rose and fell with the rhythm of his breathing.

"What is it?" she asked finally.

"Go back inside with Nick," he said, pushing the chair out from under him and thrusting his cell phone into his pocket.

"I asked you a question," she continued, walking right behind him.

He turned so fast she bumped right into his massive chest. He grasped her arms and pushed her back. "Not now, Caprise. You do not want to be near me right now."

His eyes were so dark Caprise could only describe them as black. He held her so tight she wanted to gasp at the pain.

"I'm not leaving you," she said in a quiet voice. "Whatever it is, we can deal with it together."

"No!" he shouted. "It's my problem. I'll deal with it alone."

Behind her, Caprise heard the door open. Of course Nick would hear X yelling and of course he'd come barreling through the door first.

"What the hell's going on?" he asked.

X let her go so fast she stumbled. Kalina moved quickly to keep her from falling. As for X, he still stood there looking like some sadistic maniac about to go the hell off. Still Caprise moved to his side. She looked at Nick and said in as calm a voice as she could muster, "It's fine. He's fine."

"The hell he is," Nick said, taking a step closer. "What's going on, X?"

X shook his head and looked away. "I'm just gonna go for a while. I'll be back later."

"We'll come with you," Rome said, standing beside Nick.

Again X was shaking his head. "No. I gotta do this alone."

"I'm going with you," Caprise said.

"You're staying here with Nick," X said.

She shook her head. "I'm not. Either I'm riding in that truck with you to wherever it is you're going or I'm getting in one of those jeeps and following you. You're not going alone and that's final."

His curse was long, loud, and fluent, but when X stomped out the door Caprise was right on his heels.

Chapter 25

He hadn't looked back, hadn't spoken a word on the long drive from Havenway to his apartment in the city. And as they did the hide-the-truck in the underground parking garage and boarded the elevator, he still remained quiet. Caprise was biding her time. Whatever was ticking around inside of X was about to blow completely. Veins bulged in his arms and hands. The tattoos on his neck pulsed with the rush of blood going on beneath. He walked with long purposeful strides, slid the keycard into the base on the door with a quick motion.

The moment she walked into his apartment Caprise was smacked with the cold. She shivered, hating this place for what it represented and how it made her feel. And yet at this moment there wasn't any other place she'd rather be. For the first time in her life there was someone who needed her and not the other way around. Of course he wouldn't admit it—would probably rather pull his eyeballs out than admit that he needed her right now. It didn't matter. She was determined not to run this time.

"You don't listen, do you?" he said, heading back to his bedroom. "Every goddamn time I tell you to do something, you do the opposite."

Following him into the room, Caprise stopped at one

side of the bed and shrugged. "Then you should probably stop telling me what to do."

He turned to her then, his neck snapping around so quickly it was almost comical. His eyes, however, were still ominously black, so she didn't dare crack a smile. This wasn't a laughing matter, she knew. X was in deep trouble. Caprise prayed she had what it took to help him.

"Why don't you sit down and we can talk."

"I don't want to talk," he said, a growl following his words. "You wanted to follow me so you're gonna get the show you asked for."

He went to the armoire in the corner. On the side almost hidden was a keypad—Xavier loved his codes and computers. He punched in some numbers, then opened both doors so that the contents were on full display.

If someone had told her this was the type of stuff X was into, Caprise would have never believed them. Then again, she thought, blinking a couple of times, she would have. It said so much about the man standing there, staring into the open armoire. And then, it didn't say enough.

From where she stood, and looking around his muscled frame, she saw the tools of the trade, knew them because dancing in seedy clubs like Athena's introduced her to so much. There were leather whips and chains hanging neatly on the insides of the doors. Deeper inside were shelves all lined with red velvet. On them she could see a variety of nipple clamps, vibrators, and plugs.

She swallowed, because damn, she had no idea what she'd been walking herself into.

"I'm not like other men," he said, not turning to face her. "I'm not even like the other shifters."

"It's okay to be different," she said, demanding her knees stop wobbling. She would not sit down, would not cop out on him in any way. If this was the man she wanted, she would have to stand for him, no matter what the cost.

"I don't know how to stop what's inside me."

Caprise chose that moment to move. She walked up behind him, touching a hand to his back.

"Something happened," he continued, his words sounding tortured, his voice almost unfamiliar. "It changed everything and I can't take it back. I don't want to take it back."

She nodded even though he couldn't see her. Both her hands were on his back now, sliding down to his sides as she rested her forehead against him. "I know how that feels."

"No," he said slowly. "No, you don't."

Then he turned so fast, grabbing her by the arms and pushing her back until she fell on the bed.

"You have no fucking idea what I've been through. None! But since you can't follow simple instructions I'll have to show you."

Everything began happening in a blur. X's hands moved so fast, ripping at her clothes, tearing her shoes from her feet, tossing her belt and bra across the room. She was naked when he lifted her off the bed, pulled back the comforters, then dropped her back onto its center. Her heart pounded, her eyes open so wide she thought her eyeballs would pop right out. But she didn't run, didn't even try to fight back.

He put her wrists together, lifted them over her head, then handcuffed her there. Ripples of excitement twisted throughout her body and she bit on her bottom lip. If this was just going to be about sex, she could handle it. But something told her it was about so much more.

X grabbed her ankles next, stretching her legs apart and tying them to the posters at the end of the bed with

the softest silk material she'd ever felt. He moved around
the room, lighting black candles throughout, remaining
absolutely quiet afterward. He looked like a dark knight
standing at the foot of the bed, his eyes gleaming, muscles bulging. When he pulled his shirt over his head,
Caprise gasped. He unbuckled his jeans and pushed them
down his legs. As he stepped out of shoes and the jeans
she couldn't tear her eyes away from him. And when he
stood before her totally naked, the golden candlelight il-
luminating the numerous tattoos over dark brown skin,
her pussy pulsated.

"Death," he said slowly tracing his finger over the tattoo of the moon dripping with blood at the bottom of his
neck. "All I could think about was dying. Every time that
bastard touched me I wanted to die."

Her eyes stayed trained on him, on his face, his mouth
as he talked. Then up to his eyes as he watched her. She
couldn't tell what he thought looking down at her in this
submissive position, but whatever it was, it was enough to
keep him talking.

"He said it was what my parents wanted, why they sent
me to him in the first place. They wanted him to fuck me.
Can you believe that shit? What kind of parents want
that?"

Caprise didn't have an answer, and she suspected X
wasn't really looking for her to answer him.

Instead he bent down and picked up a whip. She hadn't
seen him take it from the armoire but guessed he'd done it
before lighting the candles. He held the heavy-looking
handle in his hands, wrapping the long strip around so it
circled his wrist one time.

"They wanted me to feel pain," he said, lifting his arm.
The whip came down with a snap.

Caprise bit the bottom of her lip to keep from jumping

with the distinctive snapping sound. The whip hadn't touched her at all.

"For days and days afterward all I could remember was the pain. Then disgust would set in. Then shame. I was ashamed of who I was, of whatever my purpose was in this life."

The whip came down again, this time so close to her skin she'd felt the quick wisp of air as it hit the mattress.

"He didn't stop. My father said to man up. My mother cried. And I walked over to his house every goddamn time they told me to. I walked right into his arms. Fucking bastard!"

The whip soared through the air once more, landing on the other side of the bed. This time when it hit, Caprise didn't want to cringe; her nipples hardened.

"Bastard!" X continued to scream, bringing the whip down time and time again until finally a small part of the edge caught Caprise's leg.

She hissed and bucked up off the bed. Not because of the pain. No, while there was a bit of a sting to her skin, the ripples of pleasure that quickly spread like a disease throughout her body took the pain away. Her pussy vibrated with each strike of that whip. She was so wet her thighs were now damp.

He stopped instantly, as if it had just dawned him that she was lying there. He looked down at her, his eyes still that eerie darkness.

"I can't stop it, don't you understand. I couldn't stop him," he said quietly, his arms falling at his sides, the whip hitting the floor with a clank.

"Xavier," she said, because Caprise honestly did not know what else to say.

He shook his head, fists balling at his sides. "But I

could stop him. I did stop him when I killed him. I killed him!" he yelled, tilting his head back to let a vicious roar break free.

"You did what you had to do to protect yourself," she told him finally. "You had to protect yourself because your parents wouldn't do it for you."

"They told me to go over there," he said.

"They were wrong, Xavier. Not you. You did what had to be done to stop him."

"I'm a murderer. That's what that agent says. He told my director that I was a murderer and they suspended me."

Caprise wanted to touch him. She wriggled her hands futilely in the cuffs. She wanted to wrap her arms around him and tell him he wasn't a murderer, that he was a good man, a good shifter. Instead she took a deep breath.

"Xavier," she said, but X had looked away from her. "Look at me, Xavier."

He ignored her.

"Goddammit, you look at me!" she yelled.

His head turned slowly until those dark eyes were once again trained on her.

"You are not a murderer. You didn't kill any of those girls. Sabar and his Rogues did that. And we'll prove it."

"It's too late," he said solemnly. "I'm already a killer. I killed Jeremiah. Then I killed Rolando because he was a bastard, too, and he was scaring you. I'm a killer."

"You are not! You're a shifter, a commanding officer, and you are good." Dammit, she wanted to get up from this bed.

X knelt on the bed, coming over her like a dark cloud. She sucked in a breath and told him again. "You are good, Xavier. You are so good. So good that . . . I couldn't help but fall in love with you."

He stopped. His hands were on the bed on either side

of her breasts, his knees planted firmly between her legs.
And he didn't move another muscle.

"I love the man and the shifter that you are, Xavier,"
she told him sincerely.

"You have no idea," he started saying.

Caprise shook her head so hard she knew a headache
would soon follow. "Shut up. Just shut up! I know who you
are. You're the man who went to pick Nick up in the middle of the night when he was sixteen because Lisa Drenner
had slit all four of his tires. You're the one who stood at
my parents' funeral right next to me and my brother waiting to catch either of us if we fell to the ground in grief.
You went to the Gungi with Rome and his new mate to
look for Ary. You helped all those kids who were brought
here and sold as sex slaves. You are good, dammit!"

"You," he said, moving up until his face was hovering
directly over hers. "Have no fucking idea what you're
saying."

"I do and I'll say it again," she told him. "I love you."

X dropped his head, his shoulders slumping just
enough that Caprise could lift her head to kiss him there.
Then her lips went to his neck, to that damn death tattoo.
She kissed his skin slowly, let her tongue move in tiny
circles over the tattoo. Then she bit into his skin, let her
sharp teeth prick him. He tensed and her pussy creamed.
She knew right then she had him.

His lips took hers with a savage hunger, his tongue
swiping along her lips, her tongue, her cheeks in a display
of ownership. She wanted to laugh with the sexual excitement that bubbled inside her but he took her mouth again.
When he finally pulled away from her, Caprise was
breathless.

X climbed off the bed, headed back to that armoire, and
grabbed something from the shelves.

"Since you refuse to listen to common sense," he was saying as he climbed back on top of her, "I'll just have to show you what you're walking into."

"Show me," she said on a breathy sigh. "Show me everything, Xavier."

Without another word he clamped each of her nipples. She couldn't help the scream that ripped free, couldn't stop the pinpricks from radiating throughout her breasts, and didn't want to stop the pleasure spikes shooting right to her clit.

"This is who I am. More often than not, this is what I want," he told her as he moved down her torso. His tongue found her tattoo and stayed there for more minutes than Caprise could count.

Then he tapped the other side of her midriff, directly across from the tattoo of her son's name. "Right here," he told her, "that's where I want the *Topètenia* insignia. Right fucking here so you'll know who and what you are."

"Fine. Fine. Can you just . . . just," she said, trying to squirm, to get some sort of friction going near her clit. It was unsuccessful.

"Calm down," he told her, looking up to her with his cat eyes glowing. "I've got this."

Caprise let her head fall back on the pillow. Her teeth bit into her bottom lip as she reached for patience she knew damn well she didn't possess. She felt his palms beneath her buttocks and wondered, what now? He had to stop with all this playing and foolishness.

Instead X lifted her so that her pussy was in his face, being served like a platter. He licked her hungrily, the sound of his tongue moving through her slippery center echoing throughout the room. She jerked at the cuffs holding her arms, wiggled her legs, and stifled a moan. He held her still, using his fingers to spread her open wider, his tongue to lick her deeper. The first ripples of release hit her like a boulder and Caprise fell back, her entire body convulsing.

X laughed, a deep guttural sound that was masculine and proprietary. "After the *Topètenia* insignia, X gets inked right here." He tapped the line of skin just above her juncture, where her hairline would be if she hadn't shaved completely.

She could barely speak when she said, "Whatever."

He chuckled again before his fingers slid back, back, his thumb touching the tight bud of her anus. She sucked in a breath.

"No. Breathe. I just need you to keep breathing," he told her.

She nodded, tried to do what he told her.

"Breathe, babygirl," he whispered as one finger slipped deeper inside her. "You can do it. You can take whatever I give you. Your strength is the sexiest part about you. I love how you can take whatever, deal with it, and throw it right back. I love it," he said, sighing over her.

"Xavier," she whispered.

Then there was a different feeling, a fullness she hadn't expected. Opening her eyes she could see him staring down at her, his hands still working between her cheeks. "A little pressure, then pleasure," he said licking his lips. "So much pleasure, babygirl."

Caprise sighed with him, felt him snap the plug deep inside her anus, and licked her lips.

The second X saw that she'd taken it and the clamps without qualm, he was over her, guiding his thick erection into her center. He watched with pleasure unbound as his dick separated the saturated folds, sinking into her with tender ease. The connection itself was arousing; the sight of her lighter skin wrapped securely around his darker complexion had him gasping. The tightness with which she sucked at him caused his cat to growl. When he began to move they both moaned, and sighed, and hissed with pleasure.

He closed his eyes, let the feel of her and the scent of their mating engulf him. In that moment he had accepted, had known exactly what the scent was and precisely who this woman was to him. As he pumped deeper and deeper still he called her name, then waited.

"Yes! Xavier. Yes!" was her loud reply.

He loved the sound of his name on her lips, loved the tendrils of pleasure that floated down his spine when he heard it.

"Come for me, baby," was her next instruction.

X almost smiled. They were two of kind—both of them scarred, both of them guilty of running from a past they couldn't change, both of them struggling to find their place in this world that was their own. And finally, both of them falling through the hazy fog of mating as shifters and loving as humans.

Sabar awoke to sweat pouring down his face, his chest heaving, legs aching as if he'd been running for miles and miles. His mouth was dry and his vision was blurry. He tried to speak but words wouldn't come. Then, just when he thought he was losing his mind and was about to shift just to feel a semblance of normalcy, the lights switched on.

"You okay, baby?" Bianca asked.

She was across the room, had turned on the main light using the switch by the door. There were two lamps on either side of the bed; he wondered momentarily why she hadn't turned on one of those, why she wasn't in the bed next to him.

"Get me something to drink," he told her using the back of his hands to rub against his eyes.

It took effort to steady his breathing, but he was determined to get it right. Beneath the blankets he moved his legs just to make sure the damn things still took his command.

In a few minutes she was beside him, extending her arm with a glass. Sabar grabbed her arm because his vision was still a little off and the glass wobbled in front of him. He closed his eyes for a few seconds, then opened them again, looking up at Bianca to see if they'd work right on her.

She was beyond beautiful, even in the middle of the night. That much could be seen, he figured, even if he were blindfolded with a bag over his head. Her hair was pulled to hang over one shoulder, eyes glittering when she stared down at him, full lips puckered as they spread into a smile.

"Serve me," he said to her because he didn't fully trust his own hands to grab that glass and put it to his lips without making an embarrassing mistake.

Besides, he had a feeling she needed a reminder. She was looking at him as if she wanted to laugh. There was the air of knowing something he didn't know as well that hovered over her like a drape. Even the way she smiled down at him was different than it had been before.

"Of course, Sabar. Did you have a bad dream?" she asked as she leaned forward slightly, putting the glass to his lips.

"I'm fine," he told her before taking a long, greedy swallow.

His mouth felt like cotton. It even hurt to swallow. But there was no mistaking the distinct taste as he finally managed to do so. "This isn't water," he said looking up at Bianca once more.

She shook her head. "No. You didn't ask for water."

"What did you give me?" he asked licking his lips and blinking uncontrollably fast.

"We thought you needed to get more rest so we fixed you some tea," she told him.

The glass was gone and Sabar's hand had dropped from her arm. He'd tasted this tea before, at dinner he thought. Or maybe it was lunch yesterday, he couldn't remember, but knew it was familiar. He fell back on the pillows as if someone had pushed him. Attempting to turn to look at Bianca again wasn't easy. His head felt like lead.

"What did you put in the tea, bitch? Are you trying to kill me?"

She leaned in closer. He couldn't really see her clearly, but he smelled her, the rich intoxicating scent of her pussy filling his nostrils as he inhaled slowly.

"We would never hurt you, Sabar, baby. We're only trying to take care of you so you can continue to lead us."

"We?" he said his voice becoming slurred. "Who the hell is we?"

He heard her laughing then, a deep-throated chuckle that echoed throughout the room. Then her lips were at his ear, her tongue lapping along his lobe.

"Sweet dreams," she whispered in his ear. "Sweet fucking dreams."

Chapter 26

Rome and Kalina had just finished a hot shower. Their just-dried bodies lay entwined on the cool silk sheets of their king-size bed.

He wrapped his arms around his wife, loved the feel of her backside pressed firmly into his front. As his palms cupped her breasts—their favorite resting spot each night—he'd kissed her neck and muttered a sleepy, "Good night, my *gato inferno*."

She'd sighed into his embrace. She loved his nickname for her, loved to hear him whisper it while they made love and afterward. He never let her down. Kalina was the other half of him he'd yearned for but hadn't the good sense to search for, wasting far too much time without her. But now that he had her, Rome was determined to keep her safe. He was determined to keep them all safe.

And as he slowly drifted into the place just before sleep where he thought about his duties and responsibilities and the conflicts that waited in the distance, his cell phone rang.

Not letting Kalina go, Rome reached one arm behind him to fumble on the nightstand until the sleek device was in his hand. Sliding his hand across the screen in the security pattern he'd memorized, he accepted the call.

"Reynolds," he answered.

"Sabar's making a buy tonight. You want to stop this war you need to stop him now! RSE Warehouse in Woodland. Midnight."

The call was disconnected before Rome could say another word. At the mention of Sabar's name he'd shot straight up in the bed. Kalina, light sleeper that she was, sat up beside him. The moment he pulled the phone from his ear she was talking.

"Who was that? What's wrong?"

Rome was already dialing another number. "Got a lead on Sabar, meet me at the door in ten. Get three teams to go with us, and find X."

Kalina was throwing back the sheets, climbing out of the bed. She'd already reached for her robe when Rome grabbed her arm.

"You're not going," he told her firmly.

She opened her mouth to speak and he kissed her lips hard. Resting his forehead against hers for a few seconds after the kiss, he said, "It's too dangerous. You stay and help Ary get the medical center ready in case there are injuries."

"Rome," she started.

He shook his head. "No, Kalina. I don't care how much training you have on these streets. There's no way I can do this if I'm worried about you getting hurt. I need you to stay here. I need you to do this for me, baby. Please."

Rome understood her need to work, to fight beside him; he knew that urge and respected it. But she was his wife, his First Female, and he would not risk her for anything in this world.

When she nodded her agreement, cupping his face

and kissing his cheek, he realized how much he truly loved this amazing woman.

"I'll be waiting," she told him quietly. "I'll be right here waiting."

"Caprise is with X," Nick said the moment he disconnected the call.

Ary had already gotten out of bed and was slipping into dark blue scrubs and black Alegria nursing clogs.

"Then she's safe," she told him as she pulled her hair back and secured it tightly in a ponytail.

Nick was already dressed. He reached into his closet, all the way in the back where he kept his personal firearm. Nick was accustomed to carrying his weapon when they were out at public events, and even more so lately. He checked the nine-millimeter for bullets and made sure to put the safety back on before tucking it in the back band of his dark jeans.

"She should come here to wait with you and Kalina," he said, moving toward the door, then stopping to wait for Ary.

She walked slower these days, her stomach protruding a little more each day. Despite the circumstances, as he watched her, Nick's excitement piqued. He couldn't wait to see what he and Ary had created.

"Do you really think Caprise is going to come back here to twiddle her thumbs with us?" she asked, moving by him and looking up with a smile.

Nick shrugged. "I can only hope."

X disconnected the call with Nick and instantly got out of bed. Caprise, of course, was right behind him. They hadn't been asleep, far from it actually. After their lovemaking, which she was intent on calling it no matter what

X said, they'd showered together. When he'd had that shower designed, he never imagined he'd enjoy it so much more with a female beside him. But not just any female; it only worked because it was Caprise. He knew that now without any doubt.

"What's happening?" she asked, standing in front of him as he tried to make his way to the door.

She was gloriously naked, not a modest bone in her entire body. God, he was crazy about this woman.

"Rome got a tip about Sabar making a deal tonight. We're going to head him off," he told her honestly. There really wasn't any other way to be with Caprise. For a woman who hadn't wanted to tell him about her own past, she'd been like a pit bull trying to get the details of his, and she hadn't done background checks and phone searches like him. She'd simply gotten in his face and hadn't backed down. He had to respect a woman for that type of tenacity.

"Okay, I'll get dressed," she said immediately.

Her bag that Seth had brought over a week ago still sat in the corner of his bedroom. X had a feeling more of her things would soon occupy the space and miraculously wasn't bothered by that fact.

"Caprise, this is going to be dangerous," he told her, reaching for his own jeans out of the closet.

"I know. I'll get my gun."

X hadn't been facing her, but he turned quickly at her words. "Your what? You have a gun?"

She nodded as she pushed her leg into her jeans. Her breasts were still bare and for a minute distracted the hell out of X.

"Yeah, I carry a Glock 19. I don't like to carry heavy. This fits my hand like a glove. Don't worry, I'm good," she said after pulling the weapon from her purse.

He was already shaking his head. "No."

"No, what?"

"No. You're not going. Take my truck and go to Haven-way. I'll get Nick or one of the guards to swing by here and get me."

"That's ridiculous. We're going together," she said, pulling a shirt over her head.

Oh, hell no, she was out of her mind if she thought she was going to this fight with him. And wearing no bra at that. Shit, he'd never keep his mind straight knowing that.

"Caprise, listen, you're not a trained guard."

"I'm going with you," she said simply, pulling her hair back and twisting it into some kind of knot with one of those elastic bands she had a ton of.

"No, you're not," he said adamantly.

"I am." She nodded and turned away from him to pull boots out of her bag. She sat down to lace them up, and X moved closer to her.

"Look, we're cool on the mating thing now. You're a part of me that I don't want to lose just yet. So I'm asking you nicely to go to Havenway and wait for me there."

She looked up, a smile spreading quickly over her face. He liked seeing her smile, liked the way her dark eyes lifted with the action, how her teeth were all white and straight, her pert nose spreading only slightly. She was fucking beautiful. But hardheaded as hell.

She kissed him quickly on the lips. "I'm going. If you're coming you better hurry up and get dressed."

X was still standing there wondering what he was going to do with her when she'd left the bedroom.

Chapter 27

They'd driven through a neighborhood that looked like it had seen better days. Even in the dark of night Sabar could see the remnants of urban decay. He picked up the scent of alcohol and urine and cringed. Sitting in the back of his Hummer he admitted only to himself that this headache he'd been carrying around for the last two days was a bitch. Not to mention the bouts of memory lapse he was suffering. Anything before two days ago was crystal clear. It was the last forty-eight hours that seemed like he'd walked around in a daze. He remembered meals and he remembered Bianca—nothing and nobody else. When he'd climbed into the vehicle tonight he'd caught a glimpse at Darel. The man barely looked at him, and his scent was of pure hatred. That wasn't out of order for a Rogue, but tonight it seemed more along the offensive lines than ever.

He'd asked Bianca to come along, but she'd declined. In the back of his mind he knew he should be suspicious about that, but had decided to focus more on closing this deal. On the seat between him and Darel were two suitcases. Both were filled with cash, proceeds from their drug operation that had been growing steadily. Even in the midst of the raid on Athena's, they were still receiving orders for shipments. Norbert Hanson was still running the lab back at Sabar's headquarters on the outskirts of the city. Their facility there had been a steady work in progress. Darel had put a lot of time into the structural issues, picking up the security, while Sabar had planned the layout and financed the entire project. Now their lab was fully functional and they were shipping about half a million dollars' worth of merchandise each week. The savior drug was the drug of the future and Sabar was going to make a fortune as the only supplier.

However, his plans to rule needed to be bigger, their territory expanded. Hence this deal with Kensington and his boys with the guns. Once he made this purchase he'd probably have to get rid of Kensington—that guy definitely knew too much. And he wasn't above running his nasty mouth about Sabar and his plans and their existence. Not that Sabar was against having the existence of the Rogues known—it would happen in due time anyway—still, everything had to be planned perfectly.

"We're almost there," Black, the huge dark-skinned shifter that now traveled everywhere Darel did, said from the driver's seat.

"Good," Sabar heard himself replying. He shifted in his seat, his clothes feeling more than uncomfortable. It had been like that the last two days: Clothes were too much for him to bear. Each time he'd been awake he'd worn his silk robe and nothing else, the cool softness rubbing against his skin in a soothing manner that turned him on and baffled him at the same time. "When we get inside I'll do all the talking," he said.

Darel nodded.

"You carry the money and don't give it to anyone until we see the product."

Darel nodded again.

"And stop acting like a fucking mute!" Sabar screamed, his patience wearing thin.

When Darel's head snapped around and he glared at Sabar, not with human eyes, but the dark green-rimmed eyes of his cat, Sabar growled back. He was sick of Darel's bitch-ass attitude. If he had a problem with Sabar or this operation, the shifter could very well walk out the door. He was tired of giving a damn.

The corner of Darel's mouth lifted, his eyes glinting. "Sure thing, boss," was his reply, his New York accent a little more fluent than Sabar had ever heard it before.

It was about fifteen minutes to midnight when they pulled up to the eight-foot metal gates that looked like they surrounded the entire premise. When the Hummer drove slowly up to the speaker, everyone was quiet. Black pushed in the code that Sabar had given him, and they drove through without any problems. Kensington had given Sabar a detailed list of things for them to do tonight.

"Wasn't the gate supposed to close?" Thunder asked, looking back as the vehicle continued forward.

"Probably staying open to let us out afterward," Black said.

Five minutes later, after they'd parked as close to the door as they could without running up on the sidewalk, the four Rogues were entering the building, using a side door entrance that had also been outlined in Kensington's notes. Thunder reached for the doorknob. When it turned and the door was open, Black went in first with Darel right behind him. Sabar went in next, and Thunder locked the door before following them.

It was dark and chilled in the open space. Darel used a penlight from his pocket to illuminate the way to the elevator they'd been told was at the far end of the left hallway. They boarded the elevator without any issues. By the time they stepped off, Black and Thunder were both gripping huge black guns in their hands. Sabar walked ahead of them, empty-handed.

Darel watched him move with his cocky air of superiority. He was shorter than Darel by a couple of inches, but in his ass-kicking boots no one could tell. He walked in front of them while Darel carried the two briefcases full of money. There was half a million dollars in each bag; they'd counted it for the third time about an hour ago. Sabar was buying two hundred UK79865 rifles. Once the deal was made, Sabar was hopping on a private plane and heading to Albuquerque, where he was setting up another base for his business. There were already ten Rogues there waiting for him and the shipment. Those were details Darel made sure he knew.

"They should be down here, in the last room," Sabar said, turning down yet another long hallway.

This place seemed to be linked by one long-ass hallway after another. Darel felt like they were walking in a maze, even though they were following Kensington's map. The place was huge and located just far enough down the winding road they'd traveled to be discreet, which he suspected was the reason Robert Slakeman had built the facility that manufactured all of his weapons here.

Sabar stopped at the door. Behind him Darel also stopped. He figured Sabar was waiting for someone to open the door. He was, after all, the boss. And Darel was so fucking fed up with this particular boss. He nodded and Thunder took a step forward, moving in front of Sabar. He touched the knob, then looked up in question before opening it.

"Well, open it, goddammit! I don't have all night to get this done," Sabar yelled.

Over Sabar's head, Thunder met Darel's gaze. With a smile, Darel nodded and Thunder pushed open the door.

* * *

Sidney Pierson was the only son of General Oscar Pierson, who had been forced to retire from the US Marine Corps amid allegations of torturing POWs during his last tour in Iraq three years ago. Sidney, however, had never wanted a career in the armed forces. What he wanted, and what his father had been doing a damn good job of providing despite all his other letdowns, was any- and everything he wanted, when he wanted it. He was used to living a certain lifestyle, one he wasn't about to lose because his father was no longer a general in the marines.

General Pierson had lots of sponsors, as he liked to call them. These were people in very high places with very deep pockets, who needed favors only the general could grant. It was his father who had introduced Sidney to Bob Slakeman and it was Sidney who through his father had been brokering international deals for Slakeman. It was Ralph Kensington's job to keep said dealings off the radar. So far, the overweight senator-elect had held up his end of the bargain.

But this time, this deal, had Sidney and his father a little shaky.

"He's going to show," Kensington said for the third time since they'd been holed up in this office.

Sidney was lighting his third cigarette in the last hour. On his left arm was a nicotine patch and in his back pocket were gum chunks that tasted like stale paste. And in his fingers on its way to his lips was a newly lit Newport—bad habit, too damn hard to quit, so he figured to hell with it.

"He'd better show," he said after his first puff. "And he'd better have the money. We don't have room for mistakes. Not tonight." He was shaking his head, thinking of all that was riding on this deal.

His father had something else going on, something big

with the government—or covertly with the government since anything on the up-and-up, the general couldn't be involved with. The country was still at war, which meant the Piersons were still in business.

Standing to Kensington's left was a new player, one he'd met tonight for the first time. Palmero Greer was from somewhere on the West Coast. He'd been introduced as a regional facilitator, which to Sidney meant he was a mole sent by the bigwig to make sure everything went as planned. Since he knew Bob Slakeman personally, Sidney was more than a little peeved at the man's need to oversee one of his buys by sending Kensington and this thinly built guy wearing the shiny-ass tight suit.

He puffed on his cigarette again, long and hard.

"So where is he?" he asked, shifting from one foot to the other. He'd never liked the waiting game. Besides, most of his buyers seemed anxious to get the deal over with, showing up at least ten to fifteen minutes early, ready to rock and roll. Lifting his arm, he looked at the clear face of his watch and frowned. Five minutes after twelve.

"He'll be here," Kensington said. "I got a text from him about twenty minutes ago saying he was on his way and not far from the building. Just calm down. You look like you're about to have a fucking baby over there. Sucking on those sticks like a dick."

Sidney had been just about to put said stick to his lips. He looked over at Kensington with a fuck-you glare and proceeded with his next puff.

"We're too open here," Greer said quietly. "We should have done this somewhere more secure."

"What the fuck are you talking about, more secure? We're in a secluded warehouse, dammit. What's more secure?" Sidney asked with disgust.

Greer didn't frown, didn't do more than give him a

tired glance. "A secluded warehouse that belongs to Slakeman. You might as well have put out an APB letting every law official in the city know what's going down."

Sidney felt like he was getting sick. His nose kept running and he'd been swallowing some nasal crap all damn day long. He choked up something, leaning over to cough and spit on the floor. When he returned upright he saw the two bozos sent to watch him both giving him a look of thorough disgust. He almost laughed at how comical their faces were.

"Nobody cares what we're doing out here. This is private property; they can't just come in here whenever they feel like it. So this is the safest place in the city to move the amount of steel we're moving tonight."

Greer shook his head. "Amateur."

"Who are you talking to? Man, I'm no stranger to this game. I've been doing it for years." Sidney talked to the back of the guy's head since Greer had started walking toward one of the large windows on the other side of the office.

"And that's why he called me in," Greer mumbled.

"Look, Sidney, just calm down," Kensington said. "We'll be done with this deal in a few minutes, then you can go get yourself more drugs or more smokes or whatever the hell's got you so strung out tonight."

"I don't do drugs," Sidney said adamantly. He was telling the truth. Drugs would hamper his thinking and that would fuck up his money, which was not an option. He'd smoke on these cancer sticks until hell froze over but he wasn't snorting shit or sticking no goddamn needles in his arm to get high. He didn't even want to move that shit, which was why he'd become Slakeman's buyer instead of taking on other financially lucrative ventures through his father's connections.

"Whatever you say, just be the fuck quiet and we'll get

this over with." Kensington had now joined in with the yelling.

"Shhhhh," Greer hissed.

He extended a hand toward them, pointing a finger as if they needed to know he was specifically telling them to shut the hell up.

"Someone's coming," he continued and moved toward the door. He plastered his back to the wall so that when the door swung open he'd be standing right behind it. Digging into the waistband of his pants he pulled out a gun, clicked the safety off.

"Whoa, wait a minute. This is not how my deals go down," Sidney was saying, taking a step toward Greer and the door.

He stopped when Greer lifted his gun hand, pointing the fucker right at him.

"Get in position," Greer said, his face twisting in a lethal sneer.

"Who is this guy, Miami Vice?" Sidney asked.

Kensington pulled on his arm, saying in a hushed tone, "Just get back here."

"No!" Sidney yelled. "This is not how I work. It's not how Slakeman wants business conducted."

His words died in the next instant as the door was nearly kicked off its hinges and Greer—or he should probably call him look-alike Detective Ricardo Tubbs—pointed his gun, finger on the trigger.

Chapter 28

"Something's going down," Eric said into his cell phone as he drove his Acura through the city streets like a man on a mission. "All available officers have been called down to this warehouse in Woodland."

"Drugs?" Dorian asked, already getting out of his bed, grabbing the pants he'd thrown over the chair and stepping into them.

"Weapons and drugs I hear. SWAT's even coming in. This is big. You should come down just in case," he said.

"Yeah, text me the address and I'll be there," Dorian said, disconnecting the call. If SWAT was being called in, it was big. Besides, the only warehouse Dorian knew of in Woodland belonged to Robert Slakeman Enterprises, the arms dealer suspected of making deals with the devil to accommodate his lavish lifestyle. Hell yeah, he was going out there to see what was going on.

The moment their SUV pulled up, X scented Rogues. He looked to his right where Caprise was sitting and frowned.

"I can do this," she told him, patting his knee reassuringly.

In the seat in front of them Nick shook his head and X

knew he'd heard Caprise's words. Nick had already given X the nastiest case of stink eye the moment he saw Caprise heading for the vehicle. She'd told her brother to kick rocks, or something along those lines. Rome had wisely kept his opinions to himself.

"You stay behind me," he told her.

"X—" she started to say.

He put his hand over her mouth to silence her. "You'd better be on my back like flies on shit, you hear me, Caprise? This is not negotiable or I swear you'll never see sunlight again."

She blinked and blinked, then tilted her head to the side as if to say *You can let me go now.* He removed his hand from her mouth, and she sat back against the seat.

"Just because I'm in love with you doesn't mean I have to listen to everything you say. But since we're on your turf, I guess I can bow to your infinite wisdom."

She'd said all this with the prettiest smile he'd ever seen and X was instantly hard. Damn, he thought with an inward sigh, he was in love with this woman. It hit him just like that in the instant she smiled at him. Sure, he knew now she was his mate and had accepted that, but X had never put too much stock in the word *love*. Until now.

Behind them, two black vans filled with shifter guards pulled up. When all the vehicles were parked Rome came to stand in the center of the semicircle the shadows had formed.

"The gate was open," he started. "That's not a good sign. This facility manufactures defense weapons; there should be guards and locks and alarms, the whole nine yards. But we just drove right up."

"Setup?" Ezra asked.

Nick nodded. "That's exactly the way we're going to play this. Everybody armed and ready."

"Shoot before shifting," Rome added.

There were mumbles but when Rome held up his hand they ceased. He pointed to the com link at his ear, signaling they were going quiet, no communication except through their secure com links. Nick and X already knew their jobs and motioned their separate teams accordingly.

X was followed immediately by ten guards, including his personal guard, Zach. They went around the back of the building to find an entrance. Rome and his team would go through the front door. Nick and his team would make their way to the roof.

The night air was stuffy; today had been humid with scattered showers. When X put his hand on the doorknob, it was slick but didn't turn. He hadn't figured the doors would simply open for him, so he was prepared. Pulling out a device no bigger than a cell phone, he punched in codes that searched the area for connectivity. He'd designed this device to be able to penetrate any security system, as long as said system used streaming data. Red would indicate no and green yes. For a couple of heart-stopping seconds he stared at the device in the palm of his hand. When it finally blinked green he felt partial relief, then a bigger part concern.

This building wasn't being monitored at all.

"Clear," X whispered in the com link. Rome and Nick were waiting for his go-ahead before they tried to enter.

If there had been an alarm system, X would have hacked into the computer system to disarm it. But there was nothing. He wondered if he should tell Nick and Rome, but figured they were already going under the assumption this was a setup. Which to X only meant that whoever was in this building and had brought them here under false pretenses was fair game to shoot to kill.

Slipping his device into his back pocket, X pulled another small metal tool from the utility belt designed specifically for and worn by all the shadow guards. It wasn't as big as those fanny pack things—he'd been clear, and Nick had agreed, that those were not something the guards would wear—but it held a lot of his tools of the trade. One of those trades being breaking and entering when need be. Of course this conflicted with his job as a federal agent. It also conflicted with Nick's and Rome's human jobs, as well as those of all the guards who functioned in the human world. But they couldn't deny who they were, and tonight's mission would be protecting the humans just as much as the shifters. They all understood this and would proceed accordingly.

When the knob turned in X's hand, he pulled the door open and took the first few steps inside. He was about to turn around and signal for the others to follow when he bumped right into Caprise. His gaze narrowed on her but he didn't say anything.

"What?" she asked. "I'm right behind you."

That she was, he acknowledged by signaling the others to follow suit. Once they were inside X knew he was in the basement. On the ride into town, they'd been able to find some very old blueprints of this building, as one of the guards worked for the Department of Public Works and had assigned crews to come out and inspect the plumbing after a water main break two years ago. It could have been redesigned since then, but they figured it probably wasn't.

"I'm in," X said into his com link.

A few minutes later Rome reported, "I'm in."

Jax was with Rome. This shifter's human half hadn't always been a law-abiding citizen, so X assumed he'd probably done the actual breaking-and-entering part. Should anything ever be revealed about their existence, Rome, as an FL and the Assembly leader, would be protected at all costs—even if that meant another shadow took the fall for him. One of the new standards implemented and voted on by the Stateside Assembly—which consisted of each of the Faction Leaders and two officers from their Zone—was that the Assembly leader and the First Female were to be protected to the fullest extent.

X, Zach, and two of the other guards all used the penlights from their utility belts to search their surroundings while X waited to hear from Nick.

"We're in," Nick finally reported.

With that, X motioned for his team to follow him through two large areas that looked like they were used for storage. They were taking the stairs up to the next level when loud popping sounds ripped through the com link. X and the others all stopped on the stairs the moment they heard it.

"Shots fired!" Jax yelled through the link. "Second floor! Second floor!"

Thunder had kicked the door in on Sabar's orders.

"I want these fuckers to know who they're dealing with," he'd said.

Darel knew exactly who they were dealing with and where this deal was heading. He'd shrugged, letting Thunder know from this point on it was his call.

Thunder, who didn't mind making noise and getting things started, had lifted his size-twelve foot and kicked the door with the entire force of his three-hundred-pound body behind it. The wood squealed with displeasure as it cracked under the pressure and swung open, dangling off its hinges.

They walked in like characters from one of those old mobster movies, four big-ass shifters, two strapped and one drugged almost out of his mind. The other moved with a slow swagger because he knew exactly how this episode would end.

"Took you long enough," Kensington said. He was the

first to move toward the center of the room where Sabar had stopped walking.

"I'm here, now where's my shit?" Sabar asked, his voice slurring on that last word.

Kensington's head tilted as if he, too, were questioning Sabar's stability. Darel knew Sabar was wondering what the hell was going on, had been for the last few days. He'd found a good bit of humor in the turn of circumstances himself.

"You okay?" was Kensington's question.

Sabar went to take a step forward, probably thinking to get in Kensington's face, maybe threaten the guy again, possibly scare him a little.

Not.

Tonight was definitely not Sabar's night. Inside Darel there was a flicker of regret for what he knew was about to come. On the outside there was a smile, like a dying ember in Darel's dark cavernous form.

"I'm fuckin' . . . fuck . . . I'm fine. Where's my shit?" This time when Sabar went to take a step his legs gave out.

Before he could hit the ground, Palermo was behind him, catching Sabar in his arms. When Sabar looked up it was into Palermo's face. Darel knew the moment recognition hit Sabar.

"This guy's a joke, man. Get him out of here," Sidney said. "I'm not doing business with no druggie."

"You're doing this deal," Kensington said, using both his hands to push Sidney back as the younger man had already started for the door. "Part of that money's mine and I'm not letting it walk away just because this fool decided to get high before he got here. You got the money?" he asked Darel over his shoulder.

Darel put down the briefcases he carried. He lay them both flat on the floor, flicking the clips that held them closed and pushing the tops open one at a time.

"What the fuck?" Kensington said the moment he saw what was inside.

"I told you! I told you!" Sidney yelled, breaking away from Kensington and rushing toward the door.

"Let him go. I'll need him later," Darel said with a look to Palermo.

"Crates are already in the truck," Palermo, the Rogue shifter, told him.

"Good. Tie him up," Darel told Black. "And kill him," he told Palermo, nodding toward Sabar.

The shifter smiled, an evil grin spanning the width of his face. "With pleasure."

"You . . . you sonofabitch . . . ," Sabar whispered. "All of you fucking basta . . ." The words were lost as he began to choke. It looked like on his own vomit.

"What the hell is going on here?" Kensington asked as his arms were pulled behind his back.

"I've got a message for Slakeman and anybody else who wants to know who's running things around here," Darel said, setting the timer on each of the briefcases in front of him.

"Wait! Wait!" Kensington argued. "We can work something out. I don't have to report this to Slakeman. We can fix this! I can work it out!"

"You can die like the lying piece of shit you are," Darel spat. He was about to turn and leave the room when Sabar shifted, his cat jumping immediately onto four legs. It lunged for Darel, who didn't hesitate to shift himself. Now the two beasts faced each other, finally. This little standoff had been brewing with them for a few weeks now, ever since they'd fought the Faction Leader and his COs, when Sabar had basically ordered Darel to die while waiting for medical treatment. The arrival of Bianca and Sabar's immediate fixation and shift of loyalty to her was the last straw. From that moment on Darel had known the two of them would never be the same again. Only one of them could walk out of this warehouse breathing tonight. And it wasn't going to be Sabar.

When Sabar's cat came up on its hind legs to swipe at Darel, shots rang out. Sabar's cat took two in the upper quadrant and fell on its front paws with a thump. Two more bullets went into its flanks from one side, one gun. On the other side, another gun fired off two more rounds into the cat, until it lay still on the floor, blood quickly forming in a pool beneath it.

Darel watched the slow, labored heaving of the cat he'd once followed, the man he'd thought could bring him the salvation he wanted. He should have listened to his mother's warnings. She'd said to never put your faith in a man, to not idolize a man as his god. Darel should have never idolized Sabar, should have never followed him blindly. But he had, because Sabar had been the only one there for him when he needed it most. Life changed, people changed, shifters turned, and women, like Bianca, who knew their worth always played the odds.

"Holy shit!" Kensington gasped.

The breathy words caught everyone's attention.

Darel was still in cat form, Black and Thunder stood on either side of Sabar, while Palermo looked down on the cat, his gun still in hand. All three guns were instantly aimed at Kensington who, because he hadn't been completely tied up before Sabar's strike, had drawn his own weapon and was now pointing it directly at Sabar.

Thunder fired off one round, the bullet piercing through the wrist that held the gun. It clattered to the floor as Kensington grabbed his wrist, howling and screaming like a newborn baby. Darel jumped at that moment, catching the man completely off guard, knocking his large frame off balance. When they hit the floor Kensington tried to squirm away, but it was futile. Darel's teeth were already digging into the man's skin, clamping down at the base of his neck. He held on for endless seconds then finally pulled away, letting the blood drip from his teeth as he moved back over to the briefcases. Through the cat's eyes it saw the red blur of numbers, heard a chirping.

"Yeah, we should get the hell out of here now," Black said to him.

Palermo, the shifter that had come to him on loan from Bianca, looked down at his cat. "Let's go. I've got an unmarked truck downstairs with all the ammo in it."

Darel's cat head moved, a chuffing sound slipping from its mouth. He was just about to shift back into human form when there was a loud roar and two cats came running into the room.

Chapter 29

At the sound of gunshots, X had taken the stairs two at a time. He was just pulling open the door to the second floor when he saw a cat charging down the hallway. Behind him were two shadow guards, guns aimed at the cat, bullets flying.

He instantly put an arm back behind him to block Caprise but she wasn't there. As he looked back trying to see past the guards on his team, he didn't glimpse her.

"There!" Zach yelled, pointing past X's shoulder.

Caprise had already shifted and was chasing after the cat that had disappeared into one of the open doorways.

"Fuck!" X yelled, taking off behind her.

Inside the room a window was open, a thick stifling breeze mixing with the stale smell of carpet and air-conditioning. There was no one there. No cat. No Caprise.

Rome and his team came rushing in behind him. "Two down in the other room. Two on foot, they may have shifted by now."

"Caprise went after the cat," X said, his chest heaving as he inhaled and exhaled deeply. "They went that way."

There was a smaller door that looked like it linked the two suites. X took off through the door, heard the growling, and shifted without another thought. Rome had yelled his name but X was too far gone. His mate was in here fighting another cat, hell if he was going to stay in human form and hope for the best.

The moment he entered the other room he saw them, near a window in what looked like a standoff. Caprise's cat was sleek, her perfectly honed muscles bunching with each step she took. In the dark room her eyes looked like melted honey. Her opponent was a slim cat with a yellow coat and large distinctive rosettes. He watched Caprise carefully, moving only slightly to one side. Caprise followed suit. The male came closer to the window, its nose scenting the air.

He was searching for someone, waiting for his getaway. Caprise watched him carefully, stepping each step with him. So when he jumped at her, X thought he would catch Caprise off guard. He charged in only to witness Caprise come up on her hind legs and ward off the male's instant attack. Teeth bared, she swiped with vicious strength at the cat until it was falling back on its haunches. X was still going in; he wanted this cat dead, this fight over. Caprise turned to him then with a roar, one that reached beyond his usual instincts, shooting straight to his heart. This was her kill, that's what she was trying to tell him. For whatever reason, it was hers alone.

His cat stopped, even if the human inside wanted to push her back and finish this off. It paced in a semicircle, never once taking its eyes off her. She jumped through the air in one fluid movement that was picture-perfect, landing on the other cat's back and sinking her teeth into its neck. With all her strength she shook her head until the action broke the other cat's neck.

At that moment sirens blared and bright light speared in through the windows from a helicopter flying overhead.

"Company's coming," Nick said through the com link. "We need to move!"

"X," Rome called to his longtime friend as he watched his mate making what was most likely her first kill.

X moved to Caprise as she finally dislodged her teeth from the male cat. She looked up at him with another roar, a territorial one. X continued closer, butting his head against her flanks.

"We need to move now!" Rome yelled to X. Then he turned to Eli and the rest of his team. "Four of you go get that Rogue body out of the other room. The rest of you head down to the basement and find the truck. X?" he called to his friend again.

With a deafening roar X stood over the body.

"We'll take care of the body. You and Caprise need to go now! Get to the truck before they come in," Rome told them.

Police were coming in, there was no stopping that. All Rome could do now was as much damage control as possible.

They took the same steps they'd used to get to the second floor, Caprise in front and X right behind her. Funny how the positions had changed.

When they arrived at the basement door, X shifted. He instantly held up a hand. "No, not you. Not yet," he told her. "I'll get to the truck and find you something to put on first."

If she were human she would have said something, probably something sarcastic. But as a cat she simply eyed him like she'd rather have his ass for dinner. To that he laughed, then slipped through the door.

He was back in minutes. One of the other guards had already made it down here. The SUV they rode in was backed up to this door as close as they could get it. Rome was coming down right behind them. Nick and his team had already announced they were in their vehicle. Caprise shifted the moment he came through the door. X handed her the sweats and waited while she hurriedly slipped them on.

"See you covered yourself as well," she said, moving past him through the door.

"Don't want to give these cops a free show," he told her, his voice sounding a lot lighter than he actually felt.

It wasn't until they were in the back of the truck, sirens growing closer, that X was able to marginally relax. He reached for her hand and was pleased to find it right there, ready and waiting.

"I'm fine," she told him.

He could only nod, still holding on to her hand tightly.

The minute Rome was back in the truck they took off, the truck driving through a back gate that was already open. At that Rome gave X a knowing look. But X didn't say a word, just sat back in the seat and held on to Caprise.

Saturday, 2:35 AM

They were in the dining hall this time. Rome, X, Nick, and their mates at their usual table in the front of the room with the guards seated at two of the long tables, which were pulled closer to the front for the purpose of this meeting. There were too many of them to hold the debriefing in Rome's suite, and he really didn't want them in there. This had been a long night; when he retired to his suite, he wanted to be alone with his wife. Rome stood and they all looked to him with deference and respect. He was happy he could look to his side and see Kalina. Having a mate really had completed him.

"Somebody wanted us there tonight. I don't know who but I think I might know why. One of the cats we brought back with us was Sabar Tavares. At least that's Ary's preliminary finding. She was able to identify him in cat form from a photo that had been passed out in the Gungi when Sabar left. There's probably no way to trace his DNA," he said with a sigh. "One of the things I plan to propose to the Assembly is blood samples from each shifter to go into our growing database. In the future, if one of us is killed in cat form, identification will be made a lot easier."

X nodded in agreement. "I can coordinate that effort, once the Assembly has voted."

"Good. The one that Caprise killed, we don't have an identity for. When we entered the second-floor hallway, we scented already shifted cats; their angry roars were heard just before the gunshots. Once we got down to the room there were only two cats—one dead and the one that escaped us and Caprise eventually took down. The window was opened and Ralph Kensington was on the floor bleeding."

"It was Lazarus," Caprise put in. "The one I killed. I remember him from the time I was in the Gungi. I saw him meeting with Rolando and then I saw him shift. I remembered his cat because I was amazed by how bright its fur was. And when I saw him again the scent was the same."

"Rolando was the *Lormenia* shifter that X took out in the city?" Nick asked, looking at his sister.

She nodded. "Yes. He is the shifter that I met in the Gungi and who tracked me here."

Caprise didn't say anything else, and that was just fine. X had filled Rome in on the specifics of the kill and Caprise's involvement. Caprise indicated she wanted to tell Nick herself. Rome didn't see any problem with that.

"So if Rolando is gone, then what was Lazarus doing in that building?" Nick asked.

"Working for Sabar is my guess," X said.

Rome nodded. "Kensington was there, so this must have been some type of meeting with the Rogues."

"You think Kensington knew about the shadows?" Zach asked.

Nick nodded. "Melanie Keys was having an affair with Kensington. She hooked him up with Sabar. And we know he doesn't give a crap about who knows he's a shifter or not. So it's a good chance he did."

"So it's a good thing he's dead," Rome added.

"What I'd like to know is who called you down there and why?" Kalina asked.

"I've got the number that called Rome. I'll trace it and get back to you later," X said.

"Ary and Papplin are in the crematory preparing to get rid of the cat bodies," Rome said, finishing up his briefing. It had been Papplin's idea to build ovens, similar to the ones found in funeral homes, to dispense of bodies; burning was the only way to keep their secret safe. A shifter body could be dissected, researched, and basically discovered. That was one of Rome's biggest fears.

"So for now Athena's is shut down and Sabar is presumed dead," Nick said.

Rome inhaled slowly. "Yes. That's what it appears. But we're still going to keep our eyes open. Somebody definitely got out of that warehouse just like we did, because that back gate shouldn't have been open."

"None of those gates should have been open," Eli added. "That place should have been locked up tighter than Fort Knox."

Ezra nodded. "You're right. I think it was a setup."

"But who would want us there? Who would know to call Rome and tell him about Sabar?" Zach asked.

"Inside job," X said. "Sabar had to have pissed somebody off. Kensington probably didn't know about the connection or I'm not sure he would have proceeded with this deal. He's not too keen on Rome since the law firm declined to donate to his campaign."

"At least we've confirmed that Kensington was brokering deals for Slakeman," Nick said.

"But did Slakeman know what type of people or nonhumans he was dealing with?" Rome asked. "Either way, I don't think we're completely out of the dark. There's something else going on; we just have to figure out what it is before it's too late."

Ary entered the room then, her hands in the pockets of her scrub shirt. "The bodies are done. I just heard on the news that the warehouse exploded. A couple of officers are hurt. It'll be a while before they can get inside to see who was left in there," she told them.

"Or what was taken out of there," X said thoughtfully.

"It's late. We'll all get some rest. I'll meet with Nick, X, and the guard leaders around three this afternoon. Nivea is to continue her detail on Agent Wilson. And Caprise," Rome said finally.

She looked over at him, her long raven-black hair hanging past her shoulders. She looked just like Nick, he thought. "We want to officially welcome you to the family. I'd also like to suggest—and I know at least two people in this room who might protest, but I'm in charge so I can make a declaration if I want—I suggest you be trained as a guard. Your instincts are great, you're agile and obviously able to handle yourself in stressful situations. I'll expect the training to begin as soon as you're up to it."

As Rome grabbed Kalina's hand and they started to walk away from the table he saw Nick's frown and X's totally pissed-off look. He grinned to himself as he imagined Caprise telling both of them to go to hell when they tried to stop her. As for Caprise, the smile on her face was genuine, her eyes already alight with excitement. In that moment Rome thought he'd done good, no matter the wrath of his best friends that would undoubtedly come later.

She was beautiful, that was a given. X had already accepted that fact and the one that made him just a little breathless each time he looked at Caprise. Tonight, or rather this morning, she looked different. For starters, she had more color. Her creamy complexion had a healthy glow that made him poke his chest out a little farther—he assumed it was because she was now mated. Her eyes seemed brighter, her bitchy attitude taking longer to appear. The sway to her hips, the curve of her breasts—everything seemed softer, more alluring. And his body reacted accordingly.

They'd left the dining hall, walking slowly back to Caprise's room. He would stay with her for a while, then head back into town for a change of clothes and be back for the meeting with Rome. His body was tired from the adrenaline rush, then the letdown of not really being able to do much by way of fighting. He'd wished like hell he could have taken down Sabar or at least been in the room when the bastard took his last breath. But he wasn't going to dwell on it. A hot shower, a soft bed, and a willing mate were all he needed to get past this bout of edginess.

"I'm not sleepy," she said to him when they'd stopped in front of her door.

Her hands clasped and unclasped in front of her and she shifted from one foot to the other. X didn't answer right away but looked at her eyes. Melted honey. He almost smiled because he knew just what she needed.

"Let's go" was all he said before grabbing her hand and pulling her behind him.

The hallways of Havenway were a dusky gray color,

the floor white tile. The doors were reinforced steel with control pads beside them. When they came to the door at the east entrance, the one closest to Caprise's room, X punched in a code that would bypass the alarm and let them out without sending a signal to the mainframe in the control room. Havenway's security was designed to indicate who was coming in and going out at all times. Each action was recorded on the computer and documented by the guard on duty. But this time, X didn't want anyone to know that he and Caprise were not in her bedroom.

Instead they stepped out into the damp evening air. A light trickle of rain sprinkled their skin as the door closed behind them.

"We need to get to the gate in three minutes," he told her, heading toward the back of the structure.

"Where are we going?" she asked, following behind him.

"You'll see" was his only reply before he broke into a run.

He stopped when they were at the edge of the grounds, guarded by motion-sensor gates. One hundred feet from Havenway's entrance was the starting point for the gate. It circled the building and stood seven and a half feet tall. Above were electrically charged wires.

He'd bypassed the alarm system, but that only bought him three minutes total. If they touched that gate after that time, they were going to get an electrical jolt between seventy-five and two hundred kilovolts. Then the first-response guard teams would be in their face within the next thirty seconds, guns drawn.

But they made good time, Caprise's long legs moving almost as quickly as his. He adjusted the latch and opened the gate, standing to the side so she could move past him. Upon their return he would have to use the front entrance and call the control room to be let in.

"Now I know who to come to when I want to escape," she said, not at all winded by the run.

"You're not a prisoner here, you know. And you don't have to stay here if you don't want to," he told her, leading the way through a small brush of bushes, taking them deeper into the park where the larger trees and foliage would cover them.

"Are you inviting me to move in with you?" she said, looking up at him with a sugary smile.

"I'm just letting you know you have options," X said, wondering if that smile meant she wanted to move in with him.

He'd never thought of a female in his apartment on a permanent basis.

"It probably makes sense that I'm here during the day for the guard training." She kept right on talking as if she hadn't heard the hesitation in his voice. "But then you're here almost every day, I could easily commute like real people do."

"I don't like you becoming a guard. And I don't know if I'll be out here every day. Just because I don't have a job doesn't mean I'm devoting all my time to the shifters now." Even though he'd be foolish to think they didn't need him. He was sure Rome would appreciate the help since he and Nick still had a very prominent law firm to run.

"I don't like you brooding over a job that didn't deserve you if they let you go at the first whiff of trouble. So I guess we're even" was her retort.

They'd entered the thicker trees, moonlight struggling to stream through the rich fall foliage to provide very little light. But they could see regardless. Caprise had been walking right beside him. X stopped, touching a hand to her arm. "They did not let me go. They suspended me."

She shrugged. "Well, you're the one who said you didn't have a job."

"Because," he said, knowing she was going to love his next words, "I'm not too keen about working for people who don't believe in me. I mean, there was no real evidence that pointed to me in those murders. They should have believed me."

"Did you try to talk to anyone else from the Bureau?"

"Nobody else wanted to talk to me."

She shrugged again. "Whatever, it's their loss."

He couldn't help but chuckle at how flippantly she'd said that. Like a career at the FBI wasn't worth crap anyway.

"Right," he said with a nod. "Take off your clothes."

She had been looking in the other direction, but her head snapped around at his words. "Excuse me?"

He pulled at the T-shirt he'd put on when he arrived at Havenway, then tossed it at the base of a tree. "You heard me, take off your clothes."

X kept his eyes on her as he gripped the band of his sweatpants and pushed them over his strong thighs. The boots he wore—ones that were in the trunk of the SUV they'd taken to Slakeman's place—were kicked off. Another Assembly mandate was that all guard vehicles carried extra clothes for the shifters just in case.

She stared at him another moment before kicking off her tennis shoes. The rest of her clothes quickly followed and X marveled at how gorgeous she was even in night vision.

His shift was quick and seamless as his human muscles cracked and molded to the form of a jaguar. Paws fell with grace against the dirt-padded floor of the park. Even though parts of Great Falls National Park were open to tourists, the spot where Havenway was located and the surrounding area where the shifters liked to run was hundreds of miles away from public areas. There was no fear of being seen here; the shifters could stretch and exercise in the way they were meant to.

Caprise didn't hesitate to follow suit and when she did her cat took off. X hadn't been surprised. Adrenaline was still rushing through her body even after the cool-down of the ride home and the meeting with Rome. He'd seen it in her eyes, in the way she couldn't keep still. There was still energy she needed to dispel.

He kept up with her easily as she explored the area. She would burst free in an all-out run that had both their legs stretching to cover as much territory as possible. Then she'd slow and move her body along a tree. Only once had she come up on hind legs and scored the tree's bark with her claws. X only watched, pacing slowly, remembering this spot because she would come here often now. When she broke into a run again he followed, determined to simply let her tire herself out.

Before long he heard the rushing of water, knew they were nearing the section of the park where the Potomac River poured into a seventy-seven-foot drop on its journey to the Chesapeake Bay. She would stop at the water, he knew instinctively.

Caprise shifted before X right at the water's edge. It was gorgeous here, the raging water possessively dominating this entire area. It fell in roaring waves over edges, pooling into the river that would swirl and continue out to the open sea. It was majestic, she thought as she stood there naked, looking around at the wonder that was nature.

She could see the same wonder by looking in the mirror. Shifters were an anomaly, a creation by a higher, all-knowing being. They had evolved over time until they were now all spread out over the globe, probably all looking for a home, wanting desperately to belong somewhere.

And yet, they already belonged. They were a part of the grand plan, she realized, a part of the humans and animals that all roamed this earth in their own type of harmony. The Shadow Shifters only needed to find their harmony, to carve out the spot in this big old world that belonged to them. And when they did, she thought, taking a step toward the water and dipping only a toe in at a time, she would stand with them. It was time she stood somewhere, with someone.

Speaking of someone, she turned, knowing he was there, behind her, as he had been for the entire time she'd been running. She'd felt his presence, like a coat on a cold winter's day, had scented him as the other half of her, the piece to the puzzle she'd been searching for so long. If anyone had ever told her she'd fall in love with Xavier Santos-Markland and want nothing more than to be in his arms every night she probably would have punched some sense into them. But here she was in a state she'd never thought she'd return to, running through this park in her jaguar form and absolutely loving the feel of the cool air against her fur, standing near this cool water touching her human skin, and finding herself enjoying it all.

All her life she'd rebuked her heritage, hated the very thing that made her who she was. Until now. At this precise moment she fully grasped the *Topètenia* and all that the tribe stood for. Because here, in this beast that was also a man, was all she'd been searching for. Strength, power, protection, desire, and finally compatibility. As X had told her once before, they were two of the same kind. Even as humans they were alike, having both been irrevocably scarred by people they trusted. And they'd both survived, they'd fought like hell for the life they wanted to lead until finally bumping into each other and realizing that their lives could only be led happily if they were joined. Yes, she'd admitted it, if only to herself: She wanted the joining ceremony and all the official crap that came along with it. Because there was no way she was letting this man walk out of her life, not now.

He was still in cat form, his green eyes grasping hers and holding. The intensity between them never seemed to waver, no matter where they were or in what form. She went to her knees and opened her arms to him. Her heart did an amazing flip-flop the moment the big cat began making its way to her. When he was close enough, she stretched her arms around him, laying her head against his. His tongue licked at her cheek, down to her neck, and she sighed. She was so in love with this shifter, a feeling she'd never thought to feel again.

"I love you," she whispered, her fingers buried deep in his fur.

Then he shifted. She jerked back with the force of his change. Just in time he reached out human arms, catching her before she could fall back into the rushing water. He held her there for what seemed like endless moments, just staring down at her. Her fingers flexed on his biceps, loving the firm feel of his muscles. He was so perfect in either form, brown skin marred only by the inked artwork that she'd memorized after the first time seeing him naked. She knew where each tat was precisely, knew their meaning, their feel against her tongue.

"I didn't think I'd be here," he said, his voice gruff and low against the roar of the water. "I didn't think I'd ever be mated."

Caprise shook her head. "I didn't, either."

He chuckled. "We're some pair, huh?"

"I think we're the perfect pair."

X nodded then, his lips spreading into a smile. "I think we are, too."

"You don't have to say it," she told him, biting her bottom lip. "It's okay."

"I know," he told her, then pulled her closer, touching his lips to hers, letting his tongue slide inside for a quick tussle with hers. "But I do," he whispered as his lips slid over the line of her jaw, down to the tender spot just beneath her earlobe.

"You do what?" she heard herself asking in a breathy whisper.

After a pause that had her insides churning, her breasts and center aching, she heard him say softly, "I love you."

Absolutely perfect is what she thought until he began moving. The next thing Caprise knew they were up to their waist in the chilly river water.

"Are you crazy? It's cold out here."

"I was going to wait until we were back in your room, but you couldn't keep still. And now I can't wait a moment longer."

Her arms circled his neck; his arms clasped her waist. "You can't wait for what?" she asked teasingly.

He grabbed the backs of her thighs, lifting them so that she could now clasp her feet behind his back just like her arms. And without preamble he slipped his heavy erection deep into her waiting center.

"For this," he said when she'd opened her mouth to gasp at the immediate fullness.

There was nothing like this; not ever in her life had Caprise felt anyone like this man. He was so big and so stern and yet he filled her so precisely, so sweetly, all she could do was sigh. His pumps were fast, just as she liked them, and as the water slapped around them, falling and rushing in its natural rhythm, she and X made their music. Her moans coupled with his repeating of her name, his grunts to the background of her high-pitched screams, their climax came simultaneously like a practiced concerto.

Chapter 30

Dorian downed another glass of straight scotch. He'd returned to his apartment over an hour ago, after one night of pure adrenaline. Eric had delivered more details as Dorian had driven to Woodland. There was an arms deal going down; Senator-elect Ralph Kensington was involved. The address was to Slakeman Enterprises. Dorian hadn't initially thought any of this had anything to do with the drugs he was tracking or the killings that had taken place in the last nine months, but Eric believed it did.

By the time they'd arrived, MPD were there in deep numbers. Helicopters roamed the dark evening sky, the moon hidden by ominous clouds. There had been no alarms tripped, and all seemed to be well inside the building.

Then it happened.

The explosion that killed three seasoned police officers and injured seven more. The blast had come as a complete surprise, and only by the grace of God did Dorian and Eric not get hurt. Dorian had parked outside the gates because there were so many police cars already pulled into the parking lot. He'd just phoned Eric to let him know he was there. A few seconds later Eric had come up to the car, giving Dorian more details about what seemed to be a false alarm.

It wasn't a false alarm.

Right now they had no idea who had set the bomb. Preliminary reports indicated it was a bomb and not some sort of accidental explosion—Eric had texted him that information just before he came into the house. But who would bomb Slakeman Enterprises? That probably garnered more than one suspect, especially since Slakeman's last government contract had been canceled about six months ago. Right now he was a free agent to any country and/or terrorist group that wanted to get their hands on some serious firepower. He could have pissed any of them off. Or he could have pissed off Ralph Kensington, whom Dorian didn't believe had this kind of power. Then again, Dorian wasn't past believing anything at this point.

At any rate, he didn't have any answers about tonight's occurrences. As for his current fixation with Xavier Santos-Markland, he would have to leave the man alone, at least for now. The MPD had ruled the deaths of Diamond Turner and the other two girls at Athena's accidental overdoses—even though Diamond's body had been sliced and diced, the coroner finally ruled that those injuries came after Diamond had already ingested a fatal amount of this new synthetic drug. Dorian was almost positive the labs would come back with that drug they'd taken from Athena's as the synthetic culprit.

So Xavier Santos-Markland was off the hook. It also seemed that Roman Reynolds and his other cohort were free from scrutiny once more. Dorian threw the drink across the room, watching with muted satisfaction as the glass shattered against the wall. He scrubbed his hands down his face and took a deep breath.

It didn't fit, none of it did. But maybe it was time he let it go. He wasn't about to spend the rest of his life obsessing over one case. He had a life to lead, or at least he thought he did. Still single, no girlfriend or even a prospect of a girlfriend, no male friends, no nothing except work. Pathetic, that's what he was.

He walked over to the window, pushing back the curtains with shaky hands. Maybe he'd had one too many glasses of scotch. As he looked down onto the quiet street where he lived, his vision blurred only slightly. Breathing hard enough so that he fogged the window in front of him, Dorian tried to let the memories of tonight and the previous nights wash from his mind. He was trying so hard not to concentrate on work that he almost missed it.

In a black SUV parked across the street from his building he'd seen a shadow of a person. Someone was inside, and they'd moved the moment he came to the window. On instinct—because no matter how sorry he was feeling for himself, he was still a cop—Dorian backed away from the window. He stood close to the wall, waited a beat, then leaned in slowly. Not so his body would show but so that he could still look out to see if the person in the vehicle would get out.

It was well after three in the morning. If someone in his building were expecting company, wouldn't that company have already gotten out of the car and come inside? A drizzle of rain had just begun to come down and Dorian had to shake his head to clear his own blurriness. But the shadow was still there, sitting way back in the front seat, as if the seat had been lowered all the way down. The head of the shadow moved and Dorian gasped.

Yellow eyes.

They stared back at him, right up to his window as if they knew he was watching.

"Shit!" he cursed, falling back on his ass and rubbing his eyes. "Gotta stop drinking scotch." He scrambled off the floor to the bathroom, where he proceeded to relieve himself of all the scotch he'd just consumed.

* * *

Bianca came to sit next to Darel on the couch in his apartment. Neither of them had wanted to go back to the town house in Georgetown. It had been a long night, one they'd been setting up for nearly a week, and as far as Darel could tell it had gone perfectly.

Then she opened her mouth and began to talk. Nothing good ever came from Bianca talking. Darel wondered why he hadn't subjected her to the same fate as Sabar.

"I'm so glad that's over," she said, crossing her legs. The nightgown she wore had slits up both sides, easy access for anyone who wanted a taste.

Darel had tasted so much in the last weeks, he wondered if he'd start to go into withdrawal at some point.

"Now we can really take care of our business," she continued. "We should move the headquarters in case someone still loyal to Sabar wants to try to go against us. And that chemist guy out there is the pits. We need top-notch employees."

Darel could ignore her for hours; he'd done it before. But tonight he wanted to get some sleep, so he figured the sooner he talked to her, sucked and fucked her, the sooner he could get on with it.

"I know what I'm doing. It's all going to be fine," he told her.

"Oh, I don't doubt you," she said, leaning in closer to nibble on his ear. "I'm just throwing ideas out there, seeing what sticks." With the last word she flattened her palm over his dick.

She was so predictable.

"Go ahead and take it," he ordered her. "And don't stop until I tell you to."

Bianca smiled, her tongue licking over her lips as she eased off the couch. She went to her knees, leaning between his legs.

Darel lay his head back. He reached an arm over until

he touched a remote control on the coffee table. Lifting it so he could see, he pushed the POWER button, then the red RECORD button. Putting the remote down, he closed his eyes and let Bianca do her thing. She'd be busy for about an hour, working him until he finally came. She loved when he came, or so she said. As for Darel, he loved the aftereffect. She'd fall asleep and he'd replay the tape he made of them. That was his real turn-on.

As she unbuttoned his pants and pulled out his semi-erect dick, Darel thought over the events of the night.

Bianca had been slowly poisoning Sabar with the same damiana he'd praised for making the savior drug a success. They'd thought it sort of poetic that his own creation would contribute to his demise. But they needed him out of the way while they worked the other details of the plan.

Palermo Greer was a shifter whom both Bianca and Darel knew. His appearance in DC had seemed a little strange at first; then Darel figured it out. Bianca had summoned him to take out Sabar. If Darel hadn't fucked her that day she'd snuck into his apartment, he would have probably been on their hit list as well. Funny how things worked out in the end. He'd immediately confronted Palermo about his suspicions, and the two had found common ground—neither of them truly trusted Bianca and both of them hated Sabar. So why not team up to get the job done?

At this very moment Palermo was on a private jet headed for Albuquerque where he would deliver the weapons to their new headquarters, the one Bianca knew nothing about. Palermo was going to get things set up there while Darel continued to work the money end of the business. Now, Darel didn't trust Palermo 100 percent, either; no one would ever get that type of trust from him. But the shifter had proved he had balls by getting into

Slakeman's good graces. That new connection was going to work out well for them.

As for Pierson, that little weasel was also going to end up working for Darel. Slakeman and other greedy mother-fuckers like him would all bow to Darel sooner or later.

Bianca went deep, taking his full length in her mouth and humming just the way he taught her. Spirals of plea-sure soared up his spine, and Darel let out a little gasp. He might not trust this bitch but she could certainly give good head. Absently he touched a hand to the back of her head, grabbed a fistful of hair, and yanked. "Do it again!" he yelled.

She smiled, her lips still wrapped around his length, and ducked her head once more.

This was where he wanted to be . . . for the moment. As for tomorrow, Darel would just have to see, but his future was already looking much brighter.

Chapter 31

One Week Later

X and Caprise walked into mayhem. After deciding that their home would be X's apartment and they would both visit Havenway daily to do their new jobs—Caprise as a guard in training and X as commanding officer and intel supervisor—they'd slipped into a comfortable routine.

Going back to the FBI hadn't been an option for X. Seeing the damage the Rogues could do on the streets in the last couple of months had proved to him that working from the FBI wasn't going to stop this new war that was being waged. What they learned from Elder Alamar and Baxter proved that this battle was going to grow, and for them to stop it they'd need all hands on deck. As Rome and Nick's firm provided the bulk of the finances to the Stateside Assembly so far, X figured his best contribution was to work full-time in developing new technology to help support their endeavors. And this way he could keep an eye on his mate, the one who was determined to become a guard even though she'd also accepted a part-time teaching position at the Dance Institute of Washington.

They'd been home for about two hours when Kalina had called Caprise. Ary was officially in labor.

So, packing an overnight bag, they'd headed back out to Havenway—and had just arrived to pure chaos.

Shifters stood to the side as Nick gave orders. Rome had been just coming down the hallway as they entered. He looked to X and shared a knowing sigh. Both men moved to Nick, clapping hands on either of his shoulders.

"Come on, let's go get a drink," Rome said.

"No." Nick shook his head. "I'm going back in there. I've got to be with her."

"Sure you do," X said. "Let's just get you calmed down a bit. We'll let the women go make sure she's comfortable and we'll join them in a few."

Over his shoulder X nodded to Caprise, who smiled as she started down the hallway toward the medical center.

"I don't want a drink," Nick continued to argue.

But Baxter, the Overseer who saw and knew every damn thing, had already appeared with a tray. "Have a drink, Mr. Dominick. Dr. Papplin said a couple of hours at best. You don't want to be worried out of your mind by then."

Nick, who knew just like the rest of them that ignoring Baxter's request couldn't end well, took the glass from the tray. He drank until it was empty.

"Happy now?" he asked all that were looking at him.

Rome shook his head. X chuckled.

"You're a smooth talker in the courtroom and a definite player when you were on the prowl for women, but now you seem to be losing your cool. Where is the Nick Delgado we used to know?" X asked.

"Ha. Ha. Very funny," Nick said snidely, turning so that they would be walking toward the medical center. "You have no idea how this feels. It's not like anything I've ever expected."

"A lot of responsibility comes with having a child," Rome told him.

"That's why we've got to get these Rogues in check, man. The world has to be safer for my daughter," Nick said sincerely.

"I hear that," X told him. "And we're going to get it together. We're not going to let anything happen to her."

The three men walked into the medical center side by side, ready to face whatever happened next, just as they'd always done.

Two hours later Ary pushed one last time. With a scream that threatened to break the small windows in the room and any other glass item, Shya Delgado was born.

Shya echoed her mother's sentiments by letting out a huge wail of her own.

Beside Ary, holding her hand and leaning forward to kiss her lips, was Nick. "She's gorgeous," he told his wife when Dr. Papplin held the baby up for them to see.

Ary, who was drenched in sweat, lifted her head, breath still heaving, and cried, "Perfect. Look at her, Nick, she's absolutely perfect."

"I'll bring her right back," Dr. Papplin said, taking the Delgado baby over to an incubator they had set up just in case they should need it. By this time they had four nursing assistants in the medical center. Gisela was their most experienced and she tended to Ary.

Although this was not a human baby, Papplin still performed the Apgar testing. He watched her activity, posture, breathing, behavior, and color. All looked normal at the first minute of evaluation. As he waited for the next recording at five minutes Papplin touched along her spine. He counted her fingers and her toes and looked at her eyes once more. They were blue, which wasn't terribly abnormal. Lots of babies were born with blue eyes that later changed to their permanent color. He aspirated her, checking her nasal cavity and her mouth for any blockages. She was breathing just fine and had stopped crying immediately. Now she lay quietly staring directly at Papplin even though he was sure he was nothing more than a blob to her. Except her glare looked way too clear.

At the five-minute mark he recorded her results, pleased with the perfect score. He was about to take her over to her proud parents because he knew they were getting anxious and the last thing Papplin wanted was to endure Nick's wrath. But something told him to take a blood sample—something like the fact that the Assembly had voted to store samples of every shifter's DNA. He quickly found a needle, clamped on a vial, and pricked a tiny vein in Shya's foot. He almost looked away since this was a normal task, but something kept his eyes riveted on that vial.

"Is everything all right?" Nick asked from behind him.

"Ah, yes. Yes," Papplin said, sure his tired eyes were simply playing tricks on him.

He finished, labeling the sample and setting it aside. Wrapping the gorgeous little girl in a pretty pink blanket already provided by her mother, he carried her over and placed her in Ary's arms.

"Hello, Shya," Ary said.

Nick leaned over both his lovely ladies, kissing his daughter on the forehead. "Hello, my precious little girl."

And as they cooed and ahhed over this joyous event, Dr. Papplin took the vial of blood and carried it back to his office.

Epilogue

Three Months Later

The Grand Ballroom at the Willard InterContinental in Washington, DC, was the location for the kickoff to President Wilson Reed's reelection campaign. As staunch supporters of the current president and his administration, Reynolds & Delgado had purchased a table of ten seats to the fund-raising event that started at seven thirty on a chilly winter evening.

Priya Drake, columnist for *The Washington Post,* with her sights on becoming a White House correspondent in the very near future, covered the president's first reelection fund-raiser with all the zeal of an ambitious reporter. She'd stuffed her press pass into the small beaded purse she carried, after showing it to be allowed entrance. In her palm was a small handheld recorder that she cupped expertly so when she was speaking into it—taking her notes for the column—it would appear she was only coughing or otherwise covering her mouth. Not everybody needed to know that whatever they said or did around her was subject to appearing in black-and-white print come tomorrow morning.

She'd taken position just inside the entrance, standing near a pillar that gave her access to everyone as they walked in. This way she'd get first attempts at interviews with DC's most powerful. And she was not disappointed as she stood back to watch the newest arrivals.

At seven fifty-three in the evening, Roman Reynolds, dressed in a classic two-button Gianni Versace tuxedo, entered the large ballroom with its thick white pillars, golden accents, and crystal chandeliers. On his arm was his wife and former MPD detective, the lovely and never overstated Kalina Reynolds. Mrs. Reynolds wore what Priya was certain was Vera Wang. In Priya's other life she had to have been a fashion designer, and her obsession had simply carried over. Even though she couldn't afford half the items she gawked over, she knew them all name by expensively designed name. Kalina's dress was a fabulous A-line V-neck in a very alluring teal color that accented the ex-cop's gorgeously natural golden skin tone.

The Reynoldses had been pictured before as they'd been out to dinner or at some other social event the millionaire lawyer was invited to. And Priya had to admit they made a stunning couple.

Next—and Priya could have probably predicted this— came Dominick Delgado and his adorable wife, Aryiola. The rumor mill was still abuzz with news of Nick's quickie marriage and the resulting baby girl that had been born just a few months ago. Although there had been no pictures of the baby yet, Mommy and Daddy were both looking their picture-perfect best tonight.

Nick wore an appropriate modern-cut tuxedo, while his wife sported what Priya's eagle eye nabbed as Donna Karan—a lovely tangerine dress with one capped sleeve and a crisscross pattern over her chest. Priya gave a mental thumbs-up to this obvious South American beauty for the dress but hated her for regaining that killer body so soon after having a baby.

In the back of her mind Priya noted there had never

been any photos of the pretty foreigner with a protruding belly, so the baby could always be a rumor. However, the larger-than-life diamond on her ring finger was obviously the real thing.

Next up was a face she didn't see in the tabloids often—only when he followed behind Reynolds and Delgado, which was most of the time. As Priya recalled, he was an FBI agent and looked terribly familiar. She would have sworn he was a professional wrestler if it hadn't been for the company he kept. It didn't matter who the designer of his tuxedo was, the slate-gray material fit him perfectly, adding an ideal touch to his military-like features of bald head, cold eyes, and stern jaw. His date, whom Priya could swear she'd seen someplace before as well, was likewise beautiful. Her hair was long, cascading over one shoulder in big bouncy curls. The dress was white and fit like a second skin—damnation to another gorgeous body. It hugged her generous breasts in a halter and displayed one outrageously long and equally toned leg through a split that soared upward to midthigh.

This was a new couple, one that looked as abnormally gorgeous as the former two. Really, Priya wanted to visit whatever salon these people did. Her own medium build and mocha skin tone could use a professional makeover. Even though she thought she did a damn good job of remaining stylish and sexy on her meager reporter's budget. If the offer to move up in the world dropped in her lap, she'd scoop it up faster than a bird does bread crumbs. And she wouldn't look back. Priya had vowed long ago to never look back.

The men that followed were all dressed in tuxedos, all handsome as sin, taller and broader than most of the other men in the room. Priya's gaze followed them as they moved to a table near the far left wall of the room. She wasn't sure why, but when she moved to find a seat she made sure it was at a table in close proximity to this one. And as she stared—blatantly because there wasn't a modest bone in her body—one of the men looked up and locked gazes with her. For a minute she was startled—his eyes were a dusky tone of gray—but then she kept right on staring, feeling as if she were falling into that swirl of muted color, falling so slowly but so completely she didn't have a moment to catch her breath.

Want to help spread the word
about the Shadow Shifters?

JOIN THE SHADOW SHIFTER STREET TEAM!

Visit www.acarthur.net to find out how you can help,
or simply send an e-mail expressing your interest to
acarthur22@yahoo.com and join us as we endeavor to
share this new series with readers across the world!